SO HAPPY TOGETHER

ALSO BY OLIVIA WORLEY

People to Follow

The Debutantes

SO HAPPY TOGETHER

A NOVEL

OLIVIA WORLEY

MINOTAUR
BOOKS
NEW YORK

First published in the United States by Minotaur Books, an imprint of St. Martin's Publishing Group

SO HAPPY TOGETHER. Copyright © 2025 by Olivia Worley. All rights reserved. Printed in the United States of America. For information, address St. Martin's Publishing Group, 120 Broadway, New York, NY 10271.

www.minotaurbooks.com

Designed by Omar Chapa

Library of Congress Cataloging-in-Publication Data (TK)

ISBN 9781250372307 (hardcover)
ISBN 9781250372314 (ebook)

Our books may be purchased in bulk for promotional, educational, or business use. Please contact your local bookseller or the Macmillan Corporate and Premium Sales Department at 1-800-221-7945, extension 5442, or by email at MacmillanSpecialMarkets@macmillan.com.

First Edition: 2025

10 9 8 7 6 5 4 3 2 1

For the girls who get attached a little too quickly

SO HAPPY TOGETHER

PART ONE

The Lovers

PART ONE

NOW

It's a beautiful thing, watching something die. I never understood it until now—except he was wrong, in a way, because no one's dead yet, at least not by my hand, but still, I think I know what he meant. It's this: the look in those eyes, knowing the line between life and death rests in my palm, a prophecy foretold by branches and ridges that only I can read.

And what does it say?

The truth: it was always going to end like this.

Love stories always do. To believe anything else would be delusional. But I've fallen for plenty of delusions. Another one: I told myself that I could be good.

I see it now, sharp as a blade between my ribs. I was holding so tight to something that died long ago, a corpse clutched to my chest, convincing myself that it was still breathing. In the end, all I needed was to let it go. They say that's what to do when you love something. And maybe some part of me still does. Always will.

It's what I tell myself, a new whispered mantra in the shadows of my heart, as I raise the knife.

THREE WEEKS EARLIER

1

On the night he breaks my heart for the second time, Colin is wearing my favorite sweater. It's turquoise, the bright kind of shade that most men are afraid to wear for fear of looking soft—and it is. Soft, I mean. A little faded, like it was thrifted, or at least long loved, with a fuzz of pilling that I could only see up close. He wore it on our first date, even though it was a little too warm for a sweater, and I knew instantly that he was gentle, that he takes care of things, but not overbearingly—the type who would throw his sweater in the dryer, screw the pilling, just so it will feel warm and clean. I wanted to bury my face in it instantly, make it mine.

Now, he wears it at a cozy table, across from *her*. Because it's his date sweater, and for the first time in a long time, I feel the sharp and sudden urge to watch the life drain from another person's eyes.

"So you write plays and stuff," Axel says. "That's sick."

Axel, twenty-six, consultant at the Big Five. Originally from the Bay Area. Looking for a short-term relationship, open to long, whatever that means, fan of tequila shots for the table and girls who don't take themselves too seriously. I googled him, like I google all my dating app dates, and as far as I can tell, Axel is his actual name—at least, it has been since he was in high school, which is as far back as I could find. I don't know which is worse: choosing a name like Axel on purpose for yourself or being born to parents who looked down at your wriggling pink body and said, *This boy is an Axel.*

I wouldn't ordinarily go out with an Axel on principle alone, but Axel is far from the point of tonight. They never are.

"Yeah," I say, tucking my hair behind my ear. It's part of the script I've perfected over the course of the past two months: short response, humble, because any more than that and you sound too full of your-self, too high on this idea that you're some kind of artist.

Colin never made me feel like I had to follow a script. He didn't ask me if I write *plays and stuff*, either. He called me a playwright. Like it's a given, like I don't need to earn it because I already have. To him, I wasn't just Jane, twenty-four, playwright, looking for a long-term relationship and weirdly attracted to the Oxford comma. He wanted to peel back the layers, see what's inside.

He's watching her now, drinking her in as she talks about some-thing I can't hear. First date, I decide. I've been deliberating since Axel and I sat down about an hour ago, but it must be. Colin's look-ing at her in that way of his, like she's a complicated pattern he hasn't worked out yet, his chin in his hand, and my stomach tightens. He did this exact pose in his newest profile photo, the one he added a week after breaking things off with me because we were too *serious.*

That's what he said in the text, two days after we had sex for the first time.

I thought I was ready for something this serious, but I'm not. I'm sorry.

And then he went and updated his profile, like I wouldn't see it—like he didn't feel even a shred of sadness, of mourning this loss.

So much for *sorry.*

Now, Colin laughs at something the girl has said, a crooked grin spreading like melted butter and achieving, I guess, what he wanted all along: cracking me open. Seeing inside.

"So, what do you *do*, though?" Axel asks, pulling a hand through his too-blond, too-slicked hair.

I close my hands around my glass of cider—my go-to date order because I am *chill* and *cool* but *not a beer girl, not one of the boys*. It's cold against my palms, and I keep them there to stop myself from reaching for the nearest fork to impale my own thigh.

"I also edit college application essays."

It's the only acceptable answer because it's true. I don't make a living as a playwright—I don't make any money writing at all, not yet—but I hate the way he makes me say it.

Colin never asked what I do, not the way Axel just did, with that implied *really* before the *do*. Colin accepted me as I am, no asterisk required. He wouldn't let me if I tried, and I did: the first time he asked me what I do, I launched right into my prepared dialogue. The *I'm a playwright, but.* And Colin got this look in his eyes, all serious and honey brown under those thick lashes, and told me, *But what? You're a playwright. You don't need to undercut that with something else for it to be true.*

"That's cool," Axel says, clearly uninterested. "I think it's sick how you're trying to do something artistic, though."

I clock it as the fourth *sick* of the evening. I also clock the *trying*, and I have vivid daydreams of Axel getting crushed by a window AC unit when he leaves this bar.

"My friends always told me I could have made it as a DJ," Axel continues, unaware of my seething contempt or the fact that he's a caricature of himself. "But financial stability has always been more important to me. Like, I've got mad respect for people trying to be artists, but I'd much rather have a salary and my own place, you know? You should see it, by the way. Sick view."

As Axel launches into a detailed description of his square footage in Murray Hill, clearly meant to seduce me—with no self-awareness for the fact that he lives in *Murray Hill*, the EPCOT of fraternity man-children who want to pretend they're real New Yorkers—I watch the girl. I can only see her from behind, with a hint of her profile every time she turns to admire Colin's favorite East Village date spot, probably impressed like I was the first time: it's comfortable, designed to feel like a dive, but the cocktails are pricey enough that you know he isn't being stingy.

She's pretty, with bouncy chestnut curls that she keeps raking her hand through to make them cascade over her bony shoulders like a shampoo ad, only less pristine, like she doesn't care where they fall because she knows they'll look perfect every time. She's white, my age, and I can't quite tell when she's sitting, but she seems taller than me, thin and willowy in a supermodel way. Colin, at six foot one, still probably has at least a few inches on her.

She's so pretty, in fact, that it makes my stomach hurt, makes it feel so hollow it's like I reached inside and laid my guts out on the table as a pitiful offering, all slimy tubes and a barely pumping heart.

Marketing, I think. Maybe fashion merchandising, if that's even a real thing. She has that look about her: tight white crop top and wide-leg jeans over these chunky loafers, the kind of outfit that suggests ease and unbotheredness, even though it's still trendy. She swirls a straw in her drink, something fruity and girlish.

Suddenly, my own date outfit—black slip minidress, white Doc Martens—feels too try-hard, too basic. My drink, too. Cider is what a girl picks to make a boy think she's down-to-earth but still feminine. It's the drink for someone who thinks too hard about her decisions, who's too afraid to pick up a maraschino cherry by the stem and pop it between her lips without a brush of irony.

I should just leave, I think, give up on this whole stupid endeavor,

7

but I can't stop watching them. The fear of letting them out of my sight is somehow worse than the fear of what I'll see.

And the plan. Tonight, the plan is finally working.

I notice the absence of Axel's drone, and when I glance back at him, he's taking another sip of his beer, watching me. Waiting. I should ask him a question.

"So, what's it like being a consultant?" I ask.

Axel launches into another monologue—mission accomplished—and I catch movement at Colin's table: a server bringing over the check. Colin and the girl have been here since Axel and I arrived, so I'm not sure how long their date has lasted. I hope it wasn't much longer than ours. The pit of dread in my stomach knows otherwise.

Colin sets his card down, beating the girl to the punch—she does *the reach*, even if she doesn't mean it—and instantly, my heart picks up again, my palms going slick. I brush a hand through my hair, splaying it over my shoulder.

It's torture, looking interested as Axel talks. Shaping my face into the proper expressions, my voice into the appropriate amount of *hmms* and *ohs*. The whole time, I'm too aware of the distance between my body and Colin's, like I can feel the atoms colliding, a buzz in the air.

Axel is still talking when the server comes back with Colin's receipt, and this is it. I've never been an actor, but it's time for the show.

At the first break in Axel's monologue, I lean in, painting a soft smile across my lips.

"So you have a view, huh?"

He grins like a boy who saw his Christmas presents early, leaning back in his seat.

"Sounds like a girl who wants to see."

In my periphery, I see them approaching, see her slip a leather jacket on.

Under the table, I brush Axel's leg.

"Maybe," I say, and they're closer now, almost at the door. "But you should know I'm not easily impressed."

And then I feel him see me. I don't have to look to know—that's how connected we are—and it makes me want to shiver, like the ghost of his lips on my neck, my collarbone. I wait one second, another, and then, I look up.

Colin, standing with one hand on the door and his eyes locked on mine.

He waves. A hint of a smile, his freckles lit up in the glow of the streetlights outside.

The girl looks between us, and I know she can sense it, the history crackling there, the shock and disbelief and, yes, regret on Colin's face—because I know in this moment that I was right. He misses me, he was scared of what he felt for me, and now, he's wishing he could take it all back. He's wishing it were him across this table from me.

But I'm moving on now, I'm *chill* and *cool* and a girl who looks away first, back at Axel. I smile, reaching for my cider, as I hear the door swing open and shut, hear the city swallow them back up. I don't even check to see if Colin glances back through the window, because I know he will. And I won't be waiting for it.

"Want to get out of here?" Axel asks.

I nod, smiling and silent.

"Sick," he says, and something in me has shifted, filling with so much hope and victory that I lose count of his *sick*s, that I don't think I even care anymore. He signals for the check, and when it comes, he lays his card down, making sure I can see it's one of those thick metal ones that screams *rich and corporate*. I even enjoy the sound of it, the definitive thud.

"I'm going to run to the bathroom, and then we can dip," he says.

Even better. He goes, and once he's gone, I allow myself a full grin, silly and childish. Let everyone here think it's about Axel. I don't care. He deserves love, too, doesn't he? We all do—which I guess is the kind of thought it's easy to have when you know you've found it again, or at least the promise of it, small and bright and blooming.

Eight weekends of Friday night first dates at this bar, just a few blocks from Colin's apartment, waiting for the day when he would be here to see me moving on. I wasn't expecting him to be here with a date, not this soon, but I know now that it doesn't matter. Colin was here, he *saw* me, and I looked away first—perfectly staged, perfectly executed. I know that he won't bring this girl back to his apartment, he won't even kiss her when he walks her to the train, because he'll be thinking about me. Wondering who my date was. Wondering if I'll be going back to see his view.

I shrug into my denim jacket, worn in and oversized and so much less pretentious than that girl's shiny faux leather. Then, standing, I reach for my tote bag. I could let Axel pay—he made it very clear that he can afford it—but I'm moved by a sudden generosity and love for the universe to grab two of the crumpled tens I was going to use to get quarters for my laundry. I let them fall on the table.

Then, I knock back the rest of my cider, set it on the table, and head into the night, knowing I didn't even need the drink. I'll feel buzzed on this night the whole way home.

2

When I first moved to the city, it was easy to fall in love every time I got on the train. Hurtling through the underground, I could see New York like a play: dim, flickering light and gritty tile the perfect setting for so many different characters to come together, pumped through the city's arteries. They all have stories, I thought, and they're all beautiful.

It's a philosophy that, once you've lived here long enough, New York will teach you is bullshit. The subway isn't some magical portal, some great equalizer. It's infrastructure. And infrastructure isn't romantic or sexy—it just *is*, like the dust in my apartment, the rusty-black stains caked too deep into my shower tile to ever bleach away.

Still, every so often, the romance of the city will come back to me with feverish force. Like when I was with Colin. In our nearly two months together, I tapped my toes along with every shitty subway performer, gave them whatever cash I had in my pockets, if I hadn't already spent it on chocolate from those kids with their boxes full, eating it right there, warm and half-melted from the summer heat. I could've cupped a rat in my palms and sang a stupid little song to it, like a delirious, diseased Disney princess. I didn't care. I didn't need

11

to, because I had someone, even when he wasn't there with me—because he was always there, either as my favorite phone notification or a lingering smell on my clothes.

And now, tonight, I feel it again.

As the A hurtles from West 4th to 168th, I slip my earbuds in, open up Spotify, and shuffle the playlist of songs that remind me of him.

At the first sound of the guitar intro, warmth floods my stomach. "Crash into Me," Dave Matthews Band. It's one of Colin's favorites, and when he first said so, I laughed because it sounds like a band someone's dad would be into, but somehow, for him, it's perfect. Slow and soft and sticky sweet, a little bit nostalgic, and something thrumming underneath, something building.

I don't know, he'd said. *Kind of reminds me of you.*

The subway car rattles like a drumbeat against my spine, in perfect sync with the music, and I'm not embarrassed to bob my head along. I want people to know that I'm happy, to wonder who's responsible.

I don't check my phone once, just let the playlist shuffle on, enjoying the light and the movement of the city, the comfort of knowing that when I finally do, his name will be there again. It's a game of self-restraint, almost a flirtation, deciding not to look yet.

When I climb out of my station in Washington Heights, the early November air nipping my cheeks, I leave my phone in my pocket. It stays there until I'm back at my apartment on 171st, the door shut gently behind me.

The small kitchen space is empty, air thick with the lingering smell of Anna's Trader Joe's gyoza. Judging from the light shining under her closed door, she's in for the night, studying whatever it is a Columbia med student is supposed to study.

Harmony is out, I'm assuming—she always has plans on Fridays, shows to see and clubs to hit without ever inviting Anna or me. As an actor, Harmony was particularly thrilled about living with a playwright, until she realized that I am both unlikely to write her a Tony-winning role and also a general drag to be around. A quality of mine that, fine, *maybe* I exaggerated to ward her off as soon as I realized that rooming with an actor means hearing pop songs belted with a ridiculous amount of vibrato through the thin walls every day.

But tonight, Harmony could be home screaming along to the full soundtrack of *Dear Evan Hansen*, for all I care. I'm so giddy, I even consider knocking on Anna's door to say hi, but she's busy, and I have more important things to do.

I step into my room, lock the door, and flop onto my bed, reaching for my phone and clicking to wake it up.

Nothing. My heart sinks a little, but I know it's coming—Colin probably just needs time to process what happened, to let this girl down easy. For all I know, he's still trying to explain it to her.

I'm sorry, I imagine him saying. *I've been trying to ignore my feelings for Jane, but after tonight, I just can't.*

I turn onto my side, breathing in the smell of my pillows. Even though it's been over two months since he slept on them, I'm almost certain I catch a hint of his smell, clean and bright without the unwelcome loudness of cologne.

I could text him, I know. But I'm *moving on* and *looking away first*, I'm cider and my hand on someone else's thigh, and it would be pathetic of me. I have to wait.

Lying this way, my laptop is in my direct line of vision. It's abandoned on my small, rickety desk, the fourth leg of which is still balanced on a balled-up sock because one of the pieces came broken. I could write, put my phone away and channel all this swirling energy into the Ophelia play. I've been working on my reimagining of *Hamlet* for a while now, with visions of falling petals and a claw-foot tub and other watery stage magic, but with draft after draft, I can't decide if what I have is brilliant or a contrived Sarah Ruhl rip-off.

Anyway, I'm too wired to write, floating too high to bring myself down with the solid feeling of a keyboard under my hands.

I reach for my phone and open TikTok.

I don't know how to feel about the fact that I'm a person who uses TikTok. At twenty-four, I'm hovering somewhere between too old and just young enough to understand the niche micro-brands of humor that make up this collective digital hellscape. Sometimes, they make me laugh. Sometimes, I get good hair tips.

And sometimes, they tell my fortune.

Like now—the first post on my For You page is another tarot video. I've been getting a lot of them, lately: women with candles and dangling earrings, shuffling cards with abandon until a handful slide out of the pack at random to prophesize—always—that a *divine masculine energy* will be returning to my life. So long as I like, comment, and share to "claim," of course.

Objectively, I know they're a crock of lies. They're only here because, when I was newly bruised from losing Colin, I watched enough of them to convince the algorithm that this is what I want to see. Maybe it makes me weak, but the truth is, they help. It feels good to have something to believe in, declaring I didn't make it all up: Colin felt it, too, and he'll come back to me, if only I'm patient.

And tonight, he did. A new card held up to the light, a return and a beginning all at once.

As the tarot reader croons into my ear, I scroll through the comments. A parade of women profess that their love will come back with heart and prayer emojis, and tonight, I don't feel shame or disgust at all of us for losing ourselves in this fiction. I like a few of their comments, filling up the heart outline with my support.

Sometimes, hope is rewarded.

I keep scrolling through my For You page, sinking comfortably into the sea of strangers, as soft and mindless as my pillows.

"Want to know the secret to making him obsessed?"

I jolt up, my whole body buzzing like it's just been dunked in cold water. I recognize the girl who's just appeared on my screen. It's her. Colin's date, cupped in my palms.

I pause the video and pull her closer. She's even prettier now that I can see her clearly: button nose, thick eyebrows, and long lashes, with the kind of dewy, barely there makeup look that I can never seem to achieve.

Her handle: @zophorescent. When I click to view her full profile, I can see her full name, Zoe Ember. Fake name, almost definitely. It's too attention-seeking in the way that my full name, Jane Williams, sounds too anonymous to feel real.

Zoe has twenty thousand followers and a few videos with over a million views, including the one I was just watching. I click on it again, let it play through.

"I'm serious, you guys, this works for me every single time," she says. "Try it out, and I swear to god, you'll get a text like *that*."

She snaps her fingers, showing off her manicured nails, the color of red wine, and an intrusive image invades: those nails scratching down Colin's back. I wonder if he would like that, if he wishes my nails were longer like Zoe's instead of the short stubs I maintain so I don't have to feel them tapping against my keyboard.

"All you have to do," Zoe says, lowering her voice like she's letting all one million of us in on a secret, "is take him off that pedestal. I'm serious. Sometimes, when we want someone so bad—when we're trying to manifest that Specific Person—we give them all of our mental energy. But honestly? That's the fastest way to push them away. You need to shroud yourself in that divine feminine energy. You are here to *receive*."

The logical part of my brain knows that this is more bullshit, what she's saying—the verbal equivalent of paying eighty dollars for a candle that's supposed to smell like your own vagina—but somehow, I can't stop watching. Maybe it's the unnatural green of her eyes, but something about the way she looks into the camera feels like she's looking directly at me, like she can sense my judgment and she doesn't care, only welcomes it.

"So, here's what I want you to do: first, I just want you to close your eyes and envision yourself as the most divine version of you. Picture yourself the way you want your SP to see you: smart, powerful, confident, sexy, whatever. And yeah, I know. But stick with me."

She gives a twinkling laugh, and it's smart of her—making it seem like this is a joke we're all in on, even though she clearly wants us to believe it's real. The logical part of my mind clocks it as cult leader behavior, but I lower my head back to the pillows, my eyes closing, letting my phone rest beside me on the bed as Zoe's sweet, melodic voice shimmers in my ear.

"Really *see* that version of yourself. I'm talking vivid detail. What does the highest plane of you look like?"

I try to imagine myself as Colin saw me on our first date at that East Village bar. I was wearing the same boots and denim jacket, but instead of the slip dress, I had a white halter top and a black miniskirt, and I felt cute in a bookish sort of way, my hair clipped up with my bangs falling around my face. As I was walking from the train to the bar, though, I was hit with a sudden wave of self-consciousness, wondering if I should have let my hair down, if guys like that more, and then I felt awful for even thinking that, because why should I dress for anyone but myself? But as soon as I met Colin, I knew it didn't matter.

Because when he looked at me with that goofy, wide grin, I knew he wasn't just Colin, twenty-four, software engineer, looking for a long-term relationship, into bookstores and old movies—he was someone I could fall in love with. And the way he looked at me, I knew he felt the same thing.

"Now, picture your SP," Zoe says, and she's in my head, because I already am. I like the way it feels, too, thinking of him as my *specific person*. My own. I can see him so clearly, the way he looked at me tonight: Colin, frozen in the glow of the city, that flicker of a smile, one hand on the bar door, the other raised in greeting, caught between where he is and where he's meant to be.

"I want you to picture yourself saying this mantra to them: I am loved, I am whole, and I release you. Breathe in deep. Release. Now, say it with me. I am loved."

Colin gently tucking my hair behind my ear, the look in his eyes just before he kissed me.

"I am loved," I echo quietly.

"I am whole."

Colin's chest pressed against mine, heartbeat thudding, too warm in the sheets but neither of us caring.

"I am whole."

"Now, picture them walking away," Zoe says softly. "And let yourself feel that feeling of wholeness, filling up your chest with all that energy you gave them before. Feel it filling you up like a bright white light. And tell them, right now: I release you."

Colin leaving that bar, his thoughts all tangled up with me.

"I release you."

"One more breath in. And . . . release."

When I breathe out, I'm shocked to feel tears, warm and silent on my cheeks.

"Good," Zoe says. "Now, open your eyes."

When I do, I feel reborn, somehow. The bland cream color of my walls has a new brightness, my sheets a new softness on my skin.

"Now, don't forget to leave me a comment when this method works for you. Believe me, it'll happen sooner than you think."

I wipe my cheeks, sitting upright with a sudden bubble of laughter as the video restarts.

"Want to know the secret to making him obsessed?"

I pause it again, looking at Zoe's frozen face. Her full, glossy lips, a constellation of little moles on the cheek that dimples when she smiles. Not even two hours ago, I was so jealous of this girl, the way Colin looked at her. I don't know what I believe about fate, but I can't shake the ridiculous feeling that this video was meant for me. Zoe, reaching through the noise of social media to tell me that I'm not wrong, that what I felt tonight was real. That Colin felt it, too.

With a stupid grin on my face, I click "follow" on Zoe's profile. Just as I do, a new notification lights up my screen, and for a split second, I think it's really worked, that it's him—but then reading comprehension kicks in. It's a dating app message from Axel.

Thanks for ditching, bitch

I bet your plays suck

I laugh as I unmatch him. He'll understand one day, when he's found something like I have.

I set my phone face-down and open my laptop, safe in the certainty of Zoe's mantra: I am loved, I am whole, and I've released him. The unspoken promise beneath it: and so he will come back.

3

By morning, I still haven't heard from Colin, but I tell myself to be patient. He's always been someone who thinks things through with care, trying to see every angle before he makes a conclusion.

On our second date, we went to the Met. It's pay-what-you-wish for New York residents, and Colin gave them twenty dollars—maybe to impress me, I know, but he said the number quietly, almost bashfully, like he was embarrassed to care about the greater good. As we went through the museum, he strolled between the pieces with his hands clasped behind his back like an old British man watching for birds. It made me nervous at first, how slowly we were moving, but I grew to love it, watching the little divot that formed between his eyebrows when he was thinking. Seeking to understand.

After the museum, we stopped into an indie bookshop, and I caught him looking at me that same way as I browsed the stacks.

What? I'd asked him.

Nothing, he'd said, with a smile as soft as a hand brushing the nape of my neck. *I like the way you look at words.*

Now, still curled in bed at eleven A.M., the memory feels like a hot spoon dipped into the cold mush of my insides, emptying them until they're hollow. I know this is pathetic, that I can't just lie here and wait for him to text me all day.

So instead, I do my research on Zoe Ember.

As it turns out, I was only sort of wrong when I guessed she's in marketing. Not only is she a TikTok spiritual micro-influencer, but she's also, apparently, an artist. Her work is mixed media: paintings, collage, photography, and the combination of all three. She seems to be fairly successful at it, judging from her Instagram, where she also has a small following of around ten thousand. Like TikTok, her full name is listed as Zoe Ember, so even if it's fake, she's sticking to it.

I scroll until I get to the first piece of hers that actually draws me in: a self-portrait. Zoe is photographed in water somewhere, almost entirely submerged except for her face, her chin pointing up with her lips slightly parted, rivulets of water running down her cheeks like tears as she looks dead into the camera. On the surface of the photo paper, she's surrounded herself in a menagerie of flowers—painted, drawn, three-dimensionally crafted from tissue. The effect is breathtaking.

It's also an obvious homage to John Everett Millais's *Ophelia*, and suddenly, I hate it. I hate that Zoe also feels drawn to Shakespeare's mad girl with her poems and her flowers, so misunderstood and so silenced, and I know that I hardly own Ophelia, but it feels wrong, too, like Zoe is in my head.

I scroll back to the top of her page, where the rainbow glow around her profile photo indicates a story I haven't watched yet. Unlike my TikTok, my Instagram bears my actual name—a tithe I must offer up to the church of The Theatre, where, according to my former NYU professors, playwrights are no longer allowed to be modest misanthropes; they must also, like our actors, be public brands. If I watch Zoe's story with this account, she'll see it. Zoe strikes me as the type of person who scrolls through her story views, basking in the recognition of her acolytes.

But then another thought crosses my mind: I *like* the idea of Zoe seeing my name there. It sends a little shiver up my spine, wondering if it will mean anything to her, if Colin's mentioned me yet. If, when he inevitably breaks things off, he'll be honest and tell her why, or if he'll hide the truth to spare her feelings.

I click on the story. It's a video of an empty gallery somewhere, posted about an hour ago. *Temporary new home*, she wrote over it. She tagged the gallery, too: FOCAL in Williamsburg—in all caps, for whatever reason. I open their page to find they have fifteen thousand followers. Not huge, by any means, but it's a number that feels trendy, just on the verge of blowing up but not too mainstream yet. And, according to a pinned post, they're hosting an exhibition of Zoe's work later this month, part of their series of up-and-coming local artists.

Suddenly, Zoe's art takes on a new sheen—not just TikTok trendy, but legitimate. *Up-and-coming.*

There's a second story, more recent, so I click to view it. It's a photo of a coffee cup on a cafe table, arranged so the real purpose of this photo is clear: the man on the other side, shown only from the neck down.

My heart nearly stops. He has one arm propped on the table, so his corduroy jacket sleeve rides up to reveal the freckles on his arms, the mole right in the center of his hand—one I used to trace with my thumb, feeling the little bump with the pad of my finger.

Colin.

A pit opens in my stomach, gaping until it's wide enough to be a black hole, to suck my whole room into the darkness.

Zoe is soft-launching Colin on her Instagram story, and what I saw last night was definitely not a first date. They're *together.*

Something like a growl or a scream catches in my throat, sharp-edged and animal. I press one fist to my mouth to keep it in, feeling, suddenly, a new urge to laugh at the tragic comedy of it all: Zoe has seen Colin twice in two days, already one-third of our six dates together. Six of the best dates of my life, dates that felt like the beginning of something epic and irreversible.

I stare at the screen, and a new detail emerges. The logo on the coffee cup is visible. I google the name, and sure enough, there's a Williamsburg location within walking distance of Zoe's gallery. According to my maps app, it will take me fifty minutes to get there on the train—long enough that it might be a lost cause, if I didn't know Colin and his adorable propensity for long dates, one coffee melting into another until we realize three hours have passed without us knowing, lost as we were in our favorite songs and movies and each other.

I don't know what, exactly, I'm planning as I kick off the covers and throw myself into a presentable outfit. I'll deal with that on the train. For now, I focus on brushing my teeth and making sure my hair looks decent. I grab my tote bag, which I don't fill with anything besides my lip gloss, keys, and wire earbuds, but it feels like a crutch, a weighted blanket of an excuse to explain why I'm in Brooklyn on a Saturday morning. *Running an errand*, I think. *Meeting a friend.*

As I scramble out the door and to the rickety time bomb that passes for an elevator in my building, it occurs to me that I am not following Zoe's advice. Chasing Colin down on a coffee date is hardly *taking him off the pedestal*, but nothing makes sense anymore. Two and a half months after Colin dumped me because he wasn't ready for something serious, he's sitting in Williamsburg with Zoe Ember, who is most likely his girlfriend.

I don't want to take him off the pedestal. I want to destroy it, grind it into dust.

On the subway ride downtown, I squeeze every second out of the spotty underground internet connection to build my arsenal of knowledge about Zoe. She's from Greenwich, Connecticut. She went to Pratt, no doubt financed by the wealthy parents you must have in order to be from Greenwich, Connecticut.

I learn both of these things from her bio on the FOCAL gallery's website. For someone so online, it's surprisingly hard to find anything else about Zoe's early life. She doesn't seem to have a LinkedIn, Facebook, or Twitter profile—apparently, her preferred style of social media is purely aesthetic. When I google her name and Pratt together, there are a handful of hits: student shows she was a part of, little mentions on some student blogs. She's also credited there as Zoe Ember, which doesn't assuage my suspicions that it's some kind of stage name—it only makes it more likely, like this new persona is one she took on the moment she set foot in Brooklyn, a Zoe that sprouted from the Pratt campus, photosynthesizing in the glow of art and pretension. I can see right through her.

Maybe because I did the same thing.

Not turning myself into an art girl influencer, obviously, but using New York to reinvent myself. I'm intimately familiar with the old cliché, how this is the perfect place to become someone new, but if you ask me, that fact has nothing to do with this being the "city of dreams," or *concrete jungle wet dream tomato*, whatever the hell the kids are saying these days. It's because it's big, and no one asks questions, at least not the right ones. It's as easy to slip into a new life as it is to push through the subway turnstile: mechanical. Mundane.

The exit stairs spit me onto Bedford Avenue, the cool air welcome against the anxious blush that's worked its way under my skin. The cafe is a four-minute walk from here. I'll use it to try to calm down, to seem like I have a reason to be here.

I *do* have a reason to be here, I tell myself, as it calcifies in my mind: Colin is making a huge mistake. Screw Zoe and her pedestal theory. He needs to see me, to remember the way he feels about me, that chemical response in his body enough to let him know that he was wrong. It's not that he wasn't ready for something serious with me. He was, he wanted it, and that made him afraid.

I walk to the coffee shop with the buzzing nerves of a first date. When I'm a block away, I check my reflection in my selfie camera, then slip my earbuds in and open my playlist, going straight to "Crash into Me." The gentle thrum of guitars fills my ears, and I take a deep breath in and out.

I am loved, I am whole, and I release you.

I push through the coffee shop door.

What's essential here is that he sees me first. I can't look like I planned this—it has to be serendipitous, a second unplanned run-in in two days that maybe, *hopefully* is enough to feel like a sign. As I step into line, I force myself not to look for him, instead smiling down at my phone like I just got the sort of text that will maybe, *hopefully* make Colin jealous.

The line moves, and I glance up at the menu. No prices listed, which means this is definitely going to humble both my ego and my wallet. Still, I feel a fizz of hope so strong I don't think I actually need caffeine. I step up to the counter and order a chamomile tea. Six dollars—for a *small*—but I guess it's worth it for what this is going to do. I even tip a whole dollar on the iPad the cashier turns my way, her face blank and gaunt in a way that suggests either an aspiring model, anarchist, or both, and I give her a genuine smile.

And now, I know it's time. I step to the side to wait for my order, heart fluttering and palms going hot and slick with anticipation, and then—

"Jane?"

I recognize the voice, warm and feminine. Not Colin's.

Fighting to keep my hand steady, I pluck out an earbud and turn around.

Zoe Ember smiles at me from an empty table. Colin is nowhere in sight. For half a second, I'm frozen, trying to process the sight in front of me. I knew she was here, obviously, but I wasn't expecting this order of events.

I wasn't expecting her to know my name.

"I'm Zoe," she says, putting a hand to her chest. "You were at the bar last night, right?"

My brain is a rapid-fire assault of questions. Why does she know my name? What has Colin told her about me? How is she so confident, not uttering even one automatic *sorry* like the one I can already feel rushing to my lips, an instinctual apology for being a woman who takes up space?

"Sorry," I blurt. "Yeah, hi."

My tea appears on the counter, and I take it, wishing it weren't so warm against my palm.

"Want to come sit?" Zoe asks. "Colin's in the bathroom."

A perfectly logical explanation for his mysterious disappearance. My brain returns to a somewhat normal pace. I sit across from her, conscious of the fact that Colin was here only moments before, his soft sweater brushing the back of the chair.

"I wanted to say hi the other night, but you looked busy." Zoe's eyes sparkle, but it's mischief, not malice. "That guy was cute, by the way."

I laugh, and I hate the way my cheeks heat, no doubt red, proof to Zoe that she has power over me, that she can call Axel *cute* because she's in a secure relationship and would obviously never leave it for an Axel if given the choice. Mercifully, Zoe ignores my humiliation as she swishes her coffee cup, wine-colored nails bright against the cardboard.

"But this is actually perfect," she says. "I'm dying to hear all about what Colin was like in college while he's not here to yell at me for prying."

If my face was already red, the color must drain immediately. There are two things about that sentence that make absolutely no sense. First, Colin doesn't *yell*, even a little, but Zoe seems like a friend to hyperbole. Second, and more importantly, Colin went to Penn. I went to NYU.

Before I can scrounge up an answer, Zoe's eyes lift. Like always, I feel him before I see him. His presence is like an accidental brush of a hand, warm and shocking and standing my hair on end, my skin twenty times more aware of the touch once it's absent again.

"Saved by the bell," Zoe croons.

I turn my head, and there he is. Colin, in his corduroy jacket and the glasses I love so much, one honey-brown curl falling onto his forehead as he stares at me, only this time without the gentle smile from last night. This time, it's pure, vacant shock.

"Hey," he says, cheeks burning pink. It's something we have in common, our pale skin prone to blushing. "What's up?"

"Sorry," I say again—I hate the way I can't stop apologizing—as I stand up. "Didn't mean to steal your chair."

"No, don't apologize! It's my fault," Zoe explains to Colin. "I summoned her in hopes of getting some wild stories about your Penn days. I was really hoping Jane had seen you doing a keg stand."

Colin looks panicked enough for me to know that this is no misunderstanding: he told Zoe he knows me from Penn. Part of me wants to out him, to blow the lie up in his face so I'm the only one left to pick up the pieces. But the larger part of me will always feel as soft and impressionable as an overripe peach when he looks at me like that, and so I do what I know he needs me to: I lie right back.

"Sorry." I give Zoe a performative shrug. "I've been sworn to secrecy. There may have been blood sacrifice involved."

"You can't argue with blood sacrifice," Colin tells her, his shoulders visibly relaxing.

"The toga parties, however," I add, "are fair game. The blood sacrifice was strictly for the keg stands."

Zoe laughs, and I think it's genuine, but when I glance at Colin, he looks uncomfortable again. Normally, he likes my dry humor, but now . . . *he's embarrassed*, I tell myself. Ashamed to be caught in a lie. Maybe even ashamed that he still finds me funny, that I still have the power to make him blush, when his supposed new girlfriend is sitting right across from him.

Because that's what she is, right? His girlfriend? They haven't said it, and some part of me hopes it's not true, but I know it the way you can sense a shift in the air moments before a shout explodes, the electric charge like a coming summer storm. This is not the way this was supposed to go. Any sense of the script I was writing for myself has dissipated now, as Colin looks at me like I've forgotten my next line.

"I should have said hi last night, too," I say, just to fill the silence. "But you know . . ."

"Oh, a hundred percent." Zoe grins, a dimple carving into her cheek. "I'd have been distracted, too."

Colin's face gets redder, and it scratches my little playwright itch. *There.* Things are going back on script now, characters behaving the way they should: Colin jealous of me and my date, realizing how much he misses me, how much of a mistake he's made.

So, it's time for my exit. If there's one thing I know about crafting a good scene, it's not to let it overstay its welcome.

And then, a stroke of genius.

"Speaking of which . . ." I glance down at my phone as if at a text from my hot, mysterious date, whom I'm also seeing for the second time in two days. "I actually have to run. But it was so nice to officially meet you, Zoe." I meet Colin's eyes. "And good to see you again. So random."

"Yeah," Colin says, his stare burning into my skin like a brand. "Good to see you."

He gives me the same sheepish smile he wore last night, and I try to find the subtext behind it, to catch a spark of what I saw there before.

"We'll see you on Friday, though, right?" Zoe asks, glancing at Colin.

I short-circuit.

"My birthday," Colin says, like he's reminding me. Like he's already invited me, because I'm his *friend from Penn*. "But seriously, no big deal if you can't make it."

His birthday. Nearly two months together, and I never knew his birthday. But that doesn't really matter in the grand scheme of things. He didn't know mine, either, or that it's just a week after his. We had more important things to talk about.

"You know how he is about birthdays." Zoe gives me a conspiratorial look, like we share him, like he's hers to know, too. As if to prove it, she reaches for his hand and squeezes it. "But twenty-five *is* a big deal! A quarter of a century deserves some celebration, right?"

I smile, trying not to betray the churning in my gut, a thrilling mix of excitement and dread. "Of course. Remind me what time it is?"

Colin pulls a hand through his hair, shy again. "Eight. My place."

"Right," I say. "See you guys there." I shoot Colin another glance. "Get your keg stand ready."

And then, I walk away without looking back.

I've always hated people who say love will find you when you aren't looking for it. It's almost always people in relationships who say that, especially the ones who were fortunate enough to meet organically, who've never had to rely on the algorithm and a prayer that their soulmate will appear in a sea of Axels. Tonight, though, it feels true. Because when I finally set my phone aside to finish editing a scene, disappearing into my own words for the first time all week, the text comes. Colin's name on my screen again, where it belongs.

Hey sorry if that was weird earlier, I didn't mean to lie. Zoe asked who you were when we saw you last night and it kind of just slipped out. I can explain it to her if you want me to. Hope you're doing well

And then, two minutes later—two full minutes of thinking about me, typing and deleting:

You really don't have to come to the birthday thing

I hold my phone close to my face, grinning as I bathe in the blue glow. Because now, I'm certain of why Colin lied. It wasn't because he's embarrassed of me, or because I'm not important enough to register as anything more than a friend. It's because he's still afraid of what he feels for me. Because he didn't know how to tell her.

I place my phone face-down on my nightstand, deciding not to reply until the morning—or maybe I won't reply at all. Suddenly, I have all the time in the world.

4

Friday is ages away, and then, without warning, it's here. I'm giddy all day, even through the drudgery of work: editing the essay drafts fed to me by my company, trying not to crush the hopes of students or the parents bent on micromanaging their way into the lower-tier Ivy of their dreams. I even feel a burst of genuine enthusiasm in my virtual coaching session, where I convince the student that we can find a more compelling subject than the mission trip to Africa (country unspecified) that helped her recognize her privilege as a white girl from New Hampshire.

On every break, I consider texting Colin to let him know I'm coming, but I decide against it each time. I still haven't responded to his text from Saturday, and I like the feeling of power it gives me, like I've stowed a pearl in my pocket for safekeeping, a piece of chocolate to save for when I'll enjoy it most.

I'm so serene, in fact, that it hardly bothers me when I see Zoe's latest Instagram story: another soft-launch picture of Colin's hands around a coffee mug, a plate of pancakes in front of him. *Birthday boy brunch*, the caption says.

Colin hates brunch—it's one of the things we bonded over on

our first date—but this post doesn't even make me angry. It's clarity, bright and gleaming: Zoe is beautiful and friendly and maybe even a talented artist, but she's completely, cosmically wrong for him, and tonight, I have to make him see that.

I'll think of it as a birthday gift.

I wait until 7:30 to begin my long trek down to the East Village, not wanting to be rudely late but still hoping to make him wait for me, wonder if I'll be there. I arrive at a perfect 8:35, pausing outside of his building to take it in.

I've never been inside Colin's apartment. I only know where it is because, after our first date, we passed the building as he was walking me back to the train, and he pointed it out. Unlike Axel, he didn't try to lure me inside. We didn't even kiss that night, though I wanted to from practically the first five minutes I knew him. I never feel that way about anyone I meet online—or in person, really. There's something fundamentally unsexy about dating apps, an inexplicable *ick* at the thought of a man picking out his photos, typing out his prompts, boiling down his whole existence to things like *I'm overly competitive about? Everything* and *The best way to get to know me? Just ask.*

Colin was different. Most of the men who like my profile go for a weak pickup line, an even weaker *hey*, or, worst of all, a string of emojis to decode like vulgar hieroglyphs. The first message Colin ever sent me was a response to my prompt about the Oxford comma: *I, too, am a fan—but more importantly, how do you feel about the em dash?*

One line, and I was hooked, even before I saw the rest of his profile. His answers were intentional—*I'm looking for someone who makes fall in New York feel like a Nora Ephron movie*—but also funny—*(and won't tell anyone if I cry watching one.)* He wasn't trying to show off, either. There were no gym pics or thirst traps, only photos full of sweet smiles and natural light, clearly taken by friends, plus one adorably ridiculous selfie with a dachshund I later learned was his older sister's.

Taking it all in, I felt a pluck on some string tying us together, vibrating at an unfamiliar and thrilling frequency that only intensified when I met him in person. I *wanted* him.

Still, it wasn't until our fourth date that we went back to my apartment. We ordered in, watched a movie, and then made out in my bed like teenagers, like that was all we needed. And for the night, it was. I could feel us both reining ourselves in, conscious of how special this was, a precious new thing that we had to handle with care.

We didn't have sex until after our sixth date. I think we both knew that we couldn't wait any longer, that it had to happen.

That night, as he slept in my bed, I stayed awake, wired, watching his chest rise and fall, the stray curl on his forehead shifting with his breath. *He's so beautiful*, I remember thinking, in a way I'd never thought the word before. *He's beautiful, and I'm so fucked.* Because I knew that he could break me if he wanted to.

The next morning, when we woke up together, he seemed distant. Strange. I brushed it off, telling myself he just wasn't a morning person. He'd already told me that on our third date—another thing we share. He rushed home, citing plans with his friends, and I liked that, the fact that he's a guy with friends. That he was busy, and that I felt secure enough not to be jealous.

I didn't worry until a full day had passed without him reaching out. We'd been texting regularly, but not suffocatingly—little check-ins throughout the day so we knew we were thinking about each other. Earlier that afternoon, I'd asked him how his day was going, and he'd never responded. By the second day, I was nearly sick with panic. I sent another text, a picture of a subway dog that looked only vaguely like his sister's dachshund, mostly a ploy to remind Colin that he'd forgotten to respond. For eight more hours, I got nothing.

Then, he sent the text that broke me.

I watched it whoosh onto my screen, and just before I fell apart, I thought, with a strange sense of vindication, that I was right. He could break me, and he did. I just didn't think it would happen so quickly.

Now, looking at his building, I try to push those thoughts away, focus on our future.

I'm surprised we never came back here. It's clearly a nicer place than mine. Colin lives on East 7th, on the sort of block that makes me wonder why he ever needed to look further than his front door for that Nora Ephron fall—because Meg Ryan would already feel at home here, with the brick townhouses pressed snugly against each other in warm autumn colors. Colin's building is a classic terra-cotta shade, with a small set of steps leading up to its stone base, where a column arc frames the doorway. He must be paying at least two thousand a month for it, if not more, but that's the kind of thing you can afford to do with a tech salary, I guess.

As I climb the steps, brown leaves crunch under my boots—a picture-perfect snapshot of autumn in New York, the season of re-birth in death. I pause to check my reflection in the glass of the front door. I look good, I think. I went with a cropped sweater, black boot-cut jeans, and my denim jacket, hoping to emulate some of Zoe's coolness but with my own literary bent. I gave my hair a loose ironed wave, which I'm regretting now, wondering if it might read as me trying to copy Zoe's natural curls. But my bangs are falling nicely, my hair is somehow shinier than its usual limp light brown, and it's too late to worry about it now. Taking a deep breath, I adjust the six-pack of IPAs under my arm and press the buzzer.

The door rumbles, beckoning me inside.

Colin's building is a walk-up, and I take my time climbing the stairs to the third floor, trying to settle my adrenaline as it hums like the buzz of the door in my rib cage. When I get there, I give myself one last moment to collect myself, and little pinpricks of doubt break through my excitement. Colin said he would tell Zoe the truth about us if I wanted him to. He might have even told her already. Is that what I'm walking into?

But even that thought is thrilling, in its own way, because the lie is another thing tying Colin and me together, something that's *ours*. Besides, I doubt he told her. On the flip side of Colin's gentleness is a distinct aversion to conflict—part of why he ended things when his feelings got too intense, I'm assuming. No, I know. Because I *know* him, and tonight, I have to prove it.

I knock on the door.

When it swings open, Zoe stands in the threshold. She looks like a Free People catalogue in this tiny tie-front sweater that's barely a sweater, thin and split down the center like stage curtains to reveal the flat plane of her stomach above her jeans, the sort of trendy low-waist that no one can pull off except, clearly, Zoe Ember.

"You came!" She grins, pulling me into a tight hug, and, of course, she smells amazing, like a pink fluffy cloud.

"Hey," I say into her armpit.

When Zoe releases me, I understand two things: this party is a lot smaller than I was anticipating, and Colin is not happy to see me. He's sitting in the cozy living room with three guys I don't recognize, a look of utter surprise on his face—one that doesn't melt into relief or excitement or even nerves. Instead, in the split second after he sees me, it fades into confusion.

Swallowing my mortification, I give him a wave. "Happy birthday." I hold up the six-pack, grateful to have something in my hands. "I brought these."

Colin's eyes flicker to the IPAs, his favorite brand, but instead of looking flattered that I remembered, that I *pay attention* to what he likes and doesn't like, he glances at Zoe, cheeks turning pink.

"Thanks," he says. "That's awesome. But, um . . . I've kind of been on a break from drinking."

I clench my teeth to hide my surprise. Zoe gives me a sympathetic smile, and instantly, I know that this is her doing.

"We've been doing it together," she explains. "I saw this documentary about how bad it is for you, and I've been off it ever since then. Colin's sweet to do it with me."

If I have to hear Zoe talk about him in the context of *doing it* one more time, I am going to throw an IPA at the wall, but instead, I nod understandingly.

"Yeah, of course," I say, with a tone I hope conveys that I'm not the alcoholic Zoe probably thinks I am. "Sorry, I didn't know."

"Oh my god, no worries at all." Zoe takes the six-pack with a smile that still feels completely genuine, which makes me hate myself for being so angry at her. She sets it on the dining table, right next to a pack of nonalcoholic beer. "We haven't even been doing it that long. What has it been, babe—a month?"

She looks to Colin for confirmation, and a little fire starts to lick at my insides, burning away at my stomach lining. *Babe.* That's new. I wonder if she's putting on a show, and for whom—me? Colin's friends?

In the part of my brain that isn't latched onto the *babe*, I'm doing the math: a month. They've been together for at least a month, probably more. Colin ended things with me the last week of August. At best, that leaves a month, maybe a little more, before he met Zoe. I'd already guessed as much, but hearing it out loud is like hot coals pressed to my skin.

One of Colin's friends gets up from the couch and walks over to the table. He's white and stocky, maybe five-ten, with sandy hair, a scruffy beard, and a button-down-over-a-T-shirt look that screams *the funny friend*.

"I, however," he announces, grabbing one of the IPAs I brought, "am not on a break from drinking. And these are my favorite." He lifts the can to me in a toast with a goofy smile. "Excellent taste, mysterious friend of Zoe's."

I'm hardly a *friend of Zoe's,* and I think I hate this man, whoever he is, even if he's clearly trying to make me feel better.

"Her name is Jane," Zoe says. "And, while I find her effortlessly cool and am aspiring to become her friend, she actually knows Colin from college."

There it is again, the lie. But clearly, none of these guys went to Penn, either, because no one calls Colin on it.

"Ben," the IPA guy introduces himself. "Colin's roommate. Want one?"

He holds up an IPA for me. I hate IPAs, but out of spite, I want to ensure that every last one of these is consumed.

"Hit me," I say, and he tosses it over.

"Hand-eye coordination." Ben eyes Colin with a teasing expression. "Good sign. Clearly, none of that rubbed off on the birthday boy."

I laugh, sinking briefly into the version of this night where I'm Colin's girlfriend and Ben is my boyfriend's roommate, and he likes me, approves of me, as we share this joke together. Colin is, famously, a bit of a klutz—it always endeared him to me, the way he'd fumble his keys or trip halfway up the stairs. He needs someone there to steady him, to catch things when they fall. I wonder if Zoe does that, if she's better at it than I was.

"Wait, we should introduce everyone else," she says. "Jane, this is Peter." Zoe points to a short, skinny white guy with stick-straight brown hair and an ill-advised mustache. "Colin's friend from work. And this is Sam, Colin's friend from home." She gestures at a tall, handsome South Asian guy who looks like he came straight from his finance job—which he probably did, I guess, because the finance industry seems to look down upon plebeian concepts like the standard work week. "Some more people are coming by later, but for now, this is the crew. So, go ahead, make yourself comfortable. We have snacks and stuff in the kitchen."

Zoe slips into the spot between Colin and Sam on the couch, leaning into the crook of his arm, and I hate the way she's carrying herself—like a hostess, like she's in charge of this. She probably *did* plan it, but I don't like how she's flaunting it, like she wants to prove to Colin that she's perfect just because she remembered two whole names and offered me a snack.

Or maybe she *is* perfect, and I'm choking on my own internalized misogyny.

I sit cross-legged on the floor and crack open my can, determined to focus on the party and not my own burning jealousy.

"So, you went to Penn?" Sam asks, and I detect a hint of skepticism in his voice. "I don't think Colin ever mentioned you. Were you computer science, too?"

Okay, maybe more than a hint.

"No," Colin answers for me. "Jane was in theatre. We were in the same dorm, though."

Maybe I like this game we're playing, this conspiracy between us, as much as it makes my blood boil.

"Are you an actor?" Peter asks me. He gives it same connotation you'd probably give to *convicted felon*, and instantly, I'm enjoying it less.

"Playwright," I say, glancing at Colin. I wonder if he notices the absence of the *but*.

"Oh, cool," Ben interjects. "I do standup."

As if those are even in the same category of thing.

"Cool," I echo, going for genuine. "I could never do standup. I'm definitely a behind-the-scenes kind of girl."

"A behind-the-scenes girl with killer taste in beverages," Ben says, with an almost-shy smile, and oh no. I understand where this is going. "What kind of stuff do you write? Anything I would have seen?"

He's flirting with me—bold, seeing as though I've barely been here five minutes—and he doesn't know it, but he's just asked me my least favorite question in the world. But I won't let him know that. Because actually, I think, glancing at Colin and his unreadable expression, this could be good. It'll prove to him how much I've moved on.

"Nothing major yet," I say, tucking my hair behind my ear. "Just a couple readings." And then, an idea: "I'm working on something right now, though. It's sort of a retelling of *Hamlet* but focused on Ophelia."

I don't look at Zoe when I say it, but I get a little thrill, like I just admitted that I Instagram-stalked her, even if she can't possibly know that. She takes the bait.

"Oh, no way! I'm obsessed with *Hamlet*," Zoe says. "I've always thought Ophelia was the most interesting character, too. I actually did a series of self-portraits inspired by her last year."

"That's awesome." I mirror her excited posture, leaning my weight forward, elbows on my knees. "You're an artist?"

"Yeah," Zoe says, without a trace of my hair-tucking deference. Like it's simple. Like she's never even thought of introducing herself as an *artist, but.* And just like at the coffee shop, her confidence is magnetic.

"An incredible one," Colin says, tugging gently on one of her curls. "Her stuff is amazing."

All the hope I felt only moments ago shrivels up and wilts like petals submerged. I try my best to hide it behind an interested look at Zoe.

"Okay, so, Colin and I obviously haven't had a chance to catch up in a while, or I'd have known not to bring these," I tease, with a little lift of my IPA. "So, I'm dying to know. How did y'all meet?"

It's bold of me. I watch the question settle onto Colin's face, turning his lips into a hard line. Too bold, maybe, but I don't regret it, if only because it wiped his stupid smile away.

Zoe threads her fingers through his, and I want to chop off both their hands at the wrist, like one of those ancient societies that doled out punishments cruelly on the nose for their crimes.

"I'm always joking that we should come up with some sort of romantic story," she says, giving him a knowing look. "Like we locked eyes on the train or reached for the same avocado at Trader Joe's. But really, it was just on the apps." She rolls her eyes a little. "The epitome of modern romance."

I watch Colin's face for any sign of guilt, any acknowledgment of his hypocrisy, and I think I catch a glimmer of it as his eyes meet mine before he reaches for his nonalcoholic beer.

"Honestly, just finding a decent person on the apps sounds romantic," I say, watching Colin take a sip. "It's a cesspool out there."

"Amen to that." Ben lifts his IPA.

"You met *someone*, though," Zoe says, with a mischievous twinkle in her eyes, and it takes me a moment to realize she means Axel.

"Right." My ears heat, and I hope it comes off as shyness instead of me getting caught in a lie. I make a face. "I don't know. I'm not exactly hearing wedding bells there yet. But seriously, you're lucky," I tell Zoe as I glance at Colin, bold again. "You found a good one."

Colin meets my eyes for just a second. Then, he stands quickly.

"We should bring some of the food in here, yeah? Want to help me out, Zo?"

Zo. It's not *babe*, but it's a nickname. He never gave me a nickname. Jane isn't even really a name you can diminish, unless you call me Janie, which I'll never let anyone do, ever.

"Sure." She jumps up to follow him. "Wait, oh my god, I totally forgot we got stuff for a cheese board! I'll put that together, too." She points to the rest of us with a devious look in her eye. "Prepare your taste buds. We're about to *feast*."

They disappear down the hall and into the kitchen, and a feverish heat creeps across my chest, under my arms. I made Colin uncomfortable again. It's not something I wanted to do, and it feels like both a victory and a loss.

And now, I'm alone with the Three Stooges. Sam and Peter get chatting about some inane football thing, and, feeling Ben's attention back on me, I brace myself.

"So, where are you from?" he asks.

Another least favorite question of mine, but it's not Ben's fault he's two for two.

"I clocked a 'y'all' earlier," he adds. "I'm guessing somewhere in the South?"

My irritation morphs into a cold splash of dread. He's right. I said *y'all*, didn't I? *Shit*. I've spent years rehearsing any trace of an accent, of my past, out of my voice—too long to mess up like this so easily, without even noticing.

"We moved around a bit," I say quickly. "Nowhere exciting, though. What about you?"

Despite my slip-up, my usual tactic—deflection—works. It always does.

"New Jersey," Ben says. "Which I guarantee is even less exciting than anywhere you've been."

I can tell he's hoping for a laugh, so I toss him one.

"I don't know, it's pretty tough competition," I joke. "Did you grow up near Colin, then?"

"Yeah. Me, Sam, and Colin all grew up in Bergen County. We went to high school together. And then I became the semi-employed comedian in a group that also includes a software engineer and a financial analyst, so my parents are pretty stoked about how things turned out."

I glance toward the kitchen. No sign of Colin and Zoe. How long does it take to put a cheese board together?

"That's super cool that you're a playwright, though," Ben continues, clearly sensing my lapse in attention. "How'd you get into that?"

There's a question I don't hate, mostly because I can answer it honestly.

"I always liked reading plays more than books," I say. "They just feel so much more immediate, I guess. You know, reading something that was designed to be brought to life."

Usually, that's enough to put guys half to sleep, little more response than a noncommittal *Oh, cool.* When I first explained it to Colin, though, he didn't leave it there. He asked follow-up questions, like he wanted to get inside my brain and look around.

"Oh, cool," Ben says, right on cue. "How'd you go from reading them to writing them? Like, what made you decide to do it for real?"

Fascinating. I wasn't expecting this much genuine interest from Ben. So, I do something else unexpected: I give him a real answer.

"Writing is the only thing I've ever really been good at. And writing a play, you get to be in a bunch of different characters' heads at once. Like having an argument with yourself. I was alone a lot as a kid, so a play felt like a good way to—I don't know, work through all the thoughts in my head on my own, I guess. To make them make sense."

It's strange to be saying these same words again, almost exactly as I told them to Colin, like a line of practiced dialogue, only with a new scene partner making me more aware of the way it feels in my mouth.

Ben nods emphatically. "I'm the same way with comedy. It helps me work out the dark thoughts. Makes 'em feel less dark."

Oh no. Ben thinks we're really *connecting*, and maybe we are. Maybe that shouldn't be a bad thing, because he's sort of sweet and cute, and there's nothing wrong with him, except for the fact that he's not Colin. I need to switch gears, fast.

And then, emboldened by the loudness of Sam and Peter's conversation, I get an idea.

"So, not to pry," I say, lowering my voice and leaning closer to Ben, "but what do you think about . . . you know?" I glance toward the kitchen. "Obviously, I don't know her all that well yet, but I'm curious."

I keep my tone neutral, light-hearted, like I'm genuinely interested in my *friend* Colin's new relationship.

Ben scratches his neck, averting his eyes. "Yeah, I mean, they seem great."

He glances over his shoulder, and I sense a *but*, one that I want to rip out of him with my bare hands.

"I don't know," he says. "It just seems a little . . . quick, is all."

"What does?" Peter interjects, apparently forgetting about football. He looks toward the kitchen with a look that says, *Them?*

My heart starts to pound, and I wonder if they'll hear us from the kitchen, if they're about to stroll in to catch us red-handed, so Colin will think I'm some kind of toxic gossip corrupting his friends.

Ben winces. "Maybe we shouldn't, you know . . ."

"What *I* think," Peter says, leaning forward, "is that it's weird."

"Dude." Sam hides a surprised laugh with his fist, eyes darting toward the hallway. "Come on."

"Sorry, but you know I'm right," Peter says, and I get the impression that he often likes to play devil's advocate on Reddit. "They made things official, like, three weeks in. That's some *Single White Female* shit."

"That's not what that movie's about, bro," Sam says.

"Still." Peter holds up his hands, leaning back into the couch cushions. "Point stands."

Hope shudders through me, replacing any guilt I feel about prying. Maybe it should sting that Peter just confirmed that they're *official*, but it doesn't—because even Colin's best friends can see that this is all wrong. I take a long sip of my IPA, enjoying the cold fizz of it on my tongue.

"Well, I'm still stoked for this cheese board," Ben says at a normal volume, clearly trying to steer the conversation away from the people who aren't in the room.

And then, like he summoned them, their footsteps thud down the hall again.

"We come bearing snacks!" Zoe announces, appearing with an artfully organized spread of cheese, jam, and crackers. Colin's trailing behind her with a bowl of chips and a jar of salsa. Unless they're both excellent actors, I don't think they overheard us talking.

As they set the snacks down on the table, I search for clues in Colin's face, proof that whatever just happened in the kitchen was less about cheese and more about *me*, but he won't meet my eyes.

Still, I can't shake the hope that's started to settle inside my chest like the first snow of the year, soft and light. Colin's friends don't think he and Zoe are right together, and I know how important they are to him, which can only mean one thing: Zoe's days are numbered, even if she *does* put together an immaculate cheese board.

"Wait, before we dig in, I need to be the most annoying person in the world," Zoe says, holding her phone over the spread and snapping photos.

I fight the urge to roll my eyes. Of *course* she's a phone-eats-first kind of person.

"Okay," she says, satisfied. "Now, one more with Colin and everyone. You guys get together. Come on, I know you hate it, but you all look so cute."

We all squeeze together in Zoe's frame, me perching on the arm of the couch right beside Colin, close enough that I could reach out and touch him. But I won't, not yet. He needs time, and now that I know it's only a matter of it, I'm willing to be patient. I smile into the flash.

When Zoe's done with pictures, I reach for the cheese knife and cut off a slice of Brie, laying it on a cracker with a spread of fig jam. I place it all on my tongue, so salty and sweet and rich that I'm tempted to swallow it whole.

5

The party wears on, metastasizing: by a quarter to ten, the guest list has doubled, some more of Colin's work friends and buddies from his rock-climbing gym joining the fray. Still no one from Penn, which Colin and I should both be grateful for, but now, the number of people is awkward—too small for me not to feel like an interloper, but big enough that I'm starting to fade into the background.

Even Ben has lost interest, at least for the time being. He, Colin, and the climbing boys are deep in a chat about some mutual friend of theirs. Zoe disappeared to the bathroom a few minutes ago, and the energy in this room is becoming distinctly masculine, and not quite in a *divine* way.

I wish Colin would talk to me, look at me, but he doesn't, and I won't beg. I know I've put him in a weird position, being here, and like I said, he needs time. So, I grab a second IPA from the table and crack it open, distracting myself with the details of Colin's living room.

It's more thoughtfully decorated than most twenty-five-year-old boys' living rooms, with framed art prints hanging on the exposed brick: mountain scenes, a poster for the Met. I wonder if that one is Colin's, if he thought of me when he hung it up. There's a bookshelf, too, with a clear divide between Ben's books—graphic novels, memoirs of white male comedians—and Colin's—well-loved copies of Stephen King and Tolkien but also Toni Morrison and Joan Didion, because he's not one of those assholes who only reads white men.

I'm still thumbing through the books, considering what would happen if I just got up and left, when I hear Zoe approaching behind me.

"Hey," she says, squatting down to my level. "Want to go make sure this party passes the Bechdel test?"

I'm surprised at the genuine laugh that bubbles out of me.

"And let the feminists win?" I joke drily.

Zoe grins. "Come on."

She stands, clearly used to people following her, and I'm not exactly eager to hang around in this living room.

"There's a fire escape in Colin's room," Zoe explains as she leads me down the hallway.

A thrill shudders through me as we approach his bedroom door. Part of me doesn't want to see it this way—I'd rather him invite me in on his own, Zoe nowhere a part of that picture—but she's already opening the door, and we're here.

The first thing I notice is that it smells like him. I want to curl up inside that smell like a cozy blanket, like his arms around me. His bed looks soft, with a gray comforter that isn't quite tucked in right, but he made an effort. I fight a smile, because it's just so Colin. All of it—the whole room is tidy, with a faint air of haphazardness, like he cleans it regularly but hasn't quite figured out how to tend to all the details: the socks dangling out of his dresser drawer, the slightly shriveled succulents on his desk.

Zoe is already at the window, wresting it open like she's done this countless times. She probably has. I wonder how often she's slept here, nuzzled against his neck.

Chilly air cuts into the room as Zoe slides one leg out and turns back to face me. "You smoke?"

"Like . . . ?"

"The devil's lettuce. Reefer. Or, in this case . . ." She reaches into her pocket and takes out a vape pen, smirking. "Good ol' cannabis concentrate."

"Sure," I say.

I don't really like weed, to be honest—I don't like much of anything that makes me lose my grip on my own brain, so even two drinks is usually past my threshold—but I'm too intrigued by the opportunity for more insight into Zoe to pass this up.

"I *did* have a cigarette phase for a minute," she says as she climbs out.

"Really?" I ask, following her.

"Cliché, I know." She rolls her eyes. "But in my defense, it was practically a survival mechanism at art school. Sometimes I'll still crave a cigarette when I'm high, but Colin hates it."

My disbelief must be written all over my face, because Zoe quirks an eyebrow and asks, "What?"

And maybe it's the two IPAs I've consumed so far, but I ask her, "Isn't that kind of hypocritical? You know, no alcohol, but rotting your lungs is fine?"

Zoe watches me as she sucks on the pen, and I shouldn't have said that. It was too much, too mean. But then, as she exhales, she smiles.

"You don't bullshit," she says, holding out the pen for me. "I like that."

I take it from her.

"So, tell me everything," Zoe says.

"About Colin?"

"About Jane."

I take a hit, lengthening the exhale just so I don't have to answer. *Minimize, deflect.*

"There's not much to tell," I say, finally.

Zoe gives me a stern look. "I thought you didn't bullshit."

"That's an assumption."

She smiles, and I'm surprised at how unfazed she seems by my prickliness. Like she can see right through it.

"Okay, then tell me about your Ophelia play."

I shrug. "I have a draft, but I don't know if I've really cracked it, I guess."

Zoe's eyes narrow like she's looking at some kind of abstract sculpture, trying to decide if it's art or a sellout.

"Why Ophelia?" she asks.

I'm tempted to take another hit just to fill the space, but I want to keep my wits about me. I pull my knees up to my chest, taking in the city stretched out before us, the warm, glowing windows of the other apartments on Colin's block.

"I always thought *Hamlet* did her dirty," I say. "Or maybe it's the way we read *Hamlet*. Like, we just assume that she went crazy because she lost all the men in her life, but I don't know. I always thought there was a sort of . . . freedom in it. Her madness, I mean." It's possible that this is the fastest-acting vape pen I've ever seen, but now that I've started talking, I can't stop. "And it's sort of a parallel to Hamlet's performance of madness, right? Like, what if Ophelia just looked at court life and said, 'Fuck this. All the men in my life are dead, insane, or in France, so now I'm free to sing songs and pick flowers and do whatever the hell I want, just so you'll all stop trying to force me into a cage.'"

Okay, yeah. I might be higher than I anticipated. But Zoe nods along, digesting my ideas with a studious expression.

"What do you think about her death, then?"

I pull my sleeves over my hands, wishing I'd brought my jacket out with me. The fire escape seems rickety all of a sudden, barely suspending us above the hard revelation of the ground below.

"Isn't that a kind of freedom for her, too?" I ask. "Maybe it was the only way she could really escape."

Realizing I still have the pen, I hand it back to Zoe, and she pockets it, brows furrowed.

"Hmm."

"What?"

"I guess I never really thought of it that way," she says. "A girl shouldn't have to die to be free, right? And I always blamed Hamlet. I know it's meant to be tragic or whatever, but I'm always glad when he dies at the end. Aren't you?"

She turns to me, waiting, and I get the sense that I'm being tested. It gives me an eerie tingle on the back of my neck.

"Yeah," I say honestly. "That asshole deserves it."

Zoe looks back out at the street, satisfied, and the eerie feeling passes. "Like, he gets a pass for being this brilliant, tragic character, but honestly? He's just a dick."

"The biggest dick in all of Denmark," I echo.

Zoe laughs, and I'm surprised, again, to find it catching, making me join in. I'm surprised, really, that I like her.

"So, what's your story, then?" I ask.

Zoe pauses, her tongue moving across her teeth like she's trying to taste the question.

"I moved to New York," she says. "And everything before that is irrelevant."

So I was right—about Zoe reinventing herself, and probably the fake name, too. Still, I wasn't expecting her to admit it so freely. For a moment, I wonder what it would be like to be the kind of person who responds so honestly when someone asks me about myself, instead of trying to skirt around the question or turn it back on them. I don't know if I could.

"What?" Zoe asks.

"Nothing," I say. "Just, you know . . . same."

Zoe lifts the pen. "Cheers to that."

She takes another hit, and something has shifted now, eased enough for me to risk another truth.

"So, I've seen your TikToks."

Zoe winces. "Oh, god."

"Not in a creepy way," I say. "Just, you know. I saw one or two on my For You page."

"Such is the nature of TikTok." She sighs. "Don't get me wrong, I'm not embarrassed by it. It's cool, having a following, even a small one. I've even been able to make some extra cash from one-on-one coaching and some sponsored posts. I guess it's just weird to know that it could be someone's first impression of me. You know, all the woo-woo stuff."

"You think it's woo-woo?" The expression feels weird in my mouth, foreign.

"Isn't it?"

In spite of myself, it stings, thinking of how much I bought into her manifestation technique the other night, how new and hopeful it made me feel.

"Not that it doesn't work," Zoe continues. "I think it does. And I'm definitely helping people. But to a certain extent, everything on social media is a kind of performance art, right? Like, I won't try to convince someone they can manifest themselves out of, you know, cancer or climate disaster. And sometimes . . ." She hesitates, a smirk twitching. "Sometimes, with the collective readings, I'll pick certain cards on purpose. Or at least spin the narrative to whatever I know people need to hear."

"Ah." I lean back against the wall of the building, feeling a mix of embarrassment and vindication. I'd suspected as much. "So, you're giving people false hope, then."

Zoe shrugs. "I think of it more as giving them permission to hope."

It might be a trick of the shadowy light, or maybe the high, but I think something darkens in her expression as she turns to look out at the city.

"I mean, the world is pretty fucked," she continues. "Sometimes, I think we all need that."

"Yeah," I say. "I guess we do."

It hangs between us like vapor, this small understanding floating out and dissipating into the cool night air.

"What's going on out here?"

Colin. This time, his presence is a surprise, unannounced by a spark of knowing on the back of my neck. His tone is casual, easy, but when I turn to find him walking into the bedroom, I think I catch a dash of panic in his eyes.

Good. He has every reason to be worried that I might spill the truth to his new girlfriend.

"Just getting to know my new friend Jane," Zoe says breezily. "I've also decided that I'll be stealing her from you. Hope that's okay."

It gives me a little shudder of warmth, hearing her so boldly proclaim friendship, but I'm not sure if I buy it.

She holds out the pen to Colin. "You want?"

He hesitates, glancing at me, and despite everything, I can't hate him. All I feel, really, is *sad* for him, that he's so afraid to be honest—with Zoe, with me, let alone with himself.

"Yeah," he says, taking the pen. "Sure."

He takes a hit, cradling the pen with both hands like he's worried he might drop it, and it's like my rib cage is crushing in on itself

51

with how badly I want to touch him. How badly I want to screw the cool-girl attitude and kiss him right there, in front of Zoe, throw her own manufactured TikTok prophecy back in her face: *I am loved, I am whole, and he came back.*

But even though Zoe admits to being at least a bit of a fraud, I know she had a point: I have to take Colin off the pedestal. I have to be ready to *receive* him.

So, I get up, pretending to check the time on my phone.

"I think I'm going to head out," I say.

"Oh no!" Zoe frowns, looking actually bummed. "But it's so early."

"Oh, you know . . . places to be, people to see."

I don't know why I said that—it sounded like something a cartoon businessman would say, some facsimile of a real human being, and maybe that's what I am. I crawl through the window, and Colin steps back to let me through. A little part of me deflates, wishing he would have stayed close, that he would have let us brush together.

"Nice talking to you, Zoe," I say, once I'm back in Colin's room. I let my eyes lock with his. "Happy birthday."

"Thanks." He gives me a small smile, and I feel a little rush of hope again. Unless the only thing beneath that smile is relief that I'm leaving.

I am loved, I am whole, and I release you, I think, determined to push that thought away—and it may be bullshit, but it works. I walk through the door and into the hallway without looking back.

But I've barely made it a few steps when Colin's door opens again. He stands there, flushed, and this is it—where he pins me up against the wall, cups my chin, and crashes his mouth into mine, a kiss hard and deep enough to make up for these past two months of denial.

But what he says is, "Why'd you come?"

His face is unreadable, and every part of me that had started to melt hardens again, calcifying into rough armor.

Because I miss you, I think.

Because Zoe is great, but she's all wrong for you, and that's even more clear to me now that I know I don't hate her.

Because it should be me planning your birthday party, tumbling into your bed, kissing you back into the person you were and not this stranger you're trying to force yourself to be.

All I can say is, "Zoe invited me."

Colin nods, swallowing, and I can tell he wants to say something else. I almost want to yell at him to just say it, to stop being so fucking avoidant and tell the truth for once.

"I just—" He stops, pulling a hand through his hair. "I don't know. I didn't think you would."

A dagger, right between my ribs.

"She sprang it on me," I snap. "What was I supposed to do? Tell her you lied?"

It's too much, it's all wrong, and I'm hurting him, but it feels good.

"No, you're right." Colin sighs. It's a forced release of tension, like he's eager to move past this, and now I feel guilty for escalating it. "Thank you for—" He stops again. "You didn't have to do that. Seriously."

We both know I did. We both know I would have, no matter what.

"Are we good, though?" he asks. "I mean, I wasn't sure if you . . ."

He trails off, seemingly with no intention of finishing that thought, and I want to ride out the silence until he does.

"We're good?" he asks again.

Chance after chance, and still, he's too afraid to tell me the truth.

I just stare back at him, my throat burning, but I won't let him see me cry.

"Happy birthday, Colin."

I walk straight into the living room to snatch my jacket from the couch. I pull it on quickly, trying to breathe—not only through the tears stinging my eyes, but to cool the anger that's quickly reaching a boil. Because I put myself out there tonight. I came here alone, made it as clear as I could that the door is still open, but still, he wasn't brave enough to step through. The finality blazes under my skin, flame eating at the wick, and I need to get out of here before it detonates. I'm afraid of what will happen if it does.

"Hey, you leaving?"

Ben's voice freezes me steps from the door. I turn to find him standing at the snack table with a tortilla chip in his hand and a sweet puppy-dog look on his face.

I blink, schooling my features into my best attempt at casual.

"Yeah, I've got some stuff to do, so . . ." I trail away, too focused on holding it together to come up with a less pitiful lie.

"You sure you can't stay to help me finish these?" Ben holds up the last two IPAs, undeterred. "I mean, you know what they say: the girl who brought the good beer has to share the last one with her friend's roommate."

It's not a thing anyone says, not even a little, but he's goofy, a little drunk, and looking at me like he wants me to stay. I look back at him, with his soft face and sturdy, slightly doughy build, the kind of guy who probably doesn't go to the gym but could almost definitely carry furniture up several flights of stairs—and as hopeless as I felt just seconds ago, a new plan starts to take shape. I wonder if it would be wrong to use him, if that's even what I'd be doing. Because Colin didn't want me here, and Ben does.

And maybe, *maybe*, if I truly release him, then Colin will finally come back.

I smile. "Well, that *is* what they say."

Ben laughs, but his eyes shift to the hallway, suddenly bashful.

"We could take these to my room, if you want? Or—"

"Sure." I spare him the awkwardness of finishing that thought, reaching out to take one of the beers. Ben grins, and I follow him to his room, hope crawling to life again inside of me. I give myself permission to feel it.

Sometimes, I think we all need that.

I still can't quite explain it, what was so special about sleeping with Colin. The sex itself—the first and only time we had it—wasn't particularly mind-blowing, at least not if we're using the goal-oriented metric of orgasm. That has always felt weirdly militaristic to me, anyway, like we're just checking something off a to-do list, no pun intended.

I didn't come. I almost never do, at least not from sex alone. But there was something about the anticipation of it, six dates' worth of tension building through kisses and touches on city streets, between the bookshelves, in the dark of my tiny room. There was something about the way he looked at me that made me feel seen, laid out under the microscope of his warm eyes. Piercing, but still somehow safe, because I knew he thought I was beautiful, even before he whispered it into my neck.

It felt, in so many ways, like a beginning.

With Ben, it's better than I expected. Like Colin, he wears a condom without me having to ask—otherwise a rare find in the New York dating scene—and even though we're both a little buzzed, it's not sloppy. He doesn't try to look in my eyes or anything, either, which is best, because then I'm sure I wouldn't be able to hide my thoughts. Instead, he pulls me close enough that I can look over his shoulder, around at his room.

It's not as clean as Colin's—not dirty, but I spy two empty plastic water bottles and a Coke can on various surfaces of the room. His sheets are navy, so it's hard to tell how recently they've been washed, and there's no headboard on the bed.

I wonder if Colin can hear us through the wall, if he and Zoe are in his bedroom, now that everyone else at the party has gone home. If they're doing the same thing. And then, I start to lose track of coherent thoughts at all. There's only the low sounds in Ben's throat, his cologne, and that image sharp in my mind: Colin and Zoe, intertwined. His face lifting from the white curve of her shoulder, clocking the gentle thudding on the other side of the thin plaster.

And then I lose myself completely.

Ben snores. I know because it jolts me awake too early in the morning, gray light creeping through his shoddily erected blinds. I reach for the phone on the bedside table, thinking it's mine, but the screen lights up with a picture of a geriatric basset hound—Ben's family dog, I'm assuming, which weirdly makes sense to me. It's 6:00 on the dot.

Shit. I didn't mean to fall asleep here. I wanted this to exist only as an image in Colin's mind, one that wouldn't be ruined by the reality of me, here this morning in last night's clothes, or having to kiss Ben goodbye, to admit to myself what I've done.

Slowly, I set the phone back on the table and slip out of Ben's bed. He didn't put an arm around me as we slept, thank god, and he's out like the dead with his bare back to me. Quickly and quietly, I dress myself, grab my jacket, tote, and phone from his desk, and then pick up my boots from beside the door.

That's when I notice the key ring hanging from a command hook on the wall. It's two keys, for the building and the apartment, I'm guessing—almost identical to my own, except without the lavender handheld alarm I carry to activate if I ever get attacked on the street.

Slowly, carefully, I slip it off the hook, feel the metal cool in my hand.

I glance back at Ben. His chest rises and falls, and a little cowlick sticks up in the back of his head. He'll be perfect for someone else, someday. I hope he'll forgive me when we never do this again.

I drop the keys into my tote.

Then, I inch the door open and step into the hall, face flushed with my own impulsivity, but I can't turn back now. I don't know why I did that. I don't know why I did *any* of the past twelve hours now, in the light of day. Ben is Colin's roommate. Fine for a one-night, jealousy-inducing scheme, maybe, but then there's the crude reality of them living together. If I become the girl who ghosted Ben, then that means I can't ever set foot in this apartment again, at least not without significant awkwardness. I didn't want to make things awkward for Colin, or even Ben. I really didn't.

Fucking IPAs, I think as I creep down the hall, even though I know I only had two and a half. Well, plus the hit of Zoe's pen. Maybe she's onto something with her granola approach to substance abuse.

Something clangs in the kitchen, and I freeze.

"Colin?" Zoe asks.

She appears in the doorway, and of course she looks angelic in the morning. She's wearing one of his T-shirts, her face still dewy and flawless, even without makeup. Her hair is clipped up in a claw, curls spilling out, and there's a spatula in her hand, like she's been staged for a Target ad or something, but classier.

"Oh! Morning." She leans against the doorway with an expression that's impish, but not unkind. "Had a fun night?"

I redden instantly, and before I can respond, she puts a hand to her mouth.

"Shit, don't even feel like you have to respond to that. It's none of

57

my business. I just know how into you Ben is. I think you two would be really good together."

Right, I think, *because you know me so well and you're just an expert when it comes to my dating life.* Still, I can't hate her, because it sounds genuine. Like she wants this for me.

"It was fun," I say, and then, realizing how Ben-related that sounds, I correct myself. "All of last night. Thanks again for inviting me."

Despite everything, I do mean it.

Zoe brushes a curl away from her cheek, that dimple deepening as she smiles. "You're Colin's friend. And mine, too, if you'll have me. We're glad you came."

Because they're still a *we*. I search her face for any indication that Colin told her about us, but I can't find any.

"Still," I say. "Thanks for making me feel so welcome."

"Of course."

I adjust my tote bag, achingly aware of the keys inside, and for a fraction of a second, her eyes flick to it. My heart gallops into my throat. Quickly, I angle myself toward the exit. "So, I should probably . . ."

"Wait, do you want to stay for breakfast?" Zoe asks, like she just remembered the spatula in her hand. "I'm making pancakes."

Of course she is, goddamn angel of the morning. No doubt she'd be one of those girls posting videos about her "five-to-nine before her nine-to-five," if she wasn't already clearly successful outside of the traditional workforce. I bet her pancakes are really good, too. A big part of me *does* want to stay, to sit at Colin's kitchen table with Zoe and get to know her better, to understand what makes her tick. To maybe even ask her what Colin said about me last night.

But that's exactly why I have to go. I can't face Colin and Ben this morning, either separately or together.

"Thanks, but I really have to get going," I tell her. "I'm trying to get some writing done today."

"Hell yeah." Zoe jabs the spatula at the ceiling like a foam finger. "Well, it was really nice talking to you. And hey, if you ever want eyes on your draft, feel free to send it over. I don't know a lot about plays, but I'm dying to read it. For purely selfish reasons, obviously."

I'm surprised at how thrilled I feel at the thought of it, Zoe reading my words.

"Sure," I say. "Thanks."

"Wait." Zoe scurries back into the kitchen and then reappears with her phone. "Put your number in. I'll text you."

For a moment, I hesitate. In any other situation, I'd be wary of giving a virtual stranger a direct line to my life, but Zoe's insisting, and I don't have the willpower—or maybe even the desire—to resist. I put my number in, handing the phone back when I'm done. She smiles like she's won something, a shiny new prize she can't wait to use.

"See you later, Jane."

"You, too," I say, wondering if she means it.

"And I'm serious!" She points her spatula at me. "We're friends now, okay?"

My heart stutters.

"Okay," I echo.

As soon as I step into the apartment hallway, my phone lights up with a text.

It's Zoe!! And if you feel like sending that Ophelia play (she says, fully desperate to read it) . . .

Her email address is included below.

Friends, I think.

It's not until now that I'm starting to believe it.

6

Before the elevator has hauled me up to the fifth floor of my building, I get a text from an unsaved number.

Hey, this is Ben! Colin gave me your number, hope that's chill. I know you probably had to run this morning, but just wanted to say I had fun last night. Would you want to grab drinks or dinner sometime?

I close my eyes, taking a breath as a dull headache beats behind my nose. It's not that I didn't expect this. Zoe's voice floats into my head again: *I just know how into you Ben is.* Some part of me had hoped she was wrong.

And then, as I step out of the elevator, an understanding punches me in the teeth.

Colin gave Ben my number. Either he knows about last night— probable—or Ben just asked for my number without telling him why. In both scenarios, Colin *decided* to give it to him, which means he's okay with this. He's so enraptured with Zoe that he doesn't even care that I slept with his roommate.

I dig my keys out of my tote and shove them into the lock, that same hot fury bubbling up in my chest. Colin isn't just nonconfrontational. He's downright apathetic.

Or. *Or.* Colin has to play it cool. There's his lie, remember? If he acted weird about giving Ben my number, then that would imply complicated feelings between us, which wouldn't make sense if we're just friends from Penn. And Zoe—she's there, too, another member of the audience for Colin to contend with.

Then there's Ben. Why is he so into me? I turn the question over as I walk into my apartment. It's not that I find myself hideous or fundamentally undesirable, but Ben barely knows me. We didn't connect the way Colin and I did. I couldn't possibly connect with a guy who sends a text saying *hope that's chill,* even if he was sort of sweet and was, I suppose, at least tangentially related to an orgasm.

Back in my room, I set my phone down beside me, telling myself I don't have to figure this out right now. According to all the dating advice my TikTok algorithm keeps feeding me, you shouldn't respond to a text from someone you just started seeing for at least three hours—not that Ben and I are even seeing each other. But still. He'll understand.

In the meantime, I decide to send Zoe my play. I don't know what makes me do it. Maybe because she asked and then followed up—a rare sign of sincerity in a world of NYU peers and their empty offers of *We should get coffee sometime!* that never come to fruition, the *How are yous* that never invite a real answer.

Or maybe I just need to know what Zoe thinks.

I attach the document to an email, languishing briefly over the inclusion of exclamation points or smiley faces in the body before settling on a simple, *Here it is. Hope it doesn't suck.*

I press send.

Then, I assemble a breakfast of stale peanut butter toast and sit down to google Ben. I don't know his last name, but all it takes is one search for *Ben Bergen County New Jersey comedian* for me to find it: Ben MacKenna, according to a neglected LinkedIn profile and a few scattered results from the websites of his New Jersey high school and Borough of Manhattan Community College.

On all of his social media, though, he's @bennymack. His TikTok is the first result—figures—but fearing the immediate secondhand embarrassment, I go for his Instagram instead. It's public, mostly clips from his standup sets, and he has about a thousand followers. I watch one clip, which actually has some okay jokes, as far as white guy comedians go.

Then, I scroll back farther, wading through enough selfies, reels, and standup show ads to make myself dizzy before finally latching onto the face I hope to see: Colin. He's sitting with Ben and Sam on the floor of their living room, only an unfurnished version, the three of them around an IKEA box that's understudying the role of dining table. Ben posted it over two years ago, so Colin would have been twenty-two here, fresh out of Penn. It must have been when he and Ben first moved in together. The caption reads, *"The Boys Are Back" is my favorite song from seminal classic High School Musical 3: Senior Year.* Which, in Ben's defense, is actually a little funny.

Colin looks adorable, holding up a box of takeout lo mein with a kid-on-picture-day kind of expression, like he hasn't quite learned how to smile yet. It's an expression he would still make, sometimes, when I tried to take a photo of him, like he was insecure about being on camera, so he did a silly face to make it seem ironic.

I read through the comments. First, from @samsingh, a concise three laughing emojis.

And then, from @colin_h99: *I'm an "I Want It All" man myself.*

The toast turns to paste in my mouth, a hard glob I have to fight to swallow down. Colin told me he doesn't have an Instagram. I even looked him up before our first date, and there was nothing, a fact that satisfied me. He was down to earth, I thought. Unplugged.

I click on the profile hungrily, sure this is just a glitch and the profile has been deleted, but no, it's still there. At the top, his name is listed only as Colin, no mention of his last name, Hillgrove, which must be why it didn't come up before. But the picture is undeniably him. Even worse, it's one I'm all too familiar with: Colin with his chin in his hand, smiling. It's a recent photo—the one that he made his dating app profile picture one week after he told me he wasn't ready for something serious. Wasn't ready for *me*.

The account is private, so I can't see anything besides the fact that he has around five hundred followers, but the truth is clear. Colin has had an Instagram this whole time. Maybe not one he's very active on, but he told me he didn't have one at all. Why would he lie?

And then, the other question, gurgling up in my throat like the wrath of one too many IPAs: What else has he lied to me about?

The rest of the day passes in a fever. I try to distract myself, first with the essays I'm supposed to be editing, and then with my play, but the words all swim on the page in front of me, meaningless. Mostly, I just scroll on my phone—Instagram, TikTok, Twitter, repeat—a ritual with no clear aim except hoping that something will appear: a text from Colin. An Instagram story from Zoe. A crumb, anything. All the while, Colin's private Instagram is sitting in the back of my brain, tapping at my skull.

Eventually, I give in.

Making a fake Instagram account is pathetically cliché, but at this point, there's no other recourse. The only worse choice would be

following him with my real one. So, I create Jake Smith: Penn graduate, consultant, face stolen from a random LinkedIn profile of a social
worker with no discernible connections to Colin.

It takes me a while to flesh out his page, following a bunch of
Penn-adjacent accounts and other random people. Still, with his
staggering count of three followers—a few eager people followed
back almost immediately—Jake Smith looks one hundred percent
fake. As a last resort, I change his bio to "Penn '18. Old account got
hacked . . . thanks Zuckerberg!" It's the kind of bad joke this fictional
character might make, and hopefully it's enough. I request to follow
Colin.

It's past eight P.M. now, and my stomach grumbles, reminding me
that I haven't eaten since the toast I forced down this morning. I order
delivery I can't afford and eat it on the floor of my room, curled in
front of my laptop, barely caring that the pad thai smell will permeate
my small room. I put on an episode of *Friends*—the TV equivalent
of rice cakes, bland empty calories to shove in my mouth more for
the distraction than anything—and scroll through my phone as I eat.

A person in therapy might tell me that it's not healthy to isolate
myself like this. It's a Saturday night in New York City, and I'm
young. I could go out, hit the town, but I don't really have anyone
to do that with, unless I go knock on Anna's or Harmony's door, and
anyway, after buying the IPAs, criminally overpriced tea, and pad
thai, I don't have a ton of disposable income left to waste. Hence, I
am also not paying for therapy.

So, I toggle between my screens and forkfuls of dinner, letting
the crush of loneliness anchor me to the floor and curve my spine at
an angle I'll no doubt have to pay a chiropractor to fix, if I ever start
making money at this playwriting thing.

Eventually, I migrate to my bed, where I bury myself in the covers. I leave my takeout container on the floor, too tired to bring it to the kitchen or even focus on the *Friends* episode still playing in front of me—too tired to do anything but sink into the bleary haze of the canned laughter, the sirens and horns and engines passing outside like ships on a distant sea.

And then, my phone buzzes.

I sit up, grabbing it from the sheets. An Instagram notification: @ *colin_h99 has accepted your follow request.*

A thrilling heat breaks over my skin as I tap the banner to open the app. There it is, Colin's profile, newly revealed to one Jake Smith. I grin, an almost villainous laugh bubbling out of me as I sit back to explore this trove of hidden treasure.

A small trove, I realize: there are only eight posts. Interesting, when Colin has had the account for at least two years—he must have done a scrub. The first one, posted two weeks ago, is a carousel of photos, captioned *I hear the kids are doing "dumps" now*, with a poop emoji. The caption is so Colin that I smile in spite of myself—his emoji use has always been strictly ironic—but I don't know how to feel about the fact that he's an "Instagram dump" kind of person. They're for people who want to be seen as *casual* and *not curated* while being, in reality, the complete opposite.

Colin's dump begins with a picture of his usual bagel order—plain with scallion cream cheese—and then continues through pictures of the city skyline and a squirrel in Central Park before landing on one that almost makes me choke on my own tongue. Colin, standing in front of a window display at some kitschy furniture store. He's doing an adorably awkward thumbs-up in front of a row of candles shaped, inexplicably, like corn. And in the reflection of the window glass is Zoe, frozen mid-laugh and holding her phone to take the picture with windswept curls.

My head spins. It's not an overt declaration of their relationship, but it's obviously intentional. Isn't it? Zoe is *in* the picture. Zoe took the picture. I click on the comments. There are two. First, a bunch of corn emojis from Zoe's account, and then, from @bennymack: *a hard launch, dare we say?*

It's not a hard launch, and fuck Ben, but he's not totally wrong. Colin chose this, sifting through his album and picking it, for some specific reason, to display on his grid. Maybe he liked the way Zoe looks here, so pretty and uninhibited. Maybe he likes that she wants to take pictures of him at all, something about her making him more comfortable in front of her camera than he was with mine.

Or maybe he just thought the stupid corn candles were funny.

I'm overthinking this. I'm about to scroll away from the photo when a third comment materializes, stopping me in my tracks. It was posted just now by an account called @leighhhhh. The profile picture is hard to see clearly, except that it's a girl with a curtain of reddish hair.

Her comment: *do you miss me?*

A cold feeling snakes down my back as I click on her profile. It's private, no bio. Even with the photo blown up a bit bigger, I can't quite see this girl's face. She's captured in motion, her head turned to the side so her hair blurs around her face. She has a little under a thousand followers, but I can't check if one of them is Colin because of her privacy settings.

I grip my phone tighter. Who the hell is Leigh, and why is she leaving flirty comments on Colin's Instagram? Because she *is* flirting. What else could that "do you miss me?" mean?

I take a deep breath, reminding myself that Leigh is probably the least of my problems. The top of that list would be the fact that Colin is in an actual misguided "relationship" with Zoe. He probably doesn't even know this Leigh girl.

But "do you miss me?" implies a history, doesn't it? Before I can fall deeper down this rabbit hole, a text from Colin flashes across my screen.

Leigh vanishes from my thoughts as quickly as she took hold of them. My heart beats wildly as I click on the message, certain Colin has somehow caught on to Jake Smith—but no, that's not what this is about. I read the message, my head clearing.

Hey did you happen to see Ben's keys anywhere before you left? Apparently he can't find them

I read it again, and then a third time, trying to decipher the tone tucked inside the words. *Did you happen to. Apparently.* It's classic Colin, filler words to soften any hint of conflict—something we have in common, the need to dull things, to make them palatable—but is there a hint of aggression beneath the passivity?

Does he think *I* took them?

Technically, I did, but that's not the point. Colin should trust me. Colin shouldn't *accuse* me.

I read the message again, and a new shade comes through: *before you left.* Colin's referencing my night with Ben without actually saying it.

And then, it all clicks: Colin doesn't give a shit about Ben's keys. He just wants to hear from me. He's reaching for reasons to text me because he's jealous. A grin warms my cheeks, stretching until it hurts, but then a sudden stab of sadness tugs it back down. If Colin misses me, I need him to say so. He can't hide behind excuses, not after the lies he's told—the Instagram, the *friend from Penn* story, and the one that hurts the most, because it was a lie he told himself: that he wasn't ready to be with me. I'll forgive him, of course—always—but not so easily. Not so soon.

I force myself to wait a full episode of *Friends* before writing back.

Didn't see them, sorry!

I know he wants more, and a big part of me wants to give it to him, but I won't. Not yet. I lie back on my pillows, my phone pressed against my heart.

Do you miss me?

He does, I know, the way he doesn't miss @leighhhhh, but he needs another push, a little kick in the pedestal.

I open Ben's message and text him back.

For sure! When are you free?

7

On Sunday, I wake up feeling lighter than any of Zoe's manifestation techniques could inspire in me. Even when I reach for my phone and find that Colin hasn't texted me back yet, I don't panic—because I know, now, that he misses me. He just needs the courage to do something about it.

Ben, on the other hand, responded almost immediately to my text last night. He told me he should be around next weekend, as if he might have spontaneously jetted off to Europe or something. I didn't message him back, instead letting it hang in the kind of suspense that just might force him—and Colin—past the edge of his seat.

One of the many things I've learned from Shakespeare: the green-eyed monster is an excellent motivator.

In the meantime, I have my own work to do. I get out of bed, mind buzzing with the clarity of a good night's sleep as I head to the bathroom to brush my teeth. Obviously, I have to return Ben's keys. I've been so angry at Colin for lying to me, but last night, when he asked me about them, I did the exact same thing. Taking the keys was ridiculous. Impulsive. Nothing like the person Colin needs me to be—someone he can trust. Someone good.

Colin doesn't have to know I took the keys—a fib this small won't hurt him—but I do need to fix this. I just need to do it without getting caught.

I'm spitting out my toothpaste when an idea presents itself. In the mirror, I catch a glimpse of my earrings, the silver violet-shaped ones I bought at a flea market on the Upper West Side because they reminded me of Ophelia's flower monologue.

Wiping my mouth with a towel, I reach for my phone and send Ben a text.

Any chance you or Colin are home today? I think I took my favorite earrings off before we fell asleep the other night and I forgot them when I left—I'll be in the neighborhood later if I could swing by to get them?

Maybe I should feel guilty for this new lie, but it feels worth it when Ben texts back within the minute.

Oh damn! I'm heading in to work now and Colin's at Zoe's in BK, but I'll be back tonight if you want to grab them?

I try to ignore the little sting as I picture Colin and Zoe all tangled up together in her bedsheets.

Thanks! I respond.

Obviously, I won't be back tonight to look for the phantom earrings, but I'll come up with an excuse later. For now, all that matters is that Colin's apartment is empty.

I get dressed quickly, heading out with a new sense of purpose.

On my way to the subway, though, I slow when I see the Rite Aid up ahead. It was one of the first stops I made when I moved in with Anna and Harmony—for some godforsaken reason, our landlord had only given us two keys to the unit, and this store has one of those key-copying machines inside.

I brush Ben's keys inside my tote. If I'm remembering right, it only cost a few bucks to make an extra.

Before I can talk myself out of it, I pass the subway entrance and beeline for the Rite Aid. Inside, I slip Ben's key into the machine, telling myself that it's fine. It's not even a lie, really. Ben will have his keys back, and I'll have my own, just in case.

In case of what? a voice whispers inside me, piquing my guilt.

But the machine is already churning out a metallic wail, the new key grinding to life inside. It spits it out, and I take it, the golden metal warm against my palm.

I make a promise to myself: this is the last thing I'll lie to Colin about. After this, this one little indulgence, I'll be the girl he needs again. I'll be good.

We're good? It comes back to me again, what Colin asked me at his party. I try to picture that higher-plane version of myself, the *most divine* me. What would she have done in that moment, instead of running?

She would have planted her feet. Given him an easy smile, viciously sweet, the kind that would deepen her dimple, if she had one.

We're great, she would have said. *Just you watch.*

Colin's apartment looks even better during the day. When I get there, I stand outside for a few moments, drinking in how the light hits the brick, giving it a warm glow almost like his eyes, like you could dip your finger inside and taste the sweetness. I imagine walking down these stone steps in the morning, my hair tousled and my clothes still smelling like him. I imagine walking up them again with my own set of keys—not my Rite Aid copy, but ones *he* gave me because I spend so much time here that, in a way, it's my home, too. Maybe it's just another dubious manifestation, but it feels so real, so close that I could reach out and touch it.

Permission to hope, I think, as I climb the stairs. I push my new key into the lock and twist, like I'm stepping into my destiny.

When I get to Colin's floor, my heart pounds again, alight with an irrational fear that Ben lied, that he or Colin will be waiting here to catch me. I ring the doorbell, just to be safe. If I hear footsteps, I'll bolt. But a few shallow breaths later, no one's come to the door.

I unlock it.

Sun streams into the living room, tidied up since the party. I get the sense that it's even cleaner than it used to be—mopped floors, dusted shelves—and I wonder how much of that was Zoe. It stings a little, thinking of her cleaning his space, the two of them playing house.

I walk down the hallway, glancing into the kitchen as I pass. I didn't see much of it on Friday, but it's small. Also clean, but less so—a box of cereal sits half-opened on the counter, a few dishes in the sink. Ben's, probably.

His bedroom door is open, too, but I have no interest in reliving my previous experience there. I make quick work of it, dropping Ben's keys under his bed, but sticking out just enough that he'll hopefully find them.

Then, I slip back into the hall, toward Colin's room.

I open the door.

Even though I was here two days ago, I'm almost brought to my knees by his lingering presence, the nearness of him. Nothing much has shifted here since Friday, except for a book on his bedside table, the first in the Percy Jackson series. It warms my heart, knowing Colin rereads childhood favorites. I can picture him here perfectly, closing the book and reaching over, sleepy-eyed, to shut off the lamp.

I know I should get out of here, but something moves me to stay a bit longer, to memorize every detail. The book, the glass. His desk, the succulents on top of it stretching boldly toward the sunlight.

My gaze catches on the dresser. It looks different: tidier, no socks spilling from the cracked-open drawers like before. I open the top one, holding my breath as I realize I'm expecting to see something of Zoe's—some mark on the territory, a *girlfriend drawer*. But it's only Colin's socks and underwear. I breathe out.

And then, I notice something shoved at the back, a shirt or sweater of some kind. The other things in the drawer are arranged in Colin's sweetly haphazard fashion, but this one feels deliberately hidden— stashed, like he wanted to make it disappear.

I pull it out.

It's a gray quarter-zip with the University of Pennsylvania logo on the chest, *Penn Tennis* written beneath it. Colin never played tennis. The thought is no more than a blip, though, when I realize what else is wrong here: there's a large stain on the back of the fabric. Red, but much darker than Penn's signature color—brown-tinged and thick, like dried paint.

Not paint, I realize as I finish un-balling the sweater. Blood.

And inside, tucked away like something precious, is the source.

A knife, stained the same rusty color.

It's long, deadly—the kind that comes from a kitchen block. The kind he could stick clean between my ribs, except literally, because this is not a fucking metaphor.

I shove the quarter-zip and the knife back in the drawer and shut it, staring at my hands to make sure none of the blood rubbed off on them, but it must have been dried. My palms are clean. Still, I feel the ghost of that viscous texture. *Out, damned spot.*

And then, I recover from the shock enough to form a coherent thought.

Why the fuck does Colin have a bloody *knife* in his underwear drawer?

The quarter-zip can't be Zoe's. She didn't go to Penn. So where the hell did this come from? I want to examine it more closely, but I can't bring myself to reach for it again. Instead, something pulls me back and away, toward the window, and maybe there *is* some sort of higher power at work here, because at the exact moment I glance outside, I see Colin walking up the sidewalk and toward his building.

Shit.

I spring out of his room, away from the knife and bloody quarter-zip, and fumble to the front door, so buzzed with adrenaline that it takes me a few tries to make my hand work on the doorknob, slick with invisible blood. Finally, it swings open, and I speed out into the hallway. My heart hammers, my brain working about as well as my motor skills.

I can't go downstairs. I'll pass him on the way. For half a second, I consider bolting back into the apartment and trying to scale down the fire escape, but that would be ridiculous, and I don't want to see the blood again, and also I'd probably die, which I guess wouldn't be the worst outcome at this particular moment—and then I remember that Colin's apartment is only on the third floor of a five-floor walk-up.

Footsteps sound from below, and I bolt for the fourth floor, stopping when I'm out of sight on the landing. I should keep going all the way up to the fifth, just to be safe, but then I hear his voice.

"Hello?"

I press myself against the staircase railing, stock-still.

"I know you're there," he snaps, and there's such an edge to his voice that I'd think it wasn't Colin if I hadn't studied him so closely, weren't so primed to know when he's near. He waits a moment before adding, almost tauntingly, "I can hear you breathing."

I grip the banister so tightly my fingers ache, my whole body flushed with a weightless feeling, like I'm about to collide with the ground. This is it. I'm caught. I wait for his footsteps, for the moment he'll see me, forcing me to watch the disgust washing over his beautiful face.

But the footsteps don't come.

Only his voice, sharp enough to slice through my middle. "Fine. Not feeling chatty? Then I'll make this short: if you call me one more time, I swear to god I'll track this number, come to your front door, and make sure you can never take another smug fucking breath again."

It takes me a few moments too long to register. Colin's on the phone. He isn't talking to me. There's a breath of quiet, and then—

"Fuck!" A strangled shout. Something thuds against the wall. His fist, I realize, as he growls in pain. "Ow. *Fuck* me."

Keys scrape angrily in Colin's door. It creaks open. Shuts.

I should go. I should run while I can, but I'm frozen, fingers still tight around the banister. Colin doesn't yell. Colin doesn't *hit* things. This is the man who took me to a cat cafe on our third date and sat for the full hour with a kitten sleeping on his lap, barely moving except to stroke one finger over its tiny, fragile spine. The man who kissed me with the same tenderness, who asked me what was okay, what felt good.

Suddenly, I'm not hiding on this staircase, but curled in the corner of a different room, back pressed against the wall. Flecks of spit flying in my face. A bang so loud I'm surprised, for a moment, that it doesn't physically hurt, that the force was knuckles colliding with the plaster and not my temple.

It's a beautiful thing, watching something die.

I throw off my denim jacket, overheating, commanding myself to breathe. *Breathe.* That isn't here, that isn't now, and that wasn't Colin. I ball up my jacket and force the fabric against my mouth, like I might need to muffle a scream, only I couldn't scream if I tried.

Through the ringing in my ears, a thought takes shape.

This is not the man I know—and I may know him even better than I thought.

It's not until I unclench the banister that I realize my keys are clutched between my knuckles on instinct, sharp end forward, my own little blades hungry for purchase.

8

I never know where it starts, with the boys. If it matters.

The first was in college. There had been boys before, obviously, but I'd been too afraid to do anything about it. I held my crushes close, kept them tucked under my collar like the little key I wore on a chain—the one that opened my diary, before I realized that poorly made locks for teenage girls are nothing against the power of brute force.

But then, there was Trip.

Short for *the third*, as in James Waylon O'Connor III, which should have been my first warning. My second: he was a straight boy in the drama program. Not that there's anything wrong with that, not in theory, but in practice, the ratio of women who want to sleep with men to men who want to sleep with them back is so imbalanced that straight men become gods of their BFA programs, and you can't come out on the other side of that with a normal-sized ego.

Trip was the rare sort of straight BFA boy who is both talented *and* beautiful—sandy waves, green eyes, chiseled chin with a Clark Kent cleft—and on top of that, he was six foot one, which made him the hottest commodity in all of Tisch. So, for that reason alone, I made it my personal mission not to fall in love with him. Everyone else within a ten-block radius already had.

What I didn't account for is that Trip was a very good actor.

It happened, like so many things, because of Shakespeare. We were in the same intro class freshman year, but we'd never actually spoken until we were put in the same group for our performance assignment. I'd been dreading this as soon as I saw it on the syllabus—I was a Dramatic Writing major here to analyze Shakespeare's words, not bring them to life. Worse, I was in a group with two capital-A Actors: Trip, of course, and also Maisie Detweiler, who would go on to make her Broadway debut the year after graduation.

We were given the end of Act One, Scene One from *A Midsummer Night's Dream*. Trip claimed Lysander, obviously, and because Helena ends the scene with a lengthy, lovelorn monologue, I defaulted happily to Hermia, who had fewer lines. The fact that she's Lysander's love interest was pure coincidence.

From our first rehearsal, I was doomed. It wasn't just Trip's mastery of iambic pentameter, which he delivered with an almost musical care that so many young actors neglect. It was the way he looked at me: soft and wanting, but with a fierceness burning brightly beneath. When he asked me to run away into the magical forest, I just about believed him.

I lost my virginity in his twin XL bed after a one-on-one rehearsal. He'd suggested it—the rehearsal—and I'd accepted warily, ignoring the tiny part of me that hoped he'd be offering more than tips on my delivery. When I complimented his iambic pentameter, he kissed me exactly how his Lysander would—gently, hungrily—and I knew I was more to him than the mousy playwright he was forced to share a stage with. I could be Hermia, sweet and fiery and exalted. I could be good.

We were together for four months before I realized that we

weren't together. True, we hadn't discussed being exclusive, but we were sleeping together so often that it didn't even occur to me that he'd have the time or the stamina to be with anyone else. And then, on the night of my first NYU reading, a one-act I wrote, I came to his door, buzzed from the afterparty. I was eager to tell him all about it, the full-body rush of watching my words come to life. When the door opened, I was practically breathless.

Until I realized that the person standing in the threshold was not Trip, but Maisie Detweiler. She stood there in nothing but his button-down and said, *Oh, hi. Sorry, what was your name again?*

Despite that final humiliation, Maisie was kind enough to call for Trip when I burst into tears. I didn't let him talk to me, though. Not there. I stormed down the hall until he threw on a shirt and followed me, placing a strong hand on my shoulder and guiding me into a common room. He rubbed that same hand up and down my back as I sobbed on a crumb-ridden couch like a child.

I don't understand, he'd said softly when I was done. *Where is this coming from?*

And even though I'd cried myself hollow, a new rush of disbelief swirled in my solar plexus, shooting up and out of my mouth like dragon's breath.

Maybe it's coming from the fact that I'm sort of in love with you, Trip.

His hand froze on my back before springing back to his side, like I'd burned him.

What?

A pit opened in my stomach like a trap door.

I'm not saying it again.

*No, I mean—*He paused, that classically handsome crease between his brows. *Why?*

I stared at him with tear-blurred eyes. I know, now, that he didn't actually want an answer. He was only trying to excuse himself, to prove that my love was all in my head and not the result of anything tangible he'd done—which may have been true. But back then, I was bruised and drunk and hurting, and I took words at face value. I sat there and told him.

Because you're smart, I said. Not true, not entirely, but it sounded like a good reason. *And you're sweet and talented, and I love how confident you are, and—*

Jane . . .

I was grateful for the interruption, because I was humiliated, and because I didn't even know where I was going with that list of reasons, and because some part of me believed that maybe, against all odds, I'd convinced him.

But what he said, as the shock in his eyes melted into an aching mix of pity and horror, was, *Please tell me I wasn't your first.*

I could have killed him. Even now, there are times I wonder what I would have done if I'd had the opportunity, if I'd been anything but a girl alone in a shitty dorm common room with a boy twice my size.

What I did instead was stand up, wipe the snot from under my nose, and storm off to my own dorm to sob until I felt empty again, until all that hurt and shock calcified into a hard diamond of rage inside my ribs.

It wasn't a new feeling. I was well-acquainted with it, the rage. Sometimes, I lived off it the way a body begins to eat itself when it's starving. Sometimes I let it go too far.

But I was done with that. No matter how much I wanted to hurt Trip, to *ruin* him—as much as it felt, every time I saw him with a new girl, like another little death—I couldn't. Because I was free of that now.

I had sworn to myself that I would be *good.*

And with Colin, I was.

Only now, it feels like I'm back in that common room all over again. The air is just as stale and hard to breathe as I run down the stairs, fleeing Colin's apartment—except this is worse, because I'm older now, wiser, and this was supposed to be different. But here I am, falling too fast and too hard for a delusion, a hazy outline of a man that I filled with details of my own making.

But no. *No.*

I step back into the cool air of East 7th, and my head starts to clear. The first thing I have to understand is that this *is* the man I know. What just happened in there—the shout, the fist, the blood, the knife—was all real, at least in the tangible sense, but there has to be more to the story.

Because at the brutal, beating heart of it is one truth: Colin is different. He isn't Trip, or any of the others who came after. I understand him. I know him. And we can get through this.

I don't often think of my mother—I try not to—but one thing she told me that's always stuck with me is that love isn't some kind of magical destiny, this intangible, ineffable *spark*. Love is a choice. Sometimes, it's the wrong one. But that doesn't change the simple fact: if something's going to work, it's because we *decide* that it will. If something fails, it's because we let it.

So, I won't let it.

The clarity stops me in my tracks. *I love Colin.* I've loved him since the moment I met him, all of him, and that means that this—whatever it is—is a part I love, too. I just need the full picture. I need to understand how the pieces fit together, and then I'll be able to love him fully. We'll be able to work through it.

Because the truth is, I'm the only one who can. Zoe won't understand this. Zoe wouldn't choose him if she knew. She'll run. I won't.

Just as I'm turning around to head back to Colin's apartment, my phone buzzes, and there really *is* something in the air today, some genuine power of manifestation, because it's her.

"Hello?"

"Jane, oh my god. I can't believe you didn't tell me."

I freeze, gripping the phone as my heart grows into something wild and terrified, ramming at the bars of its cage. She knows. She *knows*—

"You're a fucking playwright."

For a moment, I'm stunned, recalibrating to the awe in her voice, but she doesn't seem to notice.

"I mean, obviously I knew, but *damn*. Seriously. I've never inhaled a play so fast."

"Thank you," I manage finally, a little hoarse.

"What are you doing on November twenty-second?"

"Um, I'm not sure." That's a lie. The twenty-second is a little less than two weeks from now, and I'm not busy, but I can't think of anything right now except the completely contradictory realities of what I just saw and what Zoe just told me. *She likes my play.* "Why?"

"My show at FOCAL is that night. I'm already featuring some of my own Ophelia stuff, and I think your play is just so perfectly in conversation with all of it that I would be silly not to ask you to be a part of it. I'm thinking a scene or two, maybe a ten-minute excerpt, performed at the gallery. What do you think?"

My brain rights itself. What do I think? I think Zoe's soon-to-be ex-boyfriend is hiding a bloody knife in his underwear drawer. I think I still love him, and this would be wrong, so wrong, but—

"That sounds great," I say.

"Amazing! Oh my god, I'm so excited. Are you doing anything right now? I think I'm gonna go thrifting in a bit if you want to come. We could talk logistics and everything, too."

I don't want to go thrifting right now. What I want is to march back up to Colin's, bang on the door, and ask him what happened, tell him he doesn't have to hide from me. But Colin *was* in a state just now. He needs time to cool down. He may not want me to see him like this, not before he's ready.

Zoe, on the other hand, could be useful. She doesn't know Colin, not the way I do, but she *has* been spending quite a bit of time with him lately. Maybe she's seen something. I also can't ignore the part of me that's still a little thrilled by this unabashed invitation, her flattery. *Zoe likes my play.*

"Sure," I say.

"Yay!"

I don't think I've ever heard a more genuine *yay* out of another adult woman.

"When are you thinking?" I ask.

"Whenever you're free, honestly. I just need to throw on some real-person clothes."

I'm not sure if this implies that Zoe is naked, in pajamas, or embroiled in some sort of Pinocchio situation, but I'd rather not ask, and she doesn't seem interested in explaining.

"Want to meet me in Williamsburg?" she asks.

I cringe. It doesn't surprise me that Zoe is the type to assume that wherever she lives is the center of the universe, but I guess I'm already downtown. And this is for Colin. A mission to quell my fears before they balloon into something oversized and untenable.

"Yeah," I tell her. "I can probably be there in like forty-five."

"Amazing! I'll text the address of the first shop I want to hit. See you then!"

She hangs up, and just like that, I have a friend date with Zoe Ember. Even if I *will* be using it for ulterior motives, I can't fight the warmth buzzing through me, despite the chilly breeze that slips under my jacket.

Someone asked me to hang out. As a friend.

That hasn't happened in a long time.

It's a shame, really, that I'll have to ruin it.

9

The thing I forget about thrifting in Brooklyn is that it's not actually *thrifting*—more like sifting through racks on the side of the street or in unfinished industrial spaces only to realize that each thing is at minimum a hundred dollars, because to them, it's more of an aesthetic choice than a financial or even moral one, and thrifting isn't actually the point. But that's okay. It's not the point for me, either.

"Oh, I love this one," Zoe says, running her fingers over a bizarrely turquoise leather jacket.

It's our second store of the day. We already covered all the *logistics and everything* between the first and the walk here. Zoe's cleared everything with the gallery, who are willing to pay me a few hundred. They'll even be able to source a bathtub, which is a pivotal set piece in the play. All I need to do is find some actors—which shouldn't be too hard, given the countless out-of-work Tisch alumni in this city—and choose which scene to perform, and boom: my professional debut in New York City.

Now, shop talk is out of the way, and we're still here. It seems, against all odds, that Zoe genuinely wants to be *friends*.

She takes the jacket off the rack and holds it up. "You should try it. It feels very you."

"It feels very . . . bright," I say, scanning it for a price tag. No luck. But I can assume. The lighting in here is too good and the aesthetic too cohesive for this to be anything close to affordable.

Zoe grins mischievously. "Are you not bright?"

I look down at my outfit: black boots, black leggings, black sweater, denim jacket.

"I prefer 'tastefully melancholy.'"

Zoe laughs. "Shakespearean. I like it." She purses her lips, eyeing the jacket. "I don't know, Jane. I've got a feeling you're a lot more colorful than you give yourself credit for. I can always tell that about people." She turns that discerning look back to me. "Are you a Scorpio?"

"Yeah." I don't like that she knows that, not one bit.

"I knew it! When's your birthday?"

"Next week," I answer uneasily. I don't like to think about my birthday, either.

"That makes *so* much sense. Colin's a Scorpio, too. It's part of why we work so well. I'm a Pisces. Which actually means you and I are a great match, too—if, you know, you don't think astrology is bullshit." She raises her eyebrows like this is an inside joke between us, pulling the jacket off the hanger. "Try it? Every time I've seen you, you're in that same denim jacket. Which is such a vibe, honestly, but I feel like we can change it up."

I don't want to take off the denim jacket, especially now that she's astrologically dissecting me, but maybe Zoe's right—not about the compatibility, even if it does make me want to google if Scorpios match well with other Scorpios or if that's too much Scorpio, not that I care, but that I *do* rely too much on this jacket for protection. I pull it off and take the leather one from her. As I put it on, I catch

Zoe checking her phone with a strange look on her face, her bubbly confidence lost to a nervous flicker.

I know that look. I've *felt* it.

Zoe's waiting for a text that isn't coming. From Colin, I'm certain, and this is the perfect time to strike.

"So, what's it like dating us Scorpios?" I ask her, keeping my tone casual. "Aren't we supposed to be the super-secretive, unknowable type? That must be annoying."

Zoe's eyes snap up from her phone. I step in front of a mirror, pretending to examine the jacket as I glance at her expression. The look fades quickly, replaced with a smile as she puts her phone back in her pocket.

"You guys are actually my favorite type of person," she says. "You know, the ones who don't want to let people in at first. Maybe I'm a glutton for punishment, but I think I just love a challenge." She scans my reflection. "How do you feel?"

Clearly, she wants to change the subject, so I check the price tag. A hundred and fifty dollars.

I shrug off the jacket. "I think we might need to ease me into color."

Zoe laughs, taking it from me. "Like I said, I love a challenge." She sticks it back on the rack. "So, what are you going to do for your birthday?"

I put my denim jacket on again, feeling like I'm back in my own skin. I'm not going to forget about the slip in her mask, but I don't want to be too obvious about steering us back to the Colin discussion.

"Pretend it's not happening, probably," I answer honestly. "I hate my birthday."

She gapes. "Why?"

"I'm a playwright. We notoriously despise attention." And maybe I'm about to push my luck, but the connection is there, so I add, "Colin's the same way with birthdays, right? Could be a Scorpio thing."

There it is again—her hand brushing her phone, like she's going to check it, but then she stops herself.

"Speaking of which," she says, guiding us away from the jackets and deeper into the store, "has Ben texted you?"

It's a clumsy segue. She's obviously avoiding the topic of Colin, and I'm itching to force her back on track, but I don't want to press so hard that she closes off completely.

"Yeah," I say, busying myself with a rack of jeans. "We haven't confirmed, but I think we're going out next weekend."

Zoe squeals. Like, actually squeals in that way girls do in movies, but somehow, she pulls it off, and I'm suddenly conscious of the other cool Brooklynites around us, what they think of this strange pair in the middle of the store.

"Okay, so promise you won't tell Ben this," she says, "but I actually masterminded this whole thing. I knew he was single, and I figured you're both so smart and creative, so I may or may not have talked you up before you got to the party. It was risky, since I wasn't sure about your situation with that guy you were at the bar with, but I'm *so* glad I did."

It's a battle to keep my face neutral and unbetraying of the bitter understanding rising in my throat like bile. So, this is who Zoe is. The *matchmaker*, the girl obsessed with setting her friends up because she's just so *confident* and *secure* in her own relationship that she wants to help everyone be as happy as she is, except not *so* happy, because no one could possibly be as happy as Zoe and her Scorpio boyfriend Colin—even if he's clearly not texting her back. I almost want to tell her about the knife right here, to plunge my own metaphorical blade straight into her heart, but I can't. I fix on a smile.

"I don't know," I say. "I don't want to get too ahead of myself."

Zoe's eyes widen, her hand flying to her lips, and I must have said something wrong. She knows, somehow, exactly what I'm thinking.

"Shit," she says. "I'm overstepping again, aren't I? Colin always tells me I do this. I get so excited about something that I get these blinders on, and—shit. You didn't just agree to go out with Ben because you felt pressured into it, did you?"

I'm so caught off guard that it takes me a few seconds to respond. "No," I say. "Not at all."

It's not technically a lie. It wasn't that I was pressured. It's that I'm using Ben to shake Colin awake and force him out of his state of denial, but I can't exactly come out and say that to his *girlfriend*.

Still, she mentioned him again, and I can't pass up the opportunity.

"Colin tells you you're overstepping?"

Zoe's lip quirks, a frown revealing itself before she schools it into a smirk. "Not in, like, a bad way. Only when he's actually right."

"Huh." I knit my brows.

"What?"

Even Trip couldn't tell me I'm not an actress, because clearly, she buys my performance hook, line, and sinker.

"Nothing," I say. "He's just normally so nonconfrontational, I guess." I give her a stern look. "But seriously, if he's ever being an asshole to you, let me know. I'll whip him right into shape."

I play it off like a lighthearted joke, something you say to your friend, but it's an opening. And for a moment, I think she's going to bite. She chews her lip, running her thumbnail against the edge of her forefinger—nervous? But then, like a light switched on, she smiles.

"Well, I definitely overstepped with Ben, so I at least owe you a makeover." At what must be an obvious look of disbelief on my face, she adds, "I prefer to live my life exclusively like an early 2000s rom-com montage."

I can't help but laugh genuinely at that, because it feels so correct, and she's now literally pulling me toward a rack of dresses like a Hoku song is playing in the background, but maybe this is just what it's like to have a friend like Zoe. I don't want to give up on my investigation, especially now that there's a hint of trouble in paradise, but she's a tidal wave of energy. She fills my arms with hangers, flitting between racks with a gleam in her eyes and purpose in her step, and I get the sense that maybe she's done this before—taking the weird antisocial girl under her wing and trying to transform her into Zoe 2.0.

Only, as I start to examine the clothes Zoe's handed me, I realize she *isn't* trying to make me into her copy. They're all actually my style: understated, but with a hint of the color Zoe's so certain I hold within me, things I'll like but probably wouldn't have picked out on my own. Maybe, I realize, Zoe doesn't do this—the *matchmaker/ makeover* thing—because she wants to rub her own superiority in everyone's face. Maybe she genuinely wants to help.

"Okay." She claps her hands when my arms are fully laden. "No makeover montage is complete without the fashion show part. You ready?"

I want to ask her more about Colin, but she's on a mission, clearly, and also determined to deflect every mention of him. Her phone is still pointedly in her pocket. And so, I allow myself to be herded into a dressing room. Zoe whisks the curtain closed, leaving me alone with my reflection and the industrial lighting.

"Try the dress first!" Zoe instructs from outside. "It would be cute layered over the sweater."

"Okay," I say, embarrassed at the smallness of my own voice.

And then, there it is, crawling back into my brain like the ants that infested my apartment shower when we first moved in: the reason I feel so uncomfortable.

The last time I did this—the whole trying-on-clothes-while-someone-waits-outside-for-me thing—was the summer before my freshman year of high school, when my mom took me shopping. It was going to be my first time at a school without uniforms, and I felt paralyzed as I stared at the American Eagle racks, inhaling the cologne they pump through the store to make it smell like the boyfriend teenage girls fantasize about meeting at the beach. I chose clothes arbitrarily and fled to the dressing room, eager for it all to be over.

It was there, staring at my reflection, that I started to wonder if I'd ever had a personality, or if I was just a muted reflection of all the ones I'd come into contact with, a wooden puppet dressing up as one of the real girls. Was that why I liked writing plays so much? Because I could put different opinions in different characters' mouths without the burden of having to take an actual side?

It was also then that I started sobbing. We walked out with two shirts, a jacket, and a pair of jeans that I didn't end up trying on, and Mom bought me an Iced Passion Tango Tea from the Starbucks kiosk. It was the last time we ever went shopping together.

Choices were hard for me, but it's not like I had one, anyway. Not really.

I told Colin about that day once. Not about everything that came after—just the American Eagle, the crying, the Starbucks, the fear. I'd played it off like a silly story, but it was also a test—letting him take one of my most vulnerable days in his hands, waiting to see if he'd handle it with care or break it, toss it aside. When I finished, he laughed softly, kissing me on the forehead.

I bet I would have had a crush on you in high school, he said. *Even though you never would have talked to me, as an obviously cool teen who shopped at American Eagle and went to Starbucks.*

I laughed, because he'd passed. He'd seen my vulnerability and treated it with care and a dash of humor, a bit of flirting.

I was a theatre nerd, remember? I told him. *Hardly cool.*

Even better. I never liked cool, anyway.

Now, I throw on the outfit Zoe chose as quickly as possible and step out of the dressing room. She gasps, clasping her hands together.

"Okay, I'm officially a genius."

I don't know if I'd go that far, but I do like it, the sort of nineties grunge look she's crafted for me. I think Colin would, too. It's a little Instagram-trendy, sure—I don't think it's possible for Zoe to do anything that *isn't*—but it's miles away from American Eagle and more squarely in the camp of *I never liked cool, anyway.*

"How do you feel?" Zoe asks.

I pretend to deliberate as I search for a price tag. "I . . ."

"Don't worry about it," she says gently, seeing right through me. "It's my treat. This is my penance for meddling, remember?"

An inexplicable warmth floods my chest, even though I know Zoe is from Greenwich, Connecticut, and funding a thrift store excursion for a new friend is probably no skin off her back.

"I like it," I say honestly.

Zoe's whole face lights up. "Okay, so while you were in there, I found one more finishing touch."

She comes to stand behind me at the mirror, something in her hands. A necklace, I realize, as she holds it up. It's a silver chain with a charm dangling from the center, some kind of plant etched into a little medallion.

"It's rosemary," Zoe says. "'For remembrance.' I saw it on the table, and I was like, oh my god, that's so Ophelia. You have to have it. Here."

She steps closer, and I lift my hair as she drapes the necklace around my neck, the rosemary settling in the curve of my collarbone.

"'Pray, love,'" she says. "'Remember.'"

Her fingers brush my skin as she closes the clasp. I don't know if it's her touch or her recitation of the line, but the little hairs on my neck rise. I wonder if Zoe notices. If she likes it, having that kind of power.

"I don't know if I told you, but I played Gertrude in a high school production of *Hamlet*." She laughs, releasing me. "I wanted Ophelia so badly, but they had this future Juilliard kid playing Hamlet, and he was really short, so I towered over him. My best friend ended up getting it—she was super tiny, like you—and I was always so jealous, even though she was great. Is it narcissistic that that's where my obsession started?"

Probably. But Zoe's watching my reflection with a smile that tugs the dimple in her cheek, truly admiring her work, and I can't ruin her fun.

"No," I say, brushing the necklace. "But seriously, this is too much. You don't have to."

"Well, I want to. And I'm doing it. So there. You still have more clothes to try on." She gives an assertive little clap. "Let's get to it!"

I go back to the dressing room, but just as I'm about to shut the curtain, I catch her again. A glance down at her phone, that same dimple deepened now by a frown.

"Everything okay?" I ask.

She glances up. Caught. But with any trapped animal, you have to be careful not to spook them. I put on the same contrite look she gave me earlier.

"Shit, sorry," I say. "Now *I'm* overstepping. I don't exactly have the funds for a gift, but you can totally, like, punch me in the face if you want." The joke works, because a smile cracks through her guarded expression, so I give it one more press. "You just seem . . . preoccupied."

She groans, almost like she's relieved that I'm seeing through her bullshit, and that's it. I'm in.

"No, you're right. I'm practically attached to this thing, aren't I?" She waves her phone with a self-effacing eye roll. "It's so not like me to be that girl, but I haven't heard from Colin much today. He's been kind of avoidant lately, and . . . this is the most boring thing I could possibly be talking about. I'll stop."

I fight the vindicated smirk tugging at my lips, keeping my face neutral. *See, Zoe? Even* you *can't take him off the pedestal, use your divine feminine energy to manifest a text instead of desperately watching your phone. You're not* that girl *because* that girl *doesn't exist. She's all of us. There's no pedestal.*

The pedestal is bullshit.

"You can talk about it," I say. "You don't have to, but if you want to, I'm here."

Zoe chews on her lip, and I try to keep my face calm and open, like a friend.

"I can't really explain it," she says. "It's been a lot of little things— you know, slower responses to texts. But he's also been kind of obsessive about his phone. Like, checking it all the time, but in this way that feels secretive, where he sort of angles the screen away. And then last night . . ."

She goes quiet for long enough that I'm worried she won't continue.

"What happened?" I ask, fighting the desperation that wants to strangle the words.

"I got this call," she says. "From a girl asking for Colin. She said her name was Leigh."

The breath stalls in my chest. Suddenly, the necklace feels too tight, enough that I slide my thumb under the chain and lift it away from my skin, reminding myself that I can still inhale.

Leigh, the girl from the Instagram comment. The one I dismissed as probably nothing.

Do you miss me?

"Do you know who she is?" I manage.

Zoe shakes her head. "She hung up as soon as I asked how she got my number. I asked Colin about it, and he said he didn't know her, but he seemed really startled and weird, so I got this feeling that maybe . . ." She stops short, literally shaking herself. "I'm sure it's nothing. A telemarketer or something." She slides her phone back into her pocket as if to prove a point. "Now go on, get changed. The montage waits for no one!"

I'm glad I know now she used to be an actress, even if only in high school, because her sudden shift to chipper ease is so convincing, I could almost believe it—if it weren't for the sharp undercurrent in her eyes. The one that says *end of conversation.*

I slink back into the dressing room and close the curtain, skin buzzing with this new revelation. So, Leigh is a piece in this puzzle, a key to understanding what's going on with Colin. Eagerly, I reach for my phone and open his Instagram, going straight to the most recent post. When I click on the comments, though, Leigh's has vanished.

Like a flash behind my eyes, I see the Penn quarter-zip, the blood caked onto its fibers.

Do you miss me?

I realize I'm squeezing the necklace so tightly that the pendant has left a rosemary-shaped imprint on my thumb.

I let go. Breathe.

We all have a past to contend with. I can't judge Colin for that. I can only hope the blood in his ends with the sweater—washable, or at least disposable, not the kind that stains your hands long after it's gone.

Nothing like mine.

10

On my way home, I google her. It's hard without a last name, but I've made do with less. Usually, a first name plus a college or job title are more than enough for me to track down my dates, but even *Leigh University of Pennsylvania tennis* comes up short. I can't find her anywhere, except for the Instagram account—which I can still find by searching the username, even though her comment was deleted from Colin's post. I send her a follow request as Jake Smith.

I try to be patient.

After work on Monday, I collapse into bed and check my phone for the umpteenth time, but a full day after I sent the request, Leigh still hasn't accepted. I think about DMing her anyway, and then decide against it. I don't want to risk Leigh telling Colin that I'm going behind his back.

If she's even alive. The voice comes from a dark, shadowy part of my mind, one where the memory of the knife is still swaddled in blood-soaked cloth. But that's ridiculous. Leigh commented on Colin's Instagram two days ago. She called Zoe. She's perfectly fine. And here I am, jumping to conclusions, when there could be a perfectly reasonable explanation for all of this—like, maybe Leigh is just a jealous ex. If she's obsessing over Colin, stalking him, then that could drive anyone to the explosion of anger I witnessed in the stairwell.

But it still doesn't explain the bloody knife.

I just need to stay calm. I need to trust Colin.

And I need to know more.

The idea comes in a strike of creative inspiration, the kind I'm always chasing down for my plays. After a bit of research, I send Ben a text:

Hey! How would you feel about seeing this on Friday?

I attach a link to the website for a comedy club in Greenwich Village—one of the cutting-edge types that, according to their FAQ page, locks up all patrons' phones during performances.

He texts back immediately:

Hell yeah!

His excitement is a dig in my side, but I ignore it, focusing instead on texting Zoe. I send her the same link, along with the message, Double date this Friday? I think Ben and I are going to get tickets if you and Colin want to join!

She, too, responds near-instantly:

Yes!!! We're in.

I wonder if she even asked Colin, or if she just assumes he'll be at her beck and call. Either way, I allow myself a small smile. Things are falling into place.

Then, after deliberating for a minute too long about whether or not it's a good idea, I ask the question scratching at the back of my mind.

How's it going with him? Do I have to beat him up yet?

Zoe's typing bubble appears, then disappears, back and forth for almost a full minute. I hold my breath until her response finally whooshes onto my screen.

Nope! I'm pretty sure I was just being overdramatic haha, classic Zoe move :)

Instinct gnaws at me, telling me that response took too long—there's still something she's hiding—but the plan is almost in place.

The last hurdle is, of course, Ben. When I float the idea of turning the comedy show into a double date, he pulls a Zoe, his text bubble floating on the screen for much longer than it takes to type the eventual sounds fun!

I toss him the bone of a heart react, and then reach up to press my thumb against the rosemary pendant of my necklace, grounding myself. *This will work,* I think. It's like Zoe and all of her TikTok manifesters always say: it's about the mindset, the belief. The second our eyes locked in that East Village bar, Colin and I set off a chain reaction too powerful to undo, fissions and sunbursts all leading us back to each other, to the moment we can be together again.

I love him, and I choose to make it so.

On Friday, Ben puts on a brave face. We meet outside of the comedy club, and he pulls me into a hug with his classic puppy-dog grin.

"You look great," he says.

I blush, and I hope he doesn't take it as more than what it is: embarrassment at having my own effort clocked. I'm wearing the outfit Zoe bought me, and somehow, Ben liking it feels wrong. It's not for him.

"Thanks," I say. "You, too."

We're spared from any more small talk, because Zoe and Colin are approaching from the other side of the block. Holding hands, I notice, with a squall of panic in my gut. But as they get closer, Colin's eyes flicker between me and Ben, not quite meeting my gaze, and he drops her hand.

Hope starts to flutter again.

"Hey!" Zoe jogs my way and pulls me into a sugar-scented hug. "*Love* the outfit."

She says that last part like it's our little secret, and I mumble my thanks. She releases me, grinning.

"Seriously, you look so good. Doesn't she look good?"

She directs the question at Ben, who goes bright red.

"She does," he says.

Colin meets my eyes for a moment before his stare snaps to the ground, color creeping into his neck, and there it is again—the hope, more petals uncurling.

Then, when he reaches up to scratch his blotching skin, I see it on his hand: blood.

No, not blood. Faded brown bruises on his knuckles, probably from when they slammed into the wall. A stitch in my side, the suffocating memory of the stairwell, but I force myself to breathe. *Focus on the plan.*

"So." Zoe claps her hands like she's our fearless team captain. "Shall we?"

Colin drops his hand, hiding the bruises in his sleeve. There's nothing to do but follow Zoe through the door.

Inside, the club has the dungeon-like vibe I always love in fringy New York theatres—dark and just on this side of too warm, the club name emblazoned on a letterboard sign in a shroud of vanity bulbs. The walls are lined with framed posters and signed photos from appearances by famous comedians, which Ben geeks out on as we step deeper inside. I smile and nod along, thinking this place would be perfect if it weren't a comedy venue. The grungy, sticky temple of a New York theatre is always bastardized the moment some guy with a mic steps onstage and declares himself a *comic*.

We fall into line at the mandatory phone and coat check. I watch as, up ahead, one of the check-in workers drops a guest's phone into a pouch and snaps it shut. She hands them a ticket.

"I think it's cool that they take our phones," Ben says. "Like, it's wild how few places are left where we have to be totally unplugged and present."

It's basically every freshman theatre major's self-important take on modern-day society, but one I agree with. It's part of why I like live performance so much, too.

"I don't know." Colin's staring at the phone pouches, brows furrowed. "Don't they usually do this at shows where the comedians want to say horrible stuff and not get canceled?"

Yes, I think, but that would reveal how little I actually care about this show, even though coming was my idea, so I keep it to myself.

"Not always," Ben says, clearly a little offended. "I think it's more to keep the environment safe enough for the comics to try out new stuff without risking it getting plastered all over TikTok."

"Presumably because that 'new stuff' has at least one slur," Colin mumbles.

I almost laugh—he's right, so perceptive—but I stop myself. Because, while it could have been a joke, there's no humor in Colin's eyes. They're stony, still fixed on the phone pouches. Dread burrows in my stomach. He doesn't want to be here.

"And what are we supposed to do if there's an emergency or something?" he adds. "Seems dangerous, holding our phones hostage like that."

He's picking at the edge of his sleeve, the one that's hiding the bruises, and suddenly, I understand why Colin is so anxious about giving up his phone. Leigh is harassing him. If he locks his phone away, he'll probably come back to a barrage of missed calls and texts.

Guilt reaches under my skin, but I remind myself that this will be good for him. My plan is offering him a reprieve.

"Okay, dramatic." Zoe pokes at Colin's arm, but her playful tone is wearing. "They're not *held hostage*."

Colin pulls away from her touch, and there it is—another flash of the tension between them. For a moment, I watch it register in Zoe's eyes, a mix of hurt and frustration, but then she paints her usual calm expression back on, raking a hand through her curls.

"You can leave the show and go get your phone if you need it," I say, though whether to quell Colin's anxiety or my own, I'm not sure. "You just give them the ticket and they'll get it for you."

Colin doesn't respond, except to nod, face still wan.

The line grinds forward until we're at the front.

"Tickets?" the check-in guy asks. He's a scruffy, slouchy twenty-something, no doubt another aspiring comedian.

Ben gets out his phone and shows them ours. He insisted on paying, which I feel a little guilty about, but I can't dwell on it for too long. The worker scans our tickets as another scans Zoe's and Colin's.

"Phones," our guy instructs, reaching for two pouches.

"Oh, the four of us can be together." It comes out a little too urgently, so I add, with a corny little smile, "We're all friends here."

The guy nods, collecting our phones and passing me the check ticket. I slip it into my pocket casually, telling the others I'll hold on to it.

When no one seems to care, I let out a small breath of relief. So far, so good.

We file into the performance space, where we settle around one of the small round tables scattered in front of the stage. Ben and I sit first, and I watch Colin hesitate for a moment at the open seat next to me. My heart thuds, my whole body aching suddenly for the warmth of his side against mine, but at the last second, he steps back, gesturing for Zoe to take the seat.

My heart sinks. *It's fine*, I tell myself. *He's too afraid of feeling it, too.* Or maybe he just doesn't want to.

Before I can spiral, a server swoops in, already eager to enforce the two-drink minimum.

"Still an IPA girl?" Ben asks, nudging my shoulder.

I laugh. "Sure."

I'm not, but I want it to needle at Colin, seeing Ben order for me, watching us get the same drink. And then, because I feel Colin's eyes on me—because even though I know I'll forgive him, it doesn't soothe the part of me that wants him to sting—I reach for Ben's hand, threading my fingers through his.

When I glance at Colin again, he's staring pointedly at the menu.

Zoe doesn't seem to notice this silent warfare beside her. She's too busy blithely ordering sodas for them both and a round of fries for the table—another thing I hate about this place, the mortifying humanity of *dinner and a show*—but I force myself to look pleasant.

"So, Ben," Zoe says, when the server is gone, "has Jane told you her play will be premiering at my art show?"

Colin's shoulders tense, and it sends a prickle of worried heat down my back. Has she told him already? Is he upset that I'm working with her?

"Um, no, she hasn't." Ben grins at me, squeezing my knee. "That's awesome!"

"Thanks." I manage a fairly genuine smile. "I'm excited."

"The play is incredible," Zoe gushes. She nudges Colin. "I can't believe you have this amazingly talented friend, and you've been hiding her from me."

A muscle jumps in Colin's jaw. My own teeth grit instinctively in response.

"Yeah," Colin says, fidgeting with the corner of a menu. "She's pretty great."

It should warm me from the inside out, but it doesn't. Because

Colin doesn't even know my work. He never got the chance to. And he won't look at me.

It's brutal, enduring the rest of the chatter as we wait for the show to start. Drinks and snacks materialize, and soon, even Zoe's expert conversational skills seem to be no match for Colin's sullenness, for the awkwardness of this entire situation. I'm just about certain that this was all a terrible idea when, finally, the lights go down.

The show is about to start, in more ways than one.

I clap mechanically as the host comes onstage, doing his best to rile up the crowd, which isn't hard—some of us, it seems, have already more than fulfilled the two-drink requirement. As the first comic jogs onto the stage, I steadily sip my drink, glancing behind us at the exit. I sit through his predictably misogynistic set, and then, once the IPA is half gone and the host is coming back to introduce the second act, I lean over and whisper to Ben, "I'm going to run to the bathroom."

"Want me to come with?" he asks.

But I'm already up. "No, don't worry. I'll be back."

Before he can stop me, I go for the exit, the red beacon glowing above the door. As I step into the hallway, my heart thumps with every step. Whatever shred of acting skills I possess, I try to summon them now as I approach the check-in desk.

"Hi," I say. "Sorry."

I don't know why I'm apologizing. I guess I can't ever help it.

I swallow, fumbling for my ticket.

"Any chance I could grab my phone from the pouch? My roommate's at home with my new kitten, and I just had this total panic that I forgot to remind her to close her door because she's got lilies in her room, and they're totally toxic to cats, so—"

"Sure," the guy says, either buying my frantic cat-mom character or just eager to shut me up. "Ticket?"

I hand it over, and he grabs our pouches.

"Which one was it?" he asks.

This time, I fight the nervous urge to swallow.

"Black case," I say. "There's a little crack in the top-right corner of the screen."

He searches through the pouches until he finds the right one and hands it over.

"If you need to make a call, you can do it outside. We'll let you back in when you're ready."

"Thank you so much," I say, with my best grateful smile.

Then, I take Colin's phone and leave through the lobby doors.

Outside, the chill is a relief on my flushed cheeks. I run my thumb over the little shatter in Colin's screen, a smile playing on my lips. It's the same one he had when we were together. He really needs to take better care of his stuff.

Suddenly, my hand feels shaky as I grip the phone. I force myself to fill my lungs, blow out a breath. I can do this. It feels a little wrong, maybe—no one in a healthy relationship should ever feel like they have to go through their significant other's phone—but then I remember that we're not technically in a relationship, not yet, so maybe this is fine.

This is for him. For us.

I tap the screen to wake it up, only to be confronted with a shattering reality: Colin has a passcode.

Shit. Why didn't I think of this at any step of my grand scheming? My heart is still thudding, my legs unsteady with the adrenaline, and it's almost like the passcode is a metaphor—I'm so close and yet so far. But I can't give up.

Sucking in a breath, I type in his birthday, the four digits of the month and day.

Wrong.

My heart is in my ears now, my throat. How many tries before it locks me out?

Think. I try the full year he was born instead.

Wrong again.

Tears threaten, stinging at the back of my nose, and I'm humiliated. Of all the things I know about Colin, all the ways we're connected, not having this one little piece of him feels like the worst kind of failure.

But whose fault is that, really? If Colin had just let me in instead of running away, we never would have been here in the first place. He could have told me what's wrong, and I could have helped him, because that's what you do when you love someone. You don't run. You *stay.*

I grip the phone tight against the sudden urge to throw it against the concrete, to watch the whole screen shatter.

And then, just before I lose that battle, I hear the door swing open.

I spin around, head rushing with the certainty that it's Colin, that he's caught me.

But it's not him.

It's Zoe.

"Is everything okay?" she asks. "You looked—"

And then, before she can finish, her eyes land on the phone in my hand.

11

Panic. Deer in headlights, rabbit heart.

"What are you doing?"

"I . . ."

Think, Jane.

"I realized I left the oven on at home," I blurt. "I was going to call my roommate to ask her to turn it off, but I guess they gave me Colin's phone by accident."

It's much worse than the lie I gave the check-in guy, and I'm almost positive it won't work—especially since I've been out here long enough to have recognized and fixed the "mistake." Zoe frowns, pinched and hesitant, and I hear my pulse beating like a death march, certain she's about to call me out.

But she doesn't.

Instead, Zoe starts to cry.

For a moment, I'm stunned. I stand there, watching as the tears slip down her cheeks. My first thought: *I guess Zoe Ember is a real person after all.*

My second: *What the fuck?*

"Are you okay?" I ask. "What's . . . ?"

"I'm sorry," Zoe says. It's the first time I've ever heard her apologize. She laughs almost maniacally, wiping her eyes. "I must look so ridiculous right now."

"Not at all," I say warily. "But what's wrong?"

She takes a deep breath and sits on the comedy club steps. Cautiously, I join her.

"It's just that when I saw you had Colin's phone," Zoe starts, "my first thought was 'How can I get it so I can look through his texts?'"

It's like a lightning bolt shot straight from my head to the tips of my fingers, gripping Colin's phone tighter. It takes everything in me not to sputter out the truth and ask for Zoe's help. Instead, I rest my elbows on my knees, projecting calm and rational.

"Oh," I say. "I mean, that makes sense, with everything you've told me. I'd say it's a pretty normal reaction, actually."

It's not—looking through your partner's phone is the dying gasp of any relationship—but I won't say that. Zoe is clearly struggling right now, and there's something about her sudden vulnerability that sucks me in like a vortex.

She shakes her head sharply. "No one in a good relationship ever has to check their boyfriend's texts."

Okay, so Zoe's more self-aware than I gave her credit for.

"Did something else happen?" I ask. "With that girl who called you, Leigh? Or . . ."

She sighs, burying her face in her hands. After a deep breath, she lifts her head to face me again, and her eyes are alight with something so unfamiliar on her that it takes me a moment to recognize it: shame.

"I looked through his stuff, Jane."

My heart thrums, loud enough that I can feel it in my eardrums.

"I know," Zoe says. "I swear, I don't know what came over me. I've never done this before."

She thinks I'm judging her, I realize. But that's not what this is.

I'm a little more concerned with the fact that she may have found the knife and bloody sweater in his drawer.

I force myself into the best performance of calm that I can manage. "Did you find anything?"

She nods, face warping again like she might cry, and I clench my teeth.

Please, I think. *Please don't be what I think this is.*

"Last night," she starts, "when he went to shower, he took his phone with him. Like he literally didn't trust me *not* to look through it. And I just—I snapped. His laptop was still on his desk, so . . ."

I breathe out, relaxing just a little. So, she didn't look in the dresser. But that doesn't mean she didn't see something else. Something worse.

"What did you find?"

Zoe bites her lip. "At first, nothing. But then there was this folder on his desktop. It was kind of hidden in this other folder called 'taxes' or something. I only found it because I accidentally clicked. It didn't have a file name, and I just got this intuition, like I had to look, so I opened it." She closes her eyes. "My worst fear was that he's cheating on me or something. But this . . ."

"What was it?" I ask, too urgent to care how desperate I sound.

When she opens her eyes again, they're filled with true horror. I feel it reaching through the space between us, sinking into my bones.

"There were all these photos of this girl," she says. "She was . . . tied up. It didn't look like she was physically hurt in any of the pictures, but I don't know. It was so fucked up."

Cold grips me from the inside out, but I force myself to breathe through it. There's an explanation for this. There has to be.

"Do you know who she is?" I ask.

She shakes her head quickly. "Her face was covered with this bag, like . . . like a kidnapping victim, or something. She seemed young, though. Probably our age. Maybe younger."

The bloody quarter-zip flashes in my memory, bright as a blade.

"And you think . . ." I hesitate. "You think Colin took the pictures?"

"I don't know. He wasn't in them. For all I know, it's something he downloaded from some weird website, and I don't want to kink-shame, but he's never been into bondage or anything, and I . . ." She shudders. "I just got this really bad feeling."

I nod. It's an explanation I hadn't considered, but it sounds plausible. If all this—the pictures, the knife, even the blood—is part of some consensual sex thing, I can understand it. Get behind it, even.

But as much as I wish it would, it doesn't ring true. The same doubt that Zoe's describing is scratching at my door, a creature wanting to come inside.

"And that on top of how weird and avoidant he's been lately, and how obsessive he's been about checking his phone . . ." Zoe takes a shallow breath, and when she speaks again, her voice comes out smaller. "I think he might have done something bad."

The words reverberate through me, a string plucked and vibrating the same discordant notes. *The shout, the fist, the blood, the knife.*

I'd prepared myself for this. I knew Colin might have been hiding something truly awful, but what Zoe's describing—this tied-up girl, the methodical recording of her pain—it doesn't sound like Colin. It doesn't sound *human.*

"Something bad?" I repeat hoarsely. "Like . . . ?"

"I don't know." She looks away, out at the street. "Maybe I'm overreacting. I mean, it's *Colin.*"

It's like she's slapped me in the face. Of *course.* It doesn't sound like Colin because it isn't. There's something else going on here, something I'm just on the verge of understanding. The thought relaxes me enough to ask what I need to next.

"Did you take pictures or anything? Like, of what you saw on his computer?" I don't want to see them, but I need to know what we're up against.

She shakes her head. "I was so freaked out that I just panicked and closed everything. I even started to convince myself that I made it up, somehow. Like, I felt so terrible for even thinking Colin would hurt someone that I've got this weird guilt, like *I'm* the one who's doing something wrong. Like I don't deserve him. And—" She presses the heels of her hands to her eyes. "I feel like I'm losing my mind."

I watch her for a moment, this brazenly confident girl folded into a smaller version of herself, and a sliver of a crack widens in my heart. I know what it's like, to eat yourself alive. To be so primed for disbelief and distrust that you accept it before it even happens, contorting your own reality to fit inside what little crawl space it's allowed. I understand her, I think.

But I know where my priorities lie.

"You're not losing your mind," I say carefully. "But you're right. It's *Colin*. I mean, has he ever given you any reason to think that he would hurt someone?"

"No," Zoe says firmly. "Never." She lets out a small, airy laugh. "Once, I heard him earnestly apologize to a fly for killing it."

Warmth oozes into my rib cage. Because that's him. *That's* Colin, not any of this.

I look down at his phone, my heart picking up a nervous rhythm. I lift it, like I'd forgotten it was in my hand, and then, like the idea only just now occurred to me:

"We could look through it, if it would make you feel better."

Zoe hesitates. "Should we? I mean, that's a pretty big violation of trust."

Like she didn't do the exact same thing with his computer, I think, but I keep it to myself.

"Right, but it could also put your mind at ease, so you know for sure that nothing's wrong." I pause, letting that sink in. "But if you think we shouldn't . . ."

"No," Zoe says, reaching for the phone. "A quick check wouldn't hurt, right?"

She looks at me like she needs my answer to make it true.

I give her a small smile. "Do you know his passcode?"

Zoe types it in, and I look over her shoulder, memorizing the numbers, both relieved and envious as the phone unlocks.

She pulls up his texts, and I move in close to see the screen, trying to keep my breath steady so she doesn't feel my nerves.

And there it is, right at the top of his text conversations: a message from an unsaved number.

You can't hide forever, Colin

Zoe's eyes snap up to mine, and I can feel it rolling through us both—the terrible certainty that it's too late to turn back. She opens up the full conversation, and it's a wall of messages from the stranger, all sent throughout the day today.

I know you miss me

What would your pretty little girlfriend think if she found out who you really are?

Or are you going to kill this one too?

The knife flashes through my mind again, so sharp I can almost feel its blade against my neck.

Are you going to kill this one too?

The fries I ate at the table roil in my stomach. Colin shouting, slamming the wall, the knife and the blood . . . What other explanation could there be? Still, I grasp for one. Whoever sent this text is wrong. Lying. They have to be, right?

And then, I realize: *I know you miss me.*

It sounds a whole lot like that comment from Leigh.

"Do you recognize the number?" Zoe asks, her voice small and strained.

"No," I say. "Do you?"

She shakes her head. My mind spins, all the terrible thoughts and implications tumbling over each other like laundry from hell. This stalker—Leigh—is accusing Colin of murder. But whose? Some other girl, another ex? Another piece of his past that he hid from me?

"We have to do something," Zoe says. "Right? We have to talk to him, or—"

"No." It comes out too quickly. She looks at me, shocked, and I try to recover. "I mean, we don't know for sure what this is yet, right?"

"They're saying he killed someone," Zoe argues, eyes wide. "As in, his girlfriend, and he might do it again."

Okay, fair. I trace my thumb back and forth over the edge of the phone, thinking.

"As far as we know, they're just messing with him. You said that girl called you, right? Leigh? She could be an ex or something. Maybe she's trying to get back at him somehow. She could have even sent him those pictures."

It makes sense—maybe only if you squint—but it seems to calm Zoe down the tiniest bit.

"Maybe." She starts to chew on her long, wine-colored nail but then stops herself. "But when I told him about the call, he told me he didn't know who Leigh was." She looks at me, urgent. "Do you think I should ask him again?"

"No," I say. "Definitely not. I mean, you'd have to tell him you know about the texts."

"Shit, you're right." She covers her face. "We shouldn't have done this. This was—"

"Zoe." I reach out to touch her shoulder, an impulse that surprises the both of us. But she doesn't fight it. "You had a feeling that something was off, and you looked into it. There's nothing wrong with that. You were just protecting yourself."

She nods slowly. "Yeah, I guess so."

It's like something lodged in my throat, what I know I have to ask next.

"You love him, right?"

For a second, she's quiet, and I'm scared she can hear it, the fierce pounding of my heart as I wait for her answer.

"I do," she says.

It's a dig in the wound and a balm all at once. Because it needs to be true for the rest of this to work.

"Then I think the best thing to do is wait it out," I tell her. "Those texts and the pictures . . . I'm sure there's an explanation for both. You just have to trust him. Let him come to you when he's ready."

It's the exact advice I need to hear, too, and it seems to work for both of us. Zoe nods, her shoulders loosening slightly. Realizing I'm still touching her, I lift my hand and bury it in my pocket.

"Thank you," she says. "For listening. And for not thinking I'm crazy."

"Of course," I say, with the smallest twinge of guilt. I force it down. "Let me know if anything else comes up, okay? I don't think you have anything to worry about, but if you do, I'm here."

"Yeah." She gives me a small smile, dimple flashing, before glancing over her shoulder. "Should we go back in?"

This has, I realize, probably seemed to Colin and Ben like the longest bathroom trip in eternity. I nod, and we stand together. As we near the door, Zoe stops.

"Did you still need to call your roommate?"

I freeze. I'd completely forgotten.

"It's probably fine," I say. "Actually, now that I think about it, I'm pretty sure I remember turning the oven off. I'm just anxious. This happens every time I leave, even when I double-check."

I force a self-deprecating laugh. Zoe smiles.

"No, same." She reaches for the door, pausing again before opening it. "Seriously, thank you. You're a good friend."

The word echoes through me. *Friend.* There's an ache to it, one that deepens as I brush the rosemary pendant around my neck.

"Any time," I say.

And why not? Maybe we *can* be friends, real ones. As we step back into the murky light of the club, I envision it: I'll prove Colin isn't the monster that Zoe fears he could be, prove we're meant to be together, and Zoe will understand. Support us, even. It doesn't have to come down to the tired cliché, a girl choosing between love and friendship.

If it does, then I'll allow myself another quiet, beating hope: that she'll forgive me for what I have to do.

12

Two hours and countless red-pill, white-guy-with-a-podcast jokes later, we're finally freed from the comedy prison. As we get our phones back from the check-in desk, I watch Colin carefully, half-certain that some smudge or detail will give away what Zoe and I have done, but he slides his phone back into his pocket, unbothered.

Zoe catches my eye with a small smile. Quietly, I breathe out. I don't like going behind Colin's back, but for now, I'm just relieved we didn't get caught.

"So, what's the move?" Ben asks as we all head back onto the street. "Do we grab drinks to discuss?"

He looks hopefully at me, and I glance at Zoe.

"I might actually head home," she says. "I think I want to get some painting in tonight." She glances at Colin. "You okay if I go back to Greenpoint?"

I don't miss the *I*, the hint that he's not invited. I also don't miss the subtle wash of relief on Colin's face.

"Yeah, for sure," he says. "No problem."

Quietly, I exhale. For tonight, at least, I know Zoe won't confront

Colin. Now, the only immediate problem is Ben. I can still feel his stare, and I force myself to meet it.

"I may head home, too," I tell him. "I should catch up on sleep."

He's clearly disappointed, and guilt tugs at me as he puts on a smile.

"No worries at all," Ben says. "Can I still walk you to the subway?"

There's nothing I want more than to be alone right now—alone with Colin—but this entire date has essentially been an elaborate ruse. I can't begrudge Ben this.

"Yeah," I say. "Of course."

Zoe pulls me in for another hug.

"I'll text you tomorrow," she says, like this is a given. Like we're really friends. She pulls back, giving Ben and I another dazzling smile. "Night, you guys."

Before we part ways, I look at Colin one more time, and my breath catches. He's looking back. For a split second, we're locked together, his stare all soft and deep enough to sink inside, and I want to tell him everything: what I know. That whatever he did, I don't care. All of this ties back to Leigh. Colin could be perfectly innocent, and it's like I told Zoe: I have to trust him.

Colin turns away, leaving me colder than I was a moment ago, and follows Zoe down the sidewalk. The smell of her pink-sugar perfume still lingers on my clothes.

"So," Ben says, now that we're alone.

I gesture in the direction of the subway, shattering the moment before it can attract any unwanted meaning. "Shall we?"

We muscle our way through small talk about the show until finally, blessedly, we're at my stop. I want to scurry down the stairs as soon as possible, but that wouldn't be fair, and Ben is also directly blocking my path. I'm trapped.

"I had fun tonight," he says.

I paint on a smile. "Me, too."

He looks down at me, his pupils dancing with the light from the buildings around us, all these little pockets of the city full of other lives and stories humming alongside our own. It would be a perfect romantic moment if it weren't so wrong, but the moment has already begun, and I know my stage directions.

Ben leans in, and I close my eyes, giving myself over to the kiss. Knowing it's one step closer to the end.

I pull away first. "I should probably get going."

"You sure you don't want to come over?"

I bite down on the inside of my cheek. I knew he might try again, and a part of me likes the idea of going back to Colin's apartment, just so I can keep an eye on him. But it's clear he needs space, and I have other things to focus on.

"I wish," I say. "But I have work early tomorrow, so . . ."

Something flashes through Ben's expression—disappointment, but also something more. Frustration, I think. Maybe suspicion. He holds my gaze, like he isn't sure if he should say what's on his mind. Finally, he sighs.

"Sorry if I'm totally off-base here, but was there ever something going on with you and Colin?"

I freeze.

"No," I snap, heat rising to my cheeks. "Why?"

Ben looks like he regrets opening his mouth at all.

"No reason," he says. "I mean . . . I don't know. I'm just getting a vibe."

I'm so irritated that the lie comes out without a hitch.

"He's my friend. I'm on a date with you."

"I know, I just—forget it. I shouldn't have said anything."

"Well, you did."

Ben nods, running a hand over his stubble.

"Look, I have no problem with this being a double date," he says. "Like, at all. Colin's like my brother. Zoe's cool, too. It just caught me off guard when you asked, I guess. And then all night . . . you've kind of seemed more interested in him than in me."

A mix of guilt and anger floods my chest. He noticed. Of course he noticed.

"Is this because I don't want to go back to your apartment?"

The question burns out of me before I know if I mean it or I'm just deflecting. Ben stares at me, stunned.

"No," he sputters. "I—well, I don't know. Is that so bad if it is?"

I laugh. So, even good-guy Ben can't keep up the act when he isn't getting what he wants. I turn to go down to the platform.

"Wait," he says, stopping me. "I don't mean that. I just—I feel like we really connected the other night. But maybe I was wrong."

My throat stings, a mix of indignation at Ben's accusation and shame that he's right.

"Yeah," I say. "Maybe you were."

I turn away, but Ben reaches for me again.

"What?" I bark.

His hand falls to his side, but his gaze is locked on mine.

"I just think you should be careful," he says. "I know you're Colin's friend, but I've known him his whole life, and I know he doesn't always have the clearest head when it comes to relationships. And sometimes, there's this . . . this other part of him that comes out."

That text echoes in my head.

Are you going to kill her too?

"What do you mean?" I breathe, too stunned to remember my anger.

Ben shakes his head.

"Nothing," he says. Already, I can tell he's backsliding, that he feels like he said too much. "I just mean if there's any part of you that's into him like that, then maybe you should reconsider. For your own good."

I keep my face stone, even as dread winds its way up my spine. I should ask Ben more, *need* to, but the only thing I need more is to get away from him, from the part of him that needs me to be the vision he's created in his head. A nice, normal girl. A girl who could be his.

"Cool," I snap. "Thanks for the advice."

I turn and go, his stare like a poisoned blade in my back as I descend into the warm underground.

Long before Trip, there was Mikey Medina. He had floppy hair and a gap between his front teeth, and on the first day of second grade, he told me he liked my bright blue shoelaces. At lunch that day, Jessie Carvel had said that we were in second grade now, so we'd better have crushes, and who was mine? I told her Mikey. It felt like a good answer. She asked me if I was going to tell him, and that's when the trouble began.

I spent the better part of free play deciding how to go about things. I remembered a movie I'd watched, or maybe a book I read, where the characters wrote love letters to each other, and I thought it seemed like a decent idea.

I got to work at the art table, angling myself over my paper so no one would see before it was finished. In a menagerie of crayon colors, I confessed my love, going as far as to include a picture of us holding hands, expertly rendered with both of us in blue shoelaces. I signed the letter Jane Medina, because I suppose I was manifesting even then, and then folded it up into four neat squares. Just before bringing it to his cubby, I got the bright idea to pull my own blue shoelace out of my sneaker and tie it up around the letter like a bow.

I dropped it off with my heart full of hope.

By the next morning, I'd almost entirely forgotten. Time moves in strange ways when you're seven, and anyway, Mikey Medina's cubby had seemed like a portal to another world. Once the letter left my hand, it ceased to exist.

That is, until Mrs. McGuire pulled me aside before recess.

Did you leave a letter in Mikey's cubby, Jane?

I got the feeling that whatever was about to happen would be bad, and so I decided to lie. *No.*

She frowned at me, lines pinching around her lipsticked mouth.

It's very normal to have certain feelings, she said softly. *But sometimes, those feelings can make other people uncomfortable. Do you understand?*

I didn't, but I nodded anyway.

Good. Maybe no more letters in your classmates' cubbies for a while, okay?

She sent me off to the playground. I was vaguely aware of Mikey and some of the boys staring at me when I caught up with Jessie at the monkey bars. And then, as I swung from one bar to the other, I heard him: David Haley, Mikey's best friend.

Jane and Mikey sitting in a tree, he sang in a high-pitched voice. *K-I-S-S-I-N—*

Mid-swing, I turned to look, and that was my mistake: my hand clutched air instead of the next monkey bar, and I dropped to the ground, knees hitting the asphalt. The blood came quickly after the sting, pooling around the dirt-caked scrapes.

I knew it was smartest not to cry. Biting my cheek, I got up and dusted myself off. David was laughing, and one of the other boys, too. Even Jessie looked embarrassed for me.

Mikey just looked down at his shoes. He wasn't wearing the lace I gave him—just his own gray ones. In the end, that's what finally brought on the tears. I limped away to ask Mrs. McGuire for a bandage, their laughter a growing chorus behind me.

That night, I sat locked up in my room. My shoes were next to the door, one with its blue lace and the other still empty, eyelets staring back at me like empty sockets.

There was yelling downstairs. I knew it was about me.

I focused on the bandage on my knee. It was bright yellow, printed with Mickey Mouse's smiling face. Slowly, I peeled it off, watching the sticky part pull at my skin. Underneath, it was raw and red, scabbing over in a rusty brown.

That was the day I began to understand something essential: love is embarrassing. Delicate. Something to be tucked away, kept hidden, never shown first.

It's still a philosophy I see all around me. Just listen to the Zoes of the world. *Take him off the pedestal*, they say. *Don't respond too fast. Don't, under any circumstances, be the one who cares the most. Don't you see, you silly girl, that it's our only power here? To be chased, to make him want? To receive?*

That night in second grade, I scratched at a crusted edge of the scab until it started to peel, like another bandage. The sting was bright and clear as I pulled it off, revealing the bright gash beneath, pooling already with new blood.

It made a breathless sort of sense. It does even now, as I scroll through my old texts with Colin, reliving the banter, the planning, all of the moments when he was mine. I won't text him, even though I'm dying to know if Ben told him about our conversation tonight. It's impossible to scare off the right person, I know, and every part of me wants to stop playing this game and just call him, go downtown and bang on his door. But I can't. He needs to come to me on his own.

I am loved, I am whole, and I release him.

He will come back.

And so, I scroll.

It's like I learned back then, locked up in my childhood bedroom: you have to pick the scab, make it hurt. It's the only way you won't forget the wound.

13

Saturday is torture. I wake with a dry throat and no notifications except for a Venmo request from Anna for this month's electric bill— too much, again, because Harmony always insists on running her AC, even when it's chilly, because it *helps her sleep.* The resentment harbors in my chest cavity as I busy myself with laundry, essay sessions, and the hunt of a fly that won't stop buzzing around my room. It evades me every time.

All day, I wait for a text—maybe manifesting, maybe desperation— but none comes, not even from Ben. Leigh hasn't accepted my follow request, either, and after combing the internet once more, I still can't find her anywhere else.

The sun is setting and I'm nearly sick with longing when the universe gives me a meager win: I finally land the fly. It perches on my wall like a dare, and I catch it with my spatula, reveling in the splatter of blood and guts.

I think of Colin, and I hate myself.

I'm just about to go wash off the carcass when my phone lights up with a text.

SOS can you come to Greenpoint??

Zoe. I read it twice.

And then, my mind lurches into panic. She found the knife, I think, or she's confronted him, or—

Colin invited me to Sam's party tonight and I have no idea what to wear!

And also I need a plus-plus-one ;)

I stare at the texts with my mouth wide enough to catch any other flies that dare encroach upon my space. After last night, it's strange, how back to normal she seems. But this is good—further proof that she won't do anything impulsive, even if part of me wonders if this fashion emergency is earnest or some kind of cry for help.

Either way, after a day of nothing, this crumb of Colin is too sweet to pass up. He'll be there tonight. I'll see him, maybe even talk to him—*really* talk, if it's right, about everything he's hiding from me, everything I want to help him carry.

And, I think, with an almost masochistic curiosity, *I'll know what Zoe's apartment looks like*—another piece of her world, this girl he's convinced himself that he wants.

I wait five minutes, so I don't seem too eager, before texting back to ask what time. Her response is immediate:

ASAP! Party's in Tribeca at 9

Colin will meet us there

I clean the blood off my spatula before I get ready, scrubbing until my fingers prune with the warm water and dish soap. *A ritual,* I think. This chance to be reborn.

I don't know exactly what I expected Zoe's apartment to look like, but now that I'm here, I'm certain nothing would make more sense: a converted factory loft in Greenpoint, the old company name still painted artistically on the side. I look up the address—a compulsion I sometimes have when I see someone's apartment for the first time—and find studios going for over $3,000 a month. Zoe must be raking in more with her art, or maybe her TikTok, than I thought. Unless her Greenwich, Connecticut, parents happen to be chipping in, which I find particularly likely in the case of most hot young artists in New York.

I expect her to just buzz me in, so I'm surprised when she opens the building door herself. She's wearing a trendy lounge set, matching hoodie and sweats both stained with paint, and somehow, I still feel less put together in my jeans and sweater.

"Thanks so much for coming down," she says, pulling me into a hug. "I know it's a bit of a hike for you."

"Yeah, no problem," I tell her, hoping she can't feel the way my heart is beating through my jacket. I didn't realize how nervous I am until just now—worse now that she's acting as normal as she did in her messages, even if *normal* for Zoe is the energetic embodiment of a text smiley face.

She leads me inside and up the stairs, going on about the hundred-year history of this building until, finally, we're at her unit. She slides the key in the lock and opens the door.

It's like something out of one of those TV shows where you wonder how in god's name these twentysomethings are affording that place: a spacious studio with an exposed brick wall and rafters, hardwood floors, and pipes jutting from one side of the ceiling to the other. It's decorated like an ad from an Urban Outfitters catalogue, trendy light fixtures and accent pieces that shouldn't go together but somehow, against all odds, do. And then, there's the art stuff: a literal easel set up right in front of one of the big, airy windows; beside it, a table of paints, canvas, a digital camera, and other tools, all of it existing in a state of what I imagine Zoe describes as *organized chaos*, although I would maybe omit the *organized*.

Still, she doesn't do the programmed-into-women thing where she apologizes for the mess. Instead, she breezes right to the kitchen.

"I was just about to make coffee," she says. "You want any?"

I tell her I'm not much of a coffee person, leaving out the *especially after sundown*, but Zoe insists on serving me something. She opens her fridge and talks me through the apparently plentiful beverage menu before we settle on a Diet Coke. I crack it open, marveling at the web of contradictions that is Zoe Ember: Brooklyn art girl, a little granola, but still not afraid to indulge in TikTok and Diet Coke, things other Brooklynites would describe as *basic*. Maybe that's why she does so well in the art world, I think. Because she refuses to fit herself into their specific blueprint of coolness.

It also probably doesn't hurt that she's hot and rich.

We settle into Zoe's little sitting area—her on a fluffy white chair, me on the green velvet sofa, both of which are strewn with clothes from Zoe's apparently very real fashion emergency—and I can't take it anymore. I have to ask.

"So," I say, as casually as possible, "how's everything been since yesterday? With Colin?"

"Good." It's a little too put-on, but then she settles into a more relaxed version. "*Good.* I've been thinking about everything, and you were right. I was being ridiculous. I trust him."

I cup the Diet Coke, grateful for the coolness on my palms.

"So, he hasn't said anything else about Leigh? Or . . ."

"No. But it's like you said—he will when he's ready." She sighs. "Honestly, I'm so grateful for the way you put things into perspective. He's a great guy. A great boyfriend. The best I've ever had, really. So it makes sense, you know? That I'm looking for ways to sabotage it. It's the Zoe Ember special."

She tucks a curl behind her ear with a little roll of her eyes— maybe the first self-deprecating gesture I've ever seen on her, and it looks wrong, ill-fitting. It's also a finger in the open wound of my heart, even though I know that's ridiculous. This is what I wanted, what Colin and I need: for Zoe not to do anything rash. I just can't take hearing her talk about him like that. Like he's *hers*.

Maybe because I know that soon, he won't be.

"Good," I say, forcing a smile. "I'm glad. And if anything ever changes, you can always come to me."

"Thanks." She smiles. Then, she sets her mug down on the table, like she means business, and gestures at the mess of clothes around us. "Still in for playing dress-up?"

I want to protest—both the notion of adult women *playing dress-up* and the end of the Colin conversation—but I know it's smartest to keep things copacetic. I match Zoe's smile, and say, in her breezy tone, "I definitely owe you after the thrifting."

She laughs, reaching for some of the outfit choices from her chair. As she sifts through them, I glance down at my phone. An Instagram notification on the lock screen makes my heart jump—Colin? Leigh?— but when I click to view it, it's nothing, just a notification that I didn't ask for telling me someone I don't care about is going live.

"What's up?" Zoe asks, clearly clocking the anxious look on my face.

"Nothing," I say.

Obviously, it wasn't. I need to get myself under control.

But then, I get an idea. Zoe didn't seem to know who Leigh was before, but maybe she'd recognize her if she saw her Instagram. It's tricky territory, because I don't want to nudge Zoe back toward the ledge I just talked her down from. Still, I know I have to. Leigh is the only real clue I have about what's going on with Colin, and I can't let it go.

"Actually, I just remembered something I wanted to tell you," I say.

"Oh?" Zoe looks suddenly nervous.

"It's probably nothing," I counter. "But the other day, I saw this comment on Colin's Instagram. From Leigh."

Zoe frowns. "What did it say?"

Her posture is stiffer now, and I wonder if some part of her is jealous at the thought of this other girl in Colin's comments. Silently, I feel vindicated.

"It said, 'Do you miss me?'" I explain as I pull up Instagram—my real one—and navigate to Leigh's profile. "I didn't recognize her, but she's on private, so I couldn't see much. And when I looked again, the comment was gone. Here."

I hand my phone to Zoe.

"I tried to follow her, but she hasn't accepted," I add. "Do you recognize her?"

She scrunches her nose. "I don't think so."

My stomach knots, but I try not to show it.

"That has to be the girl who called you, right?" I say. "Maybe if we can get access to her account, we can figure out how she knows him. You know, prove she's just an angry ex, or someone he's never even met. That could put your mind at rest."

Zoe hesitates, and my heart climbs into my throat. I've played my hand too boldly, I think, and she can see right through my pale skin and into the mess of veins and arteries.

But then, she nods.

"I'll send her a follow request," she says casually, like it's nothing, and I relax. "I'm verified. Maybe that'll sway her."

As she hands me back my phone, I internally roll my eyes. As if that little blue check mark is a divine marker bestowed upon her and not something Zoe had to actively go through the process of requesting. Still, she has a point, and it's better than nothing. I watch as she pulls up Leigh's profile on her own phone and requests to follow the account.

"Okay," Zoe says. "Done." Like it really is, she gathers up her clothes again, her usual confidence flooding her expression. "Shall we?"

For the next twenty minutes, I watch as Zoe tries on different but equally bold outfits, asking for my thoughts on each one. It seems, strangely, that despite my grim lack of style, she actually wants my opinion. It's another vulnerability, another crack in the façade to file away for myself: Zoe cares what I think of her.

Or maybe, I realize, as she goes back to the first outfit she tried on—an almost-lingerie corset top, leather pants, and heeled boots, the one I could tell she liked most from the beginning—it's less that Zoe wants my opinion and more that she wants this ritual of friendship, the inverse of the thrift shop: Zoe in front of a mirror, allowing herself to be seen.

Guilt starts to nibble at me, little rat teeth in a wire on its way to sparking.

I force it down.

"Do you want to borrow something?" Zoe asks, eyes catching on my own outfit.

I tug the sleeves of my denim jacket over my hands, self-conscious of how underdressed I am next to her. I took some time with a swipe of eyeliner and my hair, clipping it up with my bangs hanging down, like it was when Colin and I first met, but I should have expected this—of course Zoe is dressed like she's going to the club. Is that what Colin likes now?

"Oh." I blanch, fidgeting with the rosemary necklace. "I wouldn't want . . ."

"No, I want to!" She clasps her hands. "What you have on right now is totally cute, but I have a bunch of other stuff that would fit you. This would be fun for me, I promise."

She's insistent, and I'm powerless. The only way out is through. And so, I surrender.

Within minutes, Zoe has me posed in front of her mirror in a black miniskirt and long-sleeved snakeskin-print bodysuit. It hugs my shape nicely, I think, giving an illusion of curves where there aren't any, but it's definitely too much.

I pull on the skirt. "I don't know. It's a little . . ."

I can't find the word.

Zoe raises an eyebrow. "You don't have to wear anything you don't want to, but you'll have to convince me first that it's not just because you're afraid to attract attention."

I'm a little dumbfounded. Never has someone reached so expertly into my mind and plucked out my exact brand of bullshit like a psychological game of Operation.

"Well, shit," I say, admitting defeat.

"Sorry. I've been told I can be a little blunt." She smirks. "Blunt, but almost always correct." She looks at my reflection with a challenge in her eyes. "So?"

I follow her gaze. I *do* look good.

I wonder if Colin would think so. If it would weird him out to see me in Zoe's clothes.

Or maybe it would remind him of what he's missing.

In spite of myself, a smile stretches on my lips. "Fine."

Zoe touches up her makeup, and then we're ready. She forgoes a jacket, saying she runs warm—of *course* she's the type of hot girl who pretends to never be cold—but I throw on my denim jacket again. It's in the high fifties, warm for November, but it's more for comfort than anything.

Zoe gives me an amused look.

"What?" I ask.

"Nothing," she says. "You're just like one of those grandparents who refuses to give up their landline, but in an absolutely chic sort of way."

I shrug, adjusting my sleeves. "I'll take that as a compliment."

She grins. "As you should."

And thus, our journey to Tribeca begins. The trains are packed with girls our age, all no doubt also headed for a night out downtown, and I can't help but lose myself in watching them—cataloguing their clothes, their movements, like an audience member of a play in a language I don't understand.

I've been out in a group of girls before, obviously—as Tisch students, we traveled in packs like prey who've convinced themselves that they're predators—but even then, I always felt like I was standing on the periphery, falling naturally to the back of the group and jogging to catch up with the leaders, with the runaway ends of stories I didn't hear. I've always told myself that it's just the curse of being a playwright and not an actor or director: this undeniable urge to be part of something bigger than myself at war with my own introversion, my duty to observe the world pushing up against the desire to live inside it.

Now, though, as Zoe tells me a story about the time some guy at a bar tried to convince her that he was Banksy, I realize that some of the riders are looking at *us*, immersed in our own site-specific performance of girls in the city, girls with somewhere to be. I know most of them are drawn to Zoe, but still, for a moment, I let myself imagine they're all Colin, taking me in. It's intoxicating, bathing in his imaginary gaze, knowing it's all for me. A bright spot of warmth, welcome in the cold.

When Sam's towering hulk of a building finally comes into view, it's pretty much exactly what I expected from a finance guy, and still, I'm floored. I always am, whenever I'm confronted with other twenty-somethings in the city who've experienced true wealth of their own making.

The lobby looks more like something from a hotel than an apartment building, with spotless tile floors, art deco lighting fixtures, and not one but *two* doormen seated behind a clean reception desk. Zoe strides inside like she belongs here, while I try not to look worried about tracking in street grime on the bottoms of my boots.

She tells them we're here for Sam, and they wave us through. When we get into the elevator, Zoe pushes the button for the roof.

"Damn," I say. "A *roof* party?"

She sighs. "If only we'd all been born with a passion for finance."

The elevator shoots upward, and I give myself one last look in the mirrored surface. I look good, I think, but as we hurtle toward the sky, toward Colin, it's starting to feel like too much.

Zoe catches me looking, and it's too late to pretend I wasn't.

"You look great," she says. "And don't say you don't, because that'll be an insult to my handiwork."

Before I can respond, the doors open, beckoning us onto the roof.

Even six years in, the city still takes my breath away from up this high. All around us, it sparkles, skyscrapers stretching up to the night like arms extending in devotion. Brightly lit windows are a portal into the surrounding luxury apartments and office buildings, and I'm stunned at how few of them have curtains, like they don't care who sees them, so long as we're elite enough to reach their heights.

It's not a huge party—maybe fifteen people clustered in different groups around the deck chairs, a table of drinks, and the balcony edges, leaning down to look at the less fortunate people below.

And then, right in the middle of it, is him: Colin, standing around a table with Sam and a few people I don't recognize, the city reflected in his glasses.

It still catches me off guard sometimes, being near him like this. After so many months of not seeing him at all, not knowing where he is or what he's doing or if he misses me, it's a wonder, being close enough to breathe his air.

He sees Zoe first, smiling as he lifts a hand to wave. And then, he notices me beside her.

I fight the urge to pull at my skirt as he takes me in, forcing myself instead to stand like Zoe: confident, daring him to look away. And he doesn't. The expression on his face is something like awe. It's the gaze I fantasized about on the subway, only at a magnified intensity, enough to burn a hole right through me.

Zoe walks toward him, and the spell breaks. His eyes are back on her.

I trail behind.

"Hey, you," Zoe says.

Colin pulls her in for a kiss, and I grit my teeth.

"I hope it's okay that I'm stealing your friend again," Zoe adds, glancing my way. "I needed backup."

I hesitate. Did Zoe not tell Colin I was coming?

"Yeah, for sure," Colin says, glancing Sam's way. "I mean, if it's cool with Sam."

My heart shrivels the tiniest bit. Zoe really didn't tell him. And she didn't prepare me for it.

"The more, the merrier," Sam booms, clearly intent on minimizing the awkwardness. I can tell he's someone who thrives on hosting, from the ragers he no doubt threw in college to the dinner fetes that will certainly become his bread and butter when he retires to the Hamptons. He shakes my hand. "Good to see you, Jane. Zoe."

He shakes her hand, too, no trace of the way he was gossiping about her with Peter just last week. It's a weird mix of guilt and exhilaration, knowing he and I have that secret between us.

"Drinks are over there," Sam says, pointing to the table. "There's also some regular seltzers and stuff, if you two are still off the sauce. Which, between you and me, maybe isn't the worst thing. Some of my coworkers have already had enough to make me wonder what my renter's insurance policy says about people falling off the roof."

Zoe laughs, twinkling. If Sam is the perfect host, then she's the perfect guest, the one who turns a gathering into a party the moment she walks in.

"Thanks," she says. "And hey, just give us the signal and we're on balcony guard duty."

"I'll have my people call your people." Sam shoots finger guns. "But seriously, enjoy yourselves! Let me know if you need anything."

He fades back into the party, moving seamlessly into another group.

"So," Zoe says, squeezing Colin's arm. "Did you miss us?"

It's a perfect girlfriend performance, but I tense at the closeness to Leigh's Instagram comment. *Do you miss me?* It was too casual for me to be sure Zoe even meant to do it, and if Colin realizes, he's hiding it well, too.

"You have no idea."

He didn't refute the *us* in Zoe's question, and it gives me a sizzling feeling just beneath my skin.

"I don't know how to talk to finance guys," Colin adds, looking around the roof with playful fear in his eyes.

That *does* seem to be the clientele here, along with a few scattered significant others. I tug at my skirt, feeling like debris tripping through a stream, unmoored. I'm always anxious in large groups, especially groups of couples, and I want so badly to reach for Colin's hand to steady myself that my palm itches.

"So, what have you guys been up to?" Colin asks. This time, he allows himself another glance my way, and my head spins with all the things it could mean. Does he want me here? Is he angry that I came?

"Just hanging out in Greenpoint," Zoe says. "Forcing Jane to give me outfit advice."

"At your apartment?" He looks surprised, and then like he's trying to hide it. "Guess you guys are really becoming friends."

It's infuriatingly toneless, a throwaway line, and it digs under my skin.

"It is now my singular aspiration to live in a former can factory," I say, almost a challenge—a confirmation that I was there. "Even if I'm not cool enough to pull it off."

Colin looks between us, and a line deepens between his eyebrows, tugging his face into something like a frown. He's just thrown off that the two of us are hanging out, I decide—his girlfriend-but-soon-to-be-ex and his ex-but-soon-to-be-girlfriend. In fairness, it *is* kind of weird.

"This place is so nice, though," I add, trying to lighten the mood. "Might shift the aspirations a bit, assuming I can pull a quick career switch into the finance world."

I need to stop talking.

But Colin, bless his heart, gives me a laugh, and my shriveled heart grows three sizes.

"Do you guys want anything?" he asks, hand on Zoe's shoulder. "I can grab us drinks."

"Yeah, sure," she says. "Actually . . . how would you feel about relaxing our no-drinking policy tonight?" She leans closer to Colin, her lips almost brushing his ear, but she speaks just loudly enough for me to hear, too. "Maybe it's all the finance guys, but I could use a real drink."

"If you're down, I'm down," Colin says, but he can't hide the relief on his face. "Vodka cran?"

Zoe kisses him on the cheek, and it makes me ache. He knows her drink.

"Thanks, babe."

He's already taken a few steps away before he remembers me. "Jane?"

"Oh, um . . . yeah, I'll do the same."

He goes, and our little space on the roof feels too big in his wake. I focus on Zoe.

"Are you really that intimidated by finance guys?" I ask, trying for teasing, even though an alarm bell is ringing in my head. Zoe's not intimidated by anyone. If she feels like she needs to drink tonight, there must be another reason, and I'm afraid it's Colin-related. But if she picks up on my suspicion, she doesn't show it.

"Honestly, a little," she says, scanning the other guests. "But I'm starting to think I might have been too hasty with the cold-turkey thing. I know Colin's stressed, and I can tell he misses it."

An irrational panic grips me. I'd pinned Zoe as a controlling girl-friend, but here she is, changing for the better. I glance at Colin over by the bar, tipping the vodka bottle carefully into a cup, like he couldn't bear to make his friend's roof messy, and I wonder if he's noticed what Zoe's doing. If he still believes she's the right partner for him.

When he returns, he's balancing our three cups with the same expert care.

"Cheers," he says, handing us our drinks. His hand brushes mine as I take the cup, and I wonder if he feels it, too—a little jolt, warm and heady. For once, I'm not sure if he does. But then, there: his hand buried in his sleeve, fist tightening around the fabric, like he's trying to protect himself. Like he's afraid of what will happen if we touch again.

"Cheers!" Zoe echoes, taking a pull from her cup.

I take a small sip, watching as Colin downs half of his in one go. Maybe he really *did* miss it—but I can excuse it, of course. He's being harassed by Leigh, this mysterious figure from his past trying to catch up with him. I want so badly to tell him that I understand, more than he knows. Instead, I take another pull of the drink he made me, relishing the burn.

The party goes on, and I come to understand that Zoe is its nexus: people flit in and out of our circle, drawn to the magnetism of her wild curls and the shoes that bring her eye-to-eye with Colin. But it's not just her looks: she's good at this. The party. People. It's mystifying to watch her, how deftly she runs a conversation, taking charge without ever feeling like she's taking up too much air. And all the while, Colin is attached to her.

We go back for more drinks, and with every refill, his touches get bolder—a brush of her hand or shoulder melting into a palm pressed to her lower back, an arm around her waist, and I don't know how much longer I can watch this. I don't know if I can survive this night without getting Colin alone.

The second drink bleeds into a third, and eventually, when the three of us end up sitting on a set of lounge chairs, it happens. The window, opening.

"I'm going to run to the bathroom," Zoe announces, standing. She looks at me. "Want to come?"

"I'm okay," I say quickly. "You go ahead."

I'm defying an ancient tenet of girl code, but Zoe, for her part, doesn't seem to be offended. She goes off on her own, heels clicking decisively on the ground.

It's not until she's gone that the magnitude of this moment crashes into me at full force. Colin and me, alone. My heart starts to pound, brushstrokes of heat down my back. It's all I've wanted since our last moment together on his birthday, but now that it's here, I'm so overwhelmed by all I need to say to him that I don't know where to start. My drink has gone lukewarm in my hands, and all I can do is sit, watching Colin's profile as he looks off after Zoe.

He takes a breath, and my heart about stops.

"What are you doing, Jane?" he asks quietly, eyes still fixed on the city around us.

Everything stutters, goes off-kilter.

"What?"

He looks at me now, finally, but it's not the way he's supposed to. His eyes are foggy, clouded by the drinks.

"Why are you hanging out with Zoe?"

It's a reasonable question, one I'd maybe also ask if our roles were reversed, but the accusation simmering beneath it makes my walls go up.

"I . . ."

I like her, I think. *And more importantly, I'm trying to protect you. I love you.*

But all of the explanations catch in my throat as Colin stands and goes, either toward the drinks or after Zoe. I can't tell, but both are bad. Both are wrong.

"Wait," I try.

He keeps going, ignoring me, and it's his birthday all over again, except even worse. This time, he won't even look at me.

I get up and reach for his arm, pathetic.

"If this is about Ben—"

He whirls around to face me. "It's not about Ben."

Finally. A little part of me is relieved—proof, at least, that I'm not invisible—but it fades quickly when I understand the rage on his face. It's an echo of what I saw in the stairwell, only this time, it's directed at me.

"I don't care if you fuck my roommate. You can fuck whoever you want."

He's louder now, some other, darker being overtaking the one I know and love. Loud enough that people are starting to stare.

"Colin—"

"Can you leave me alone? I don't know what your aim is here, what you think I want, but I swear to god, Jane—just leave us *alone*."

He shoves me back with one arm, not hard, but it's surprising enough that I stumble a few steps. I hear gasps, shock, but it's not the push that breaks me. It's that word. *Us.* Leave *us* alone, as in him and Zoe, as in I'm not a part of this anymore. He's lying to himself, trying to protect himself, and I want to help him, take his face in my hands and hold it gently until he sees that he doesn't have to fight this alone, until he remembers what we are. But that one word has dug so deep into my subconscious, has torn it apart so thoroughly that I'm empty of everything else.

Us.

Tears brim in my eyes, angry heat flooding my face, as I start to understand. It's not some otherworldly demon that's overtaken him. It's James Waylon O'Connor III, Mikey Medina, and all the other boys who have tricked me into loving them only to crush my heart like a weak little shell in their hands, discarding the pieces. For once, I think I understand them.

It's a beautiful thing, watching something die.

Those words, dredged up from the murky bottoms of my memory, the things I've tried to forget. They curdle inside me, turning into something rotten and monstrous and all too familiar. *I could do it,* I think. One quick shove, and he'd be over the balcony, hurtling to the ground below. The image is so crystal clear that for a moment, I feel my weight shift forward, my arms bracing.

No.

I love him. I'm being good. And he's confused. He's drunk.

He's lashing out in a way I know too well.

Watching him there, his beautiful face still contorted in anger, a revelation zips up my spine: I could forgive him anything, but for the first time, I wonder if I should.

It nearly takes the air out of my lungs, the simple clarity of it. If love is a choice, then so is forgiveness—and it needs to be earned. I know because I'm trying to earn it, too. Because I'm not sure if I ever will.

So, with another crack in my broken heart, I give him what he's asking for: I release him.

I turn and rush to the elevator, and it's not until the doors shut me safely inside that I let myself cry.

14

I thought I'd spent enough tears on Colin Hillgrove to last a lifetime, but here I am, discovering a new and gutting reservoir. They spill down my cheeks, hot and uninhibited, pulled somewhere from the gaping cavern of my chest. I let them blur my vision as I lean against the elevator wall, too broken to realize I haven't even pressed the lobby button before it's too late.

The doors ding open again.

Colin, I think, pathetic hope persisting even through my agony, but it's not him.

It's Zoe.

She steps inside, a little breathless, like she just sprinted over here in her heeled boots. The doors close behind her, and she wraps me in a tight hug.

"Are you okay?" she asks. "I saw you guys on my way from the bathroom. God, I have no idea what got into him."

She couldn't. She doesn't have a clue about my history with Colin, the feelings running deep and raw between us, and I almost want to tell her, just to make her hate him less—to make her hate *me* enough to let go—but it feels so good to be hugged that I can't make myself say it.

"I'm so sorry," she says. "I can't believe he did that."

"It's okay," I mumble into her shoulder.

She lets go, pressing the lobby button.

"Wait, what are you doing?" I ask.

Zoe looks at me like I've sprouted another limb. "We're leaving."

"But—"

"My good-for-nothing boyfriend just shoved my friend in front of an entire party. I can't spend another second with him."

The force of it hits me square in the chest. Zoe's choosing me. And I don't think I deserve it.

I focus on the elevator buttons as we whoosh down to the lobby, my ears popping from the rapid descent. When the doors open, I hesitate with my back against the elevator wall, an animal afraid to come out of its cage.

"What do we do now?" I ask.

Zoe bites her lip, thinking for a moment. Then, she takes my hand.

"We get the fuck out of here."

We pick up a bottle of wine at a bodega near Sam's, and then we're hurtling through the underground, two girls getting drunk too quickly on the alcohol but also the feeling of drinking it on the train, of knowing that no one will stop us, because we're young and glittering. Or maybe we're drunk on our common enemy, on the way the jagged breaks in our hearts align, marred as they are by the same hand.

It's a fantasy, and I know it. It can't last.

Still, I give myself over to it. The train rattles back down to Greenpoint, the edges of the world going soft with the wine.

When we get off, the bottle is nearly empty, and Zoe announces that pizza is the only logical recourse. I agree, so we make our way to a place near her apartment, unsteady in our shoes. It's still too early on a Saturday night to be this drunk, but it doesn't matter. We take our dollar slices and eat them on the street, the grease dripping down our chins and onto our paper plates. We wipe it away with the backs of our hands, unbothered by the notion that we should be pretty.

When the pizza is gone and we're still a few blocks from Zoe's apartment, I'm hit with the sudden and urgent need to pee, and it's hilarious, all of a sudden, how badly I have to pee, so we sprint, laughing and out of breath, to the converted can factory, which itself is now hilarious enough to make us both nearly pee with laughter.

Once we're back in her apartment, and we've both gone to the bathroom, we're lying on the floor and staring up at the ceiling when Zoe shoots upright with a gasp.

"Have you ever dyed your hair?"

"What?" I laugh because this, too, is hilarious.

"I'm serious." She reaches out to touch my hair, the warmth of her hand radiating onto my neck. "I could do it for you. I do it all the time."

Suspiciously, I eye her perfect chestnut curls.

"You dye your hair?"

"No, but I've done it for friends before. People at Pratt changed hair colors like outfits, pretty much, and no one ever wanted to shell out for a hairstylist." She lets go of my hair, and drifts back onto my shoulder. "Seriously, I could."

The question stirs a memory awake. Colin next to me on a park bench, reaching out to brush a lock of light brown.

You know, there's a little bit of red in your hair when the sun hits it, he said. *I like it.*

You think I could pull off red hair? I asked, a little self-consciously. I'd thought about it once, before college, thinking I needed a bigger change but chickening out, settling on the bangs instead.

He'd kissed me on the forehead.

You can pull off anything.

"I've thought about red," I tell Zoe now, a blush rising to my cheeks at the memory of his lips against my hair, so real it's like I can still feel them lingering there.

Zoe gapes. "Oh my god, you would *rock* red. Like, a subtle auburn . . ." She stands up suddenly, somehow still steady in those boots. "Come on. We're doing it."

I'm just drunk enough to say yes.

We stumble back out into the night, hunting through a drugstore that happens to be open until we've found the various items required: box dye, gloves, brushes like the kind you use for glazing meat. Zoe pays, refusing to let me chip in, and we forge back to her apartment, where we change clothes and set up in the bathroom.

We're both sobering up a bit now, Zoe enough that I feel like she'll probably do an okay job with the dye and me enough that I'm no longer sure this is a fantastic idea, but she's already wrapping a towel around my shoulders like I'm a child after a long day at the pool, and I feel like I can't back out. I feel like I don't want to.

She sets me up on the bathroom floor while she sits behind me on the toilet, sectioning my hair off with practiced fingers. I can't remember the last time someone else touched my hair like this—besides Colin, I mean, but this is different. That was romantic, still gentle, but this feels more like care. Capability. I'm hit with the memory of my mother braiding my hair, her hands smelling like rose lotion, but I'm sober enough now to shut that off, to focus only on Zoe. Her hands smell like citrus.

She plays music, a chaotic mix of lo-fi beats, indie girl bands, and top 40 pop, and it's like a sleepover I never had as a teenager. I'm almost lulled to sleep by the rhythm of it: Zoe dipping the brush into a bowl of mixed dye, combing it through my hair like I'm one of her canvases. When my whole head is covered, she peels off her gloves and instructs me to let it sit for twenty minutes.

Now that our only goal is stillness, time passing, I feel too sober. I'm considering asking her if she has any other alcohol when she comes to sit next to me on the edge of her bathtub and says, "What happened?"

I know she means with Colin. And I know I can't tell her, even if there's a part of me that wants to let it all out. But if I tell her that we've been lying to her this whole time, she might kick me back out onto the Brooklyn streets with a half-dyed head, so for practicality's sake, I give her a half-truth.

"I guess he was upset that we're hanging out," I say. "Or weirded out, maybe. I don't know why."

Zoe frowns, watching her own reflection in the bathroom mirror as she does. I follow her gaze, and we're really a sort of ridiculous pair: Zoe still perfect in the oversized T-shirt she's changed into, and me looking like a wet rat with my painted hair, my body swallowed in a borrowed men's button-down. It's hers, not Colin's—it doesn't smell like him—but somehow on me, it reads more like *adolescent boy at an orchestra concert* than *worldly woman post-liaison*, which is I'm sure the vibe that Zoe gives off when she wears it.

"Maybe it *is* annoying of me to steal you from him," she says finally. "But honestly, he needs to grow up. He's twenty-five. He can handle his girlfriend making friends with his friends." She pauses. "I just—in all the time we've been together, I've never seen him snap like that. I almost thought . . ."

She trails off, and it's like I can feel the dye seeping into my follicles, my scalp burning even though we didn't use bleach.

"I don't know," she finishes. "It just makes me wonder."

I want to tell her she's wrong, that this wasn't Colin, but I can't make myself say it out loud. My silence feels like a betrayal.

I force myself to break it.

"Thank you," I tell her. "For, you know, being there. And being so nice to me. And—" I hesitate, suddenly bubbling over with the kind of gratitude that makes me feel stupid for being so unable to express it.

What I want to say is I've never had a best friend before, and I think, right now, she might be mine.

"Just . . . I'm really glad you're here," I finish.

She watches me for a moment, green eyes shining. Then, she reaches for my hand. Squeezes.

"Of course, Jane. We're friends."

It feels good, at least for now, to let this be the truth.

And so we sit, waiting for the dye to take effect. My buzz sharpens to clarity as I watch my tinted hair with a kind of numb sadness, the way you feel when you leave home for the first time, watching it grow smaller in the rearview. Knowing that you've made a choice you can't undo—because even if you come back, it won't be the same.

Once our twenty minutes are up, Zoe tells me to rinse out my hair, leaving me to her shower. As she waits outside the bathroom, I let the water run down my back, making note of all the things she keeps there: custom shampoo and conditioner, curl cream, mango-coconut body wash, bright turquoise loofah, lavender razor hanging from a magnetic holder—a reflection of my own shower, but elevated, a *higher plane*. I wash out the dye, my own fallen strands mingling with hers around the drain.

After, Zoe dries my hair, refusing to let me look at my own reflection like we're on a makeover show. Then, when it's finished, she spins me around to see.

The bright light of her bathroom bounces off my new hair with a coppery shine, making me think of Central Park in autumn—of Colin on that bench, telling me I'm beautiful.

146

"Do you like it?" she asks.

"Yeah," I breathe, running my hands gently through it, half afraid it might flutter away like leaves.

I feel like a new person, someone he could love.

Like I could stand on my own pedestal, *divine*.

When we're too tired to stay up any longer, Zoe sets me up with a fuzzy blanket on her green velvet sofa. I pull it close, relishing the softness, as she turns off the light and falls into her own bed. For a while, there's nothing but a light rain starting to tap against the windows and the odd car rolling past outside.

"I'm sorry," Zoe says, quiet enough that it takes me a second to register.

"For what?" I ask, but I know she means Colin. Even though what he did wasn't her fault.

But Zoe doesn't answer. She's already drifted to sleep.

15

The sun is bright through Zoe's windows, warming me awake. For a moment, I watch it slat over my arm, the freckles and hair on my pale skin, as it dangles off the sofa. Then, I reach for my phone, somehow still alive after a night spent unplugged on the floor. No notifications. It's always a bit of a let-down, starting my day knowing that no one tried to reach me while I slept.

And then, I remember. I open my phone camera on self-view, taking in my new hair: still auburn, vibrant.

The smell of coffee beckons, even though I've never liked the taste—only the scent, which has always reminded me of bookstores, yellowed pages. I sit up, and it's like my brain shifts inside my skull, knocking against the walls. I groan, pressing the heels of my hands to my eyes. Then, once I'm certain I'm only headache-hungover and not on the verge of puking, I get up to look for Zoe.

I find her in the walled-off kitchen area, sitting at the small break-fast table while the coffeemaker gurgles.

"Okay," she says, by way of greeting, "let it be known that I'm still obsessed with the hair even in my hungover state. Truly some of my best work."

It's 8:00 in the morning, and Zoe doesn't even look mildly hungover. She looks like she slept fantastically on her fluffy cloud of a bed, which makes perfect sense to me, actually.

I give my hair a self-conscious touch. "I'll be a lot more enthusiastic once I don't feel like I've just returned from a voyage to hell."

Zoe laughs, getting up and walking to the fridge. "That bad, huh?"

"Apparently, twenty-five is the age where you can no longer pound two-thirds of a bottle of wine and feel fine in the morning." I sit down at the table. "I want my money back."

"For the wine?"

"For, like . . ." I gesture vaguely around us. "This mortal coil."

I slump dramatically onto the table.

"Wait, twenty-five?" Zoe asks.

It's there, with my forehead flopped against my forearms on the breakfast table, that I realize my subconscious understood it before I did: I *am* twenty-five.

"Oh yeah," I say, without lifting my head. "It's kind of my birthday."

"Jane!"

"Ow."

"Sorry. But Jane! How can you not tell me it's your *birthday*?"

Finally, I look up at her, squinting in the harsh morning light. She's produced a Diet Coke, which she sets down in front of me for emphasis, and it makes me feel weirdly terrible that she remembered I'm not a coffee person.

"I honestly forgot. Not into birthdays, remember?"

She laughs. "God, you really *are* just like—" She stops herself, and we both know what she was going to say. "Well, we have to do something. *I*, for one, am a birthday person, and I'll settle for nothing less than foisting my beliefs onto everyone I meet. Are you into brunch?"

I'm not, just like Colin, but she sounds so enthusiastic that I lie and tell her yes. As Zoe scours the internet for brunch places that don't require reservations—good luck with *that* on a Sunday—I think that actually, last night might have been the best beginning to a birthday I've ever had. I rang in twenty-four at home alone, fielding a grand total of three happy birthday texts from former NYU friends I hadn't seen all year.

But that's far too pathetic to even think about saying out loud, so I wait in silence until Zoe gasps at her screen. At first, I think she's found a miracle brunch spot, but then she says, "Leigh DMed me."

I put the Diet Coke down so fast it nearly spills.

"What did she say?"

Zoe's eyes widen as she reads. "She wants to meet."

I lean in close to see the message on the screen:

Hey Zoe–I'm so glad you reached out. I've seen you on Colin's Instagram, and I think there are some things you should know about him. He's not who you think he is. I don't feel safe explaining over DM, but if you meet me here at midnight, I'll tell you everything.

Beneath it, she's included a screenshot of her phone map with a pin dropped at a park next to the East River.

"Midnight?" I blurt.

It's something out of a crime show or a Taylor Swift music video, but Zoe doesn't seem to pick up on the complete and utter ridiculousness.

"We should go," she says.

I gape at her.

"She's a total stranger. We still don't know if we can trust her." The arguments come out faster than I can ask myself why I'm so resistant to meeting Leigh. If she has information about Colin, then obviously, I want it—but something about this feels wrong. Almost like a trap.

I want to say so, but the look in Zoe's eyes silences me. They're blazing in a way I've never seen before: not their usual confident spark, but a fire, raging.

"After last night," she says. "I do."

Before I can stop her, Zoe writes back that we're in.

And then, I realize.

"Wait, did Leigh accept your follow request?"

Zoe frowns. "No, just the DM. Weird."

So we can't scour her profile for any other information that would help us prepare. *Perfect.* Whoever she is, Leigh knows exactly what she's doing.

We wait, but Leigh doesn't respond again. And I know, from the determined set of Zoe's jaw, that there's no changing her mind. We're doing this. Because, I realize, we have to.

Last night, a weak and broken part of me wanted to give up on Colin, but now I understand. The knife, the bloody quarter-zip, the way he lashed out at me—it all starts and ends with Leigh. If I can prove that Colin didn't do anything wrong, that Leigh doesn't know what she's talking about, we'll be one step closer to being together again, our happy ending near enough to touch.

It's like a birthday present. The only one I've ever really wanted.

On our last date, Colin took me to the Brooklyn Botanic Garden. It was an afternoon date that spilled over into the night—dinner at a hole-in-the-wall burger joint, and then wandering until we found the train back to Washington Heights, to my apartment, to the inevitable.

After, we lay in my bed, half watching a movie on my laptop as Colin drifted off with his head on my chest. I combed my fingers through his hair, twisting them in the soft curls, thinking how lucky I was to have found someone who makes an eight-hour date feel like nothing. How lucky I was to finally have someplace soft to land.

He'd shifted, curling closer into me, and I thought, Maybe I can tell him. Maybe he can know everything, and he won't run, because he hasn't yet. Not when my hair got all frizzy from the humidity and nervous sweat on our first date. Not that night, when I'd gotten anxious and choked on my tongue a little bit as I tried to tell him what I liked. He'd only laughed, buried his face in my neck.

Just before I could make myself say anything, he looked up at me.

What are you thinking? he asked, sleepy-eyed.

And maybe I was a little drunk on the whole day, because I said, *I'm worried I might not be good enough for you.*

He made a face like that was the most ridiculous thing in the world, and then he kissed me.

Who said I wanted good?

Now, standing outside of his apartment, the memory burns so bright and close that I can feel it in my chest, flames licking out, growing too fast for my ribs to contain them.

I told Zoe I wanted to go home to rest, but I knew, even as I hugged her goodbye, that this is where I was headed. Now that I'm actually here, though, I'm rooted to the sidewalk.

For one thing, I have no idea if he's home. Worse, Ben might be. And even if I went upstairs to knock, if Colin is here, it's not like I can tell him that I'm meeting Leigh tonight, not without telling him everything else: that I made the fake Jake Smith account, that I know about the bloody knife, that whatever Leigh is going to tell me, no matter how fiercely she'll try to twist her story against him, I won't care.

I *will* tell him all of those things—the others, too, the ones from the darkest corners—but not yet. Not until I've sorted this out, until I've met Leigh and I have the full picture. Then, we'll talk, and he'll understand. He'll apologize for how he treated me at Sam's, and I'll forgive him. We always will—forgive each other. For everything.

I should go, I know, so he doesn't see me here, but I don't. Instead, I watch his window for another minute or so, the closed blinds behind the glass, aching. Silently screaming for a glance of him, so much wanting that I feel like my legs could collapse from the weight of it.

But it doesn't come.

And so, I go.

16

I usually prefer to be fashionably late, but tonight, I was too anxious to wait. When I arrive at our meeting spot a few minutes early, I'm the first one here. I double-check the pinned location Leigh chose, confirming that this is it: the waterfront, empty and desolate.

It's dark out, a bite in the air. The river spills out in front of me, lit up by the Williamsburg Bridge and the lights of Brooklyn beyond it, colors shimmering on the water like an oil slick. For all the life so nearby, this particular part of the waterfront feels barren: patchy brown grass, abandoned benches, chain-link fence separating this stretch of stone path from the cars whizzing past on FDR Drive, the wind kicking up dead leaves in their wake. The river is bordered by a railing that barely reaches me at shoulder height, a half-hearted attempt to keep us all on land. I keep a safe distance from it, wondering about what lurks at the bottom of the water. How deep it goes.

When I check my phone again, it's officially midnight. I'm about to text Zoe that I'm here when a new message from her pings on my screen.

Running late, so sorry-the trains are being annoying but I'll be there soon!!!

Worry churns in the pit of my stomach. What am I supposed to do if Leigh gets here before Zoe does? Zoe told her I was coming, but she never responded. Leigh could refuse to talk to me. She could tell Colin that Zoe and I have been going behind his back.

I take a deep breath in, out, focus on the gentle splashing of the water below me. *This is fine*, I tell myself. Better, even. Leigh will talk to me—I'll make her. I can find out what she has to say and decide what to do about it without Zoe clouding my judgment.

Footsteps approach, quiet on the stone path. I look up, heart pounding, at the shadowed figure approaching. They're tall, face hidden by the hoodie pulled over their head.

Then, I catch the glint of glasses, and I know what some part of me already knew, that string plucked somewhere inside of me whenever he's near.

Colin.

The breath rushes out of me with the pull of the river, and I don't know what to say. He stops when he sees me, mouth falling open.

"You dyed your hair."

He looks as surprised as I am that it's the first thing he said, and I just nod. I take a step toward him, the ice between us melting, but all at once, it's there again, a frozen wall.

"So, get on with it, then."

I swallow, mouth dry. "What?"

Colin stares me down, his honey eyes hardened to amber. Silent. Waiting.

It dawns on me, slow and terrible.

"Where's Leigh?" I ask.

He blinks. Still silent. I don't know what's happening.

And then, I do.

"Colin, what did you do?"

"Come on, Jane," he says, voice low and throaty. "You already know."

And I do. I don't want to, but I do. It all makes an awful kind of sense: the pictures on his laptop, the phone calls, the anger coiled tight and venomous inside him, fighting to take over. All of it has been building up to the same climax that I didn't want to see. I realize, suddenly, that it probably wasn't ever Leigh messaging us from her Instagram account. Colin must have hacked into it, set up this meeting to—what?

The thought stops me cold. The low railing, the rush of the river. He's taller than me, stronger than me. He could do whatever he wanted, and no one would be here to see it.

But still, I stay planted, not even an impulse to step back.

Whatever this is, I can understand it. We can get through it. He just needs to let me in.

"I'm not here to hurt you," I tell him.

He laughs sharply, surprising me.

"Bullshit."

"I'm not."

"Then why the fuck have you been harassing me for the past two months?"

"What?" I gape. "Wait, do you think—I'm not the one who's been calling you. I'm trying to *help* you."

It's his turn to be surprised now. He watches me, something moving slow and illegible beneath his gaze.

I take a step closer. "I know what you did." Another. "But I don't care."

I let that settle for a moment in the small space between us, but he doesn't soften.

"Where's Zoe?" he asks, glancing around like she might be hiding in the bushes, waiting to pounce.

"She's on the way," I say. "She thinks we're meeting Leigh. But we can go. I'll come up with an excuse, tell her Leigh isn't coming."

It's a betrayal, I know, but it's for her own good that she doesn't find us here together.

Colin nods slowly, moving even closer, and this is it, I think—but then he stops.

"Why are you trying to help me?"

His voice is small, young, and it breaks my heart at the same time that it sends me hurtling back to that common room, Trip's big hand stroking up and down my back as I vomited out the reasons I thought I should love him.

But this, now, is different—because I don't have to fight for my answer. I know why I love Colin. He's gentle, kind, and good at heart. He's soft hands and kisses and genuine questions and a little broken, maybe, but that's okay: I am, too. Our broken places align, prove that no matter what we've done, we're not unsalvageable. We can be each other's salvation.

"Isn't it obvious?" I ask.

He comes closer, close enough that I could kiss him now. The river races beneath us, keeping time with the pulse in my neck, and I know in this moment that whatever happens, it has to be him who decides. Not because I'm weak or powerless or destined only to *receive*, but because I can't keep chasing him like this, can't wrest my heart from my chest and lay it on the ground for him, slick and beating, until I know he chooses me, too.

Colin pushes me back against the railing, so suddenly that my breath catches. The water roars behind me as he reaches out and winds a finger with a strand of my new hair.

"Why did you do this?" he asks again, almost a whisper, his stare fixed on the auburn. "Are you trying to torture me?"

My breathing goes quick and ragged as his fingers drift from my hair to my collarbone, to the necklace. *Rosemary. For remembrance.* And I want to remember this. A distant part of my brain, the one that can think through the crush of need, knows that this is the moment—our beginning or our end. And it could be the end. He's a killer, isn't he?

He leans in, and I close my eyes, listening to the river, bracing for oblivion.

His mouth crashes into mine with such urgency that at first, I can't fully grasp what's happening. And then. *Then.* He slows down, hands finding my hair, digging into the auburn strands, and everything blurs except for this: Colin, kissing me. It's a warmth that aches, stinging my skin and then melting into buzzing contentment, like a hot shower after a day in the freezing cold. It takes everything not to let myself be overwhelmed by it—his lips, his tongue, his hands, all of him here, a manifestation made real and tangible, the best belated birthday present of all time. I want to disappear into it, crawl out of myself and into him, but I can't.

I pull back.

"Zoe," I breathe. "She's still on the way. We have to go."

Wordlessly, Colin nods, reaching down to take my hand, our fingers twining together, and we go, running away from the river and down the waterfront like the stars of a fucking rom-com, my heart beating fast and wild and in time with his. I don't even know where the train is, how I got here, but I trust him. Completely.

When we're back in the heart of the city, the waterfront behind us, I give Colin's hand a pulse.

"Let me text her," I say. "So she doesn't come looking."

I type out a message, quick and frantic, my hands still shaking from the thrill of him.

Leigh just DMed me to cancel

I'm feeling a little sketched out being here alone so I'm heading home but we can talk in the morning

I press send, and with the text, Zoe flies out of my mind. I lose track of everything except for Colin's fingers threading again through mine, the warmth of his palm.

"Back to my place?" he asks, and it's like an explosion of light and color, all the life of the city packaged up inside of my body. Everything I've wanted to hear for so long, here in front of me.

I tighten my hand around his, just to make sure he's real, and he is. I nod.

Yes.

17

It might come as a shock, but I've never been someone who believes in soulmates. Not in the sense that there's one person predestined for us all before we begin. It strikes me as fallible in the same way the concept of God does: What kind of world would that be, if there's some divine being letting children be murdered in their classrooms, letting them be born at all to parents who never wanted them, who know only how to hurt?

No, I can't stomach it, the thought that there's one person for each of us—that we're doomed to roam in search of them, hoping that all the seconds and atoms will align for us to meet them, or else we're shit out of luck, sentenced to die alone, gaslit by the universe with the same logic that all fanatics use, TikTok manifesters included.

Sorry. If it didn't happen, then you didn't believe hard enough.

But here, now, with my head resting on Colin's bare chest and his arms around me, both of us breathing together, I'm sure I believe in a certain kind of soulmate: the one you choose. The one who chooses you. Choosing each other, over and over, until the end of time.

I reach out for his bruised hand and bring it to my lips, kissing the knuckles that only days ago I'd imagined were covered in blood.

"Hey," he whispers, running a hand through my hair. "What are you thinking?"

I've never been good at it, the pillow talk that comes so easily to other people. Even now, I don't quite know how to let myself be vulnerable, how to let him into the dark cavern of my mind.

But it's okay. He's patient.

"I missed this," I say finally. "I missed you."

He kisses me again, and it's like sinking into warm water.

"Me, too," he says. And then, after another breath, his heart against my ear: "Maybe you should go, though."

I turn to look at him, a little part of me breaking, but then I understand.

He needs a chance to end it with Zoe. And I need to get out of here before Ben gets home.

I give him another quick kiss before sliding out of bed. I get dressed again, bathing in the feeling of his gaze, and then reach for my phone. Five missed calls from Zoe, the last one over an hour ago, followed by a text:

Call me when you can so I know you're ok

My heart aches, a physical pain in my chest. I knew this was coming, eventually, but it doesn't make it any easier.

When I'm ready to go, I turn and face Colin again. He's perfect there, moonlight spilling onto his skin, his freckled cheeks, and all the guilt washes away, leaving nothing but the sight of him. *Mine.*

Briefly, I let my gaze flicker to his computer, sitting shut on his desk. I wonder if the pictures are still there. If I should ask him.

The thought of Leigh, gagged and bound, sends up an alarm of doubt, but then Colin gets out of bed, sliding on his shirt and his boxers and coming to meet me, wrapping his arms around me.

"Text me when you get home?"

I nod, overcome by the question. Knowing he wants me safe.

He kisses me softly.

"Good night, Jane."

And all my doubt quiets, like heavy-lidded eyes fluttering gently to sleep.

Once I'm back out in the night air, I know I can't put it off anymore. I won't be able to fake my way through a call with Zoe, but I owe her at least a response. I send a text instead.

Sorry, I fell asleep as soon as I got home! I'm good, just kind of exhausted and not feeling great. Call you tomorrow?

It whooshes away, and I head for the subway, a big, stupid grin stretching on my face. Even with the awful swirl of guilt, I can't help it. Colin and I are back together, and everything else will fall into place, even Zoe. I'll make it true through the power of believing. She'll find her person, too, and so will Ben, and everyone else.

Except for Leigh.

Her name comes into my head, unbidden, and my smile fades. She's the one piece that doesn't fit, the only blemish in this perfect picture, and I hate myself for thinking of her that way. She was a person. A girl.

And Colin killed her.

I pull my jacket tighter, quickening my pace. I'm jumping to con-clusions again. Colin didn't actually tell me that he *killed* her. He didn't disabuse me of that notion, either, but still. Leigh had called Zoe, didn't she? I'd forgotten, but now, that detail is a beacon. She's still out there. I'm misreading this.

I have to be.

What's most important is that after tonight, I know Colin is still the person I fell in love with. He wouldn't hurt someone, not unless there was a really good reason, something that I'll understand as soon as he's ready to explain it.

He's good, and he's good for me. Curtain. End of story.

For tonight, I'll just have to be okay with not knowing every detail yet. I deserve to feel at peace, to ride this wave of joy as far as it takes me.

Tomorrow, I tell myself, walking down the subway steps, into the city's warm underbelly. Tomorrow, it will all make sense.

A buzz startles me awake. I'm in my bed—passed out here pretty much as soon as I got home. My cheeks are warm, my tongue thick in that feverish way it gets when I've been asleep for too long and yet not long enough, and I want to bury myself deeper in my duvet, go back to dreaming of Colin.

But the buzzing persists. I grope around in the sheets until I find my phone, the screen bright enough to make me squint in the darkness.

It's two thirty A.M.—I've only been out for an hour—and I have one missed call from Ben.

I sit up quickly, head rushing. *Ben?* Before I can think it through, a new text from him appears:

Hey are you around? I don't want to freak you out but I found some stuff in Colin's room and I don't know what to do. I really need to talk to someone

Shit. *Shit.* I'm fully awake now as I push the covers off me and fumble out of bed, my brain a looping racket of *the shout, the fist, the blood, the knife.*

The knife. Did Ben find the knife? Or the pictures?

Or something even worse?

My heart pounds in my throat, my palms going slick against my phone. I stare at our text conversation, watching Ben's typing bubble appear and then disappear.

It stops.

I breathe out.

Maybe this is nothing. It could be nothing, right? Maybe he found something of *mine*, and he's realized that Colin and I slept together, and this is some sort of trap.

But does that even make a scrap of sense?

I force another deep breath in and out, pacing my bedroom until my brain catches up with me, slamming into the obvious next step. Colin. I call him, but as soon as I've had an instant of hope, it cuts straight to voicemail. I try again. Same thing.

My heart picks up, uneasiness morphing into dread.

I call Ben, and it rings. I relax slightly at the sound. His phone is on, at least. But then, too many rings later, voicemail. He doesn't pick up.

"Shit," I say out loud, hanging up.

I hammer out another text, asking Ben what's going on, and then I wait. A minute passes, and then five. I can't tell if he's read my message, but he doesn't respond, and I know now that there's only one thing to do. I grab my denim jacket off the chair where I left it, swing myself into it, and then get my keys—mine, and my copy of Ben's. Shoving my shoes back on, I text Ben again.

Don't do anything. I'm coming over.

I just have to hope he listens.

The ride back downtown is unbearable, stretching to impossible lengths until suddenly, I'm at my stop. I push my way out of the train and up the stairs, breathing mechanically in and out to keep myself from holding it the whole time.

When I'm out on the street, I call Ben again. This time, it cuts to voicemail immediately.

I try Colin, too. Same thing.

"What the fuck?" I mumble, walking faster.

By the time their building comes into view, I'm out of breath, my legs burning, but I don't stop, even as I dig Ben's keys out of my bag. I force the key into the door, hand quivering, and twist, pushing it open with my full weight. Inside, I jog up the stairs, tote bouncing against my hip, until finally, I'm at his unit.

I bang on the door.

"Ben?" I call. "Colin?"

I wait a breath, and then another. No one comes. So, I give up on politeness. I unlock the door with my copy of the keys and throw it open.

"Hello?"

The living room is empty, dark. I make my way down the hall, toward Ben's room, stopping with my hand on the knob. A leaden feeling overtakes me, like I'm pushing through water.

It's too quiet.

And then, the smell. A tang in the air, sweet and murky, scratching at the back of my memory until it suddenly clicks into place. The shed at the hunting camp. A deer, shot and skinned, hanging from a hook, more meat now than animal, draining of blood. His hand on the back of my neck, like a lion carrying its cub by the scruff.

It's a beautiful thing, he told me. *Watching something die. One day, you'll understand.*

Like I'm crashing to the surface for air, I push the door open, and there. What I already knew I'd see, made real and unmistakable.

Ben, crumpled on the floor, blood spilling out of the gash on his neck into a dark pool. His eyes are open, lifeless.

And standing over him is Colin, the knife in his hand dripping bright red tears.

PART TWO

Death

PART TWO

18

Okay, clearly Colin's issues run a little deeper than I thought. I don't know why the *fuck* he's standing over his dead roommate—with a fucking *knife*—but I have to stay calm. I can handle this.

"What happened?" I ask.

Colin steps back, the knife outstretched like I might attack.

Like he doesn't trust me.

I hold out my hands, palms forward, the universal language for *I'm on your side.*

"I'm not going to turn you in," I say, just in case physical cues aren't enough. "I just want to know what happened."

"I didn't do it," he says desperately. His eyes are wide, the knife still gripped tightly.

So, he's in shock. Sure. Denial is a normal reaction to something like this.

"Ben texted me," I explain. "He said he found something in your room. What did he find?"

"What?" Colin blinks, his face crumpling into confusion before hardening again. "I don't know what you're talking about. I swear to god, I just walked in here and found him like this."

I take a careful breath, glancing down at Ben's body. I think about going over there to check his pulse, but then I remember the pool of blood on the floor, the lightless, milky look of his eyes, and I know it's a lost cause. Definitely dead.

Fuck. I look away, stomach churning. I have to stay calm for both of us.

"Here." I take a step toward Colin, hand outstretched for the knife. "Let me."

Instinctively, he pulls back.

"Colin, I need you to give me the knife."

"You don't believe me." He backs up until he's against the wall, cornered. "I didn't do this!"

I don't believe him, not entirely, but I believe that he's in a state of shock, and *he* believes it, and what kind of girlfriend would I be if I started harping on facts when he's standing over his dead childhood friend?

"Fuck." Colin digs his hands through his hair, looking down at Ben and then away again, like he might be sick. "*Fuck.* I swear to god, I didn't—"

"Colin, I believe you. But we need to think about what to do next."

His darting eyes fix on mine with a distant, stunned expression, like he hadn't considered that there's a *next* after this. I'm the only one thinking clearly right now, and I need to take charge. It hits me with an echo of something almost like nostalgia: I know how to do this.

This isn't the first time I've had to pick up the pieces.

"Has anyone else seen him?" I ask.

Colin shakes his head. "I got back here like ten minutes ago. Twenty? Fuck, I don't—"

"But no one has seen him?"

"No," he says. "I got back, and the apartment was empty. Just . . . him. Here. Like this. And the knife."

I look again at Ben's body, slumped there in the center of the room like someone staged it for a play: *Lights up on dead roommate.* Everything else looks impossibly normal: the bed rumpled slightly, the blinds and window shut.

Wait, the window. I move the blinds aside and haul it open with a rusty scraping sound. Ben's room doesn't have a fire escape, but when I stick my head out, I can see the one outside of Colin's window.

"What are you doing?" He sounds startled, like he thinks I might jump through.

"Someone could have broken in," I explain.

He frowns, confused, but then his eyes sharpen with understanding.

"Through my fire escape."

"Right." I close the window. "They could've come in through your room without realizing Ben was home."

Colin nods, but then his face goes cloudy again. "I keep my window locked, though."

"Not tonight," I say.

"What?"

I give him a careful look. "Tonight, you forgot."

Colin watches me with a gaze I can't quite read, but for a moment, I think I catch a flicker of it: awe, tinged with something sharper. Something like fear.

"It was a break-in," he says, calmer.

I nod. "So, all we have to do is make that extra clear. That way, the police will know you didn't do it."

"The police." The calm drains from Colin's face, right alongside the color in his cheeks. "Shit, the police. I can't—"

"Hey, are you with me?" I cut him off, and his eyes snap back to mine. "I'm going to help you get out of this, but I need you to stay with me."

I don't like playing hardball, but it's working. He nods, eyes still locked on me, and I think we both needed the reminder: we're in this together.

"Good." I glance around the room again, my mind spinning. If there's anything I know, it's how to set a scene, and the best ones start with the details. "The knife," I realize, noticing it in Colin's hand again. "Your prints will be on it. We can't get around that."

"Shit." Colin starts to panic again, moving to wipe the knife on his shirt before he realizes that's an even worse idea and stops himself. Good.

"Whoever killed him wouldn't just leave the weapon lying there for anyone to find, right?" I say. "So, give it to me and I'll get rid of it."

Colin starts to hand it over, and if I had any lingering hesitation, it melts away. He's trusting me again.

"Wait, actually . . ." I stop him, realizing. "Do you have gloves? So I don't get my prints on it? And maybe a plastic bag, so it doesn't get my tote dirty."

Colin stares at me for a moment longer, a question lingering on his face.

If he asks, I don't know how I'll answer.

But instead, he says, "Yeah, I should have something around here."

He goes, returning with rubber cleaning gloves and a paper Trader Joe's bag.

"They don't really do plastic anymore," he says apologetically, and it's absurd, how adorable I find him, even when we're cleaning up a murder scene.

"This is perfect," I tell him. "Thank you."

I'll make it work. I slide on the gloves and then carefully take the knife, dropping it into the grocery bag and folding it up so it fits in my tote.

"There," I say.

Now that we've solved our first problem, the creative juices are flowing. I lead Colin to his own bedroom, where I crack his window open, keeping the gloves on just in case. I look around at the rest of the room. The bed is still rumpled from how we left it, and my heart squeezes.

Focus, Jane.

"Do you have any valuables in here?" I ask. "Things that would be easy to spot? We need to think about why they'd break in."

My gaze lands on his laptop, sitting like a duck on his desk. The laptop, with those pictures hidden in a folder.

"This could work," I say as casually as possible. I'm just about to slide it into my tote when Colin's grip tightens on my wrist, hard enough to make my breath catch.

"What are you doing?" he snaps. Seeing the shock on my face, he lets go of me, but his stare is still hard. "You can't just take that."

"I'll give it back," I explain, trying to calm the pulse beating wildly in my throat. That sudden, violent surge reminded me too much of the waterfront, my back pressed up against the railing. That briefest of moments when I thought he was there to kill me.

"But if this is a break-in," I continue, pushing that thought down, "you need specific things to report as stolen. I'll just hold on to it for now." I slide the laptop into my bag. "What else do you have that someone would steal?"

Colin relents, pointing me to his nice headphones and his wallet. I drop them in my tote alongside the computer.

"Good," I say. "So, that's what they took."

There's a moment of stillness, relief breathing through us both. This will work, I think.

And then, I remember Ben's text. *I found some stuff in Colin's room . . .* It's not exactly damning, but it's something the police might question if they see it.

"What's wrong?" Colin asks.

"Ben's phone," I say. "Where is it?"

He frowns. "I don't know, why?"

"He told me he found something in your room," I say. "I just want to delete the text. Make sure it doesn't complicate our story."

We go back to Ben's room, but I don't see the phone on his bed or his desk, anywhere it should be. There's only one other option. Carefully, I move to Ben's body and bend down, patting his front pockets with my rubber-gloved hands. I try not to panic about the fact that I might be leaving some kind of DNA on him, but we *were* on a date just a few days ago, even if it feels more like years. I don't find the phone in the front, so I check his back pockets, but it's not there, either.

I take off the gloves and toss them aside, frustrated. "I don't see it."

"Maybe they took it."

I look up to find an unreadable expression on Colin's face.

"When they broke in," he says carefully.

And then, I understand: the phone isn't there because *Colin* took it. Why wouldn't he just tell me?

Maybe because he still doesn't trust you, a dark voice whispers.

I stand up, heart thudding. "Colin . . ."

The rest of that thought is stolen when Colin buries his hand in the back of my hair and kisses me, hard and deep and wanting.

"The police will ask where I was before I found him," he says, lips against my ear. "I'll tell them I was with you."

Maybe it's wrong, but that sentence starts a fire in my stomach, burning so bright and low that I want to drag him back to the bed, make him say it into my mouth.

Instead, I brush his hair behind his ear and whisper, "Of course."

Colin exhales, pressing his forehead to mine. "Thank you, Jane."

The words plant seeds in my chest, digging warm roots that wind around my rib cage. I want to stay here forever, wrapped up in each other, but we both know we can't. I have a murder weapon to ditch, and Colin needs to call the police.

At the reminder, a frantic realization jumps into my head. *Shit.*

"Are there cameras in your building?" I ask.

If there are, and the police check the footage, they'll know I was here. Worse, they'll know Colin was here a long time before calling them. Our cover story will be shot.

Panic washes over Colin's face, but then it suddenly fades to relief.

"The system's out. It has been all week. I know because—" He hesitates, looking at Ben's body with a flash of guilt, or grief, or both. "Ben went down to the super's office earlier this week to ask if anyone had found his keys, and the super got mad that he'd lost them. Apparently, they can't get someone in to fix the cameras until next week, so it's not exactly a great time to have some unauthorized person walking around with stolen keys."

I breathe out, almost limp with gratitude. The universe is on our side. How could it not be, when we've been through so much? Things are falling back into place, cosmically aligned in the way they were always meant to be, and this small comfort is our reward. In a way, me borrowing Ben's keys even saved us.

But as soon as I have the thought, there's a knife of guilt in my stomach, sharp and quick. Fucking *Ben*, with his IPAs and kind eyes and dumb jokes that would have made someone else really happy one day. He didn't deserve this, even if he was an asshole to me when I wouldn't go home with him.

But Colin didn't deserve it, either. Whatever evidence he found in Colin's room—the bloody knife, the jacket, the pictures of

175

Leigh—Ben was going to use it. It's the only explanation for what happened here tonight: Colin did what he had to do to survive. I can't begrudge him that. Not when I know too well what it's like to have your back against the wall.

Another surge of tenderness moves me to pull Colin close again, smooth the worried crease of his eyebrows with my thumb.

"We're going to be okay," I whisper. "I promise."

When he pulls me tighter to him, I know I've never believed anything more.

I walk briskly to the East River, glancing over my shoulder every so often, but I'm lucky: no one is suspicious of a small white girl with a tote bag. I dump the knife, grocery bag and all, into the water unseen.

Then, when I get home, I set Colin's laptop on my desk. I put on my own cleaning gloves—technically Anna's, but she isn't around to care—just in case, and then I sit down to open it up.

The screen prompts me for a password. I clench my jaw. I should have seen this coming. I didn't think to ask Colin for his password. Still, it's not the end of the world. If I can't figure it out on my own, I'm pretty sure he'd trust me enough to give it to me if I asked, now that we're together again, but I'll cross that bridge when I get there.

First, I go for Colin's phone password. When that doesn't work, I try a sudden whim: adding Leigh's name at the beginning.

I'm in.

A chill grips the back of my neck, but I shake it off, finding the taxes folder Zoe mentioned and opening it up. There, among various W-2s and past returns . . . is nothing. I click on every single one of them, thinking maybe Zoe was mistaken, but there's no secret folder full of evidence.

I click on Colin's trash, but there's nothing in there, either. Like, nothing at all. It's all been wiped.

I breathe deeply, trying to keep my focus clear. This is good. This was *smart*. Colin should have wiped it from the beginning. It never should have been just sitting there, on a poorly protected laptop, for Zoe to find.

My phone buzzes with a call, and I check it, expecting to see Colin's name.

It's Zoe.

Alarm bells ring in every corner of my brain, but I force myself to breathe. Be normal.

Be normal, Jane.

I take a slow breath.

"Hello?"

"Jane, oh my god. Where are you?"

My heart leaps into a frantic thump. Zoe sounds panicked.

"Are you okay?" I ask.

"I'm at Colin's."

Oh no. Bad. This is bad.

"What? Why?"

"He called me."

I clutch my phone tightly. He called her. That wasn't part of our plan.

"There was a break-in. And . . ." She sobs. "I'm so sorry."

I know what's coming, and still, my heart is pounding. "What happened?"

"It's Ben. He . . . he was hurt, and he didn't make it."

Dread lodges in my throat like a hot coal. I try to swallow it down.

"Are you okay?" I manage. "Is Colin?"

"Yeah," she says automatically. "I mean, no. We're . . . safe, at least." She sniffs. "Colin called the police, and they're here, but he can't stay here tonight because it's—" Another wet sniff. "It's a crime scene. We're going to head back to my place."

I know I should say something, but my head is spinning, a mix of relief and panic. They're both okay. Colin called the police, and it doesn't seem like they're arresting him. But Zoe . . . Zoe was not supposed to be a piece of this puzzle. And they're not supposed to go back to her apartment.

"Do you want to come over?" she asks when I still haven't spoken. "We should be back to mine within the hour, if . . . you know, if you don't want to be alone tonight."

I look at Colin's laptop, the empty folder in front of me. There are so many lingering questions, so many hidden parts of him to explore in this computer, but right now, I have bigger priorities—like the fact that Colin just murdered his roommate, and now Zoe is taking him back to her apartment. Alone.

I shut the laptop.

"Yeah, of course," I say. "I'll come." And then, after a moment: "I'm really glad you're safe."

I don't tell her that soon, I'm afraid she won't be.

19

I think about springing for a car, but I know I can't afford it. Instead, I'm condemned to MTA hell for the third time tonight, checking my phone every five seconds on the train until finally, it comes to a creaking halt in Greenpoint.

I practically sprint to Zoe's apartment. When I get there, she's already waiting outside, sitting alone on the stoop.

Our eyes meet, but before I can think of what to say, Zoe rushes over and pulls me into a fierce hug. She holds on so tightly that it feels like I'm the only thing keeping her standing, even though she's got about five inches on me. For a moment, I give over to it, letting myself be her anchor.

Then, when I can't wait any longer, I ask, "Where's Colin?"

"Asleep," she says, letting go. "He was pretty shaken up, so I gave him some of the pills I was prescribed a while back to help him rest."

"Good," I say.

I glance at the door, itching to go inside and check on him, but Zoe's right. He needs sleep. Still, it's cold out, and Zoe's not even wearing a jacket over her sweats. She looks dazed, her gaze fixed somewhere in the middle distance in a way that sets me on edge.

"Should we head in?" I ask, the uneasiness creeping into my voice.

"Yeah." Zoe shudders slightly, like she's snapping back into herself. "Yeah, I just . . ." Her eyes find mine, and now, the haunted look in them absolutely terrifies me. "He said he was with you tonight."

Everything blurs except for Zoe's face, a spotlight in the dark aimed directly at me. I blink quickly, like that might reset the image, an invisible hand tightening around my throat. I knew this would happen. I knew I would have to face this betrayal, but still, I wasn't prepared.

The shock on my face has cost me.

"I knew it," Zoe says quietly, and then again, louder, "I *knew* it. He lied."

It takes me a second to adjust to her use of the singular subject. *He* lied. Not me. This isn't an accusation. If Zoe has noticed my surprise, though, she doesn't show it. She's pacing, too buzzing with anger to stay still.

"He made up an alibi, and the police just believed it. He used you. I had a feeling something was off with the break-in story, but I was too shocked and scared to say anything. I convinced myself I was seeing things, but—*Jane.*" She stops moving, her eyes locked on mine in desperation, and I know what's coming. I know even before she says, in a small but undeniable whisper, "I think Colin might have killed him."

I don't have the words to deny it.

"Fuck," Zoe whispers, burying her face in her hands. *"Fuck."*

"We don't know that for sure," I try, but it's too late. I messed up. I waited too long.

"He lied to the police about where he was. He 'found' the body. And all of this other stuff—the texts accusing him of killing someone, and then Leigh telling us he's not who we think he is . . . What if Ben found out about it, too? Maybe he was threatening to go to the police." She looks at me, pleading. "Please tell me I'm not the only one who's seeing this."

She's not. That's the worst part. She's too smart for her own good, I know, and still, I can't let her believe this. But her voice, the look in her eyes . . . I *know* it. That seething, clawing need to be understood. I hesitate for a moment, until finally, my resolve breaks.

"I see it, too," I tell her.

Her entire body loosens with relief, but it's only a moment before she hardens again, replacing the armor she'd briefly let slip.

"We have to tell the police," she says.

I flinch, and then instantly regret it. "I don't think we should."

"Why? He might have *killed* someone."

"Right, he *might* have. We don't have the evidence to prove it."

"But we do," she argues. "You can tell them he lied. And we can tell them about the texts and the pictures, and maybe we can get in touch with Leigh again, convince her to—"

"It's not enough," I snap, my voice sharpened by the mention of Leigh. "They won't believe us."

Zoe stares back at me, unrelenting. "That doesn't mean we shouldn't try."

We're at a standstill, clearly, but I can't let her talk to the police—both for Colin's sake and, I realize, for hers. Because if Colin finds out that Zoe suspects him . . . The thought is a cold hand pressed to my spine. After tonight, I know what Colin is capable of when threatened.

An idea trickles down from the back of my mind, the place where I store things that shouldn't see the light of day.

You could try, Jane, I tell myself. *You have to.*

"I've, um . . ." I look down at the pavement as I let this little sliver of truth go. "I've had some experience with police before. There was a situation with a bad relationship."

"Oh." Zoe softens. "I'm so sorry, that's—"

"It's fine," I say quickly. "Seriously. All good now. It's just, I know how they work. You report things, and it's always the same. They won't actually do anything until you can prove your life is in danger. You know, the classic: *Sorry, we can't do anything about this guy until he actually tries to kill you.*"

I try for a laugh, but it's hollow in my throat.

"And I just know that if we go to the police now," I continue, "they won't be able to do anything. But if Colin finds out, if he's actually willing to *kill* someone to protect himself . . ."

"Shit," she breathes.

For a moment, we're silent.

"Jane, I'm—"

"It's okay," I say again, desperate to shut the lid on this conversation before any more of it can run away from me. "Really."

Her eyes drift from me to the warehouse across the street, and it's like the spotlight turns off, leaving coldness in its wake. She hugs her arms around her ribs, shaking her head in disbelief.

"Did Leigh say why she canceled?"

I'm momentarily startled by the question before I remember that it's the lie I gave her.

"No. She just said she had to bail."

"We can try her again," Zoe says, determination creeping back in. "If we tell her about Ben, that could change her mind. She'll know how serious this is."

I tense. If Colin's the one controlling Leigh's account, which I'm almost certain he is, then messaging her will tip him off. But I can make sure he doesn't see it. And waiting for a response that isn't coming *would* buy us some time.

"Yeah," I say. "Good idea."

Zoe lets out a shaky breath.

"It's just so fucked," she says. "How easily the cops believed him. I mean, they've got him at the scene of a literal murder, and still, they think some crime show bad guy is more plausible than the guy who was standing over the body."

"Maybe there's some other reason he lied," I try. "Colin's the one who called the police, right? If he killed Ben, then why—"

"Because he knew they'd believe him," she snaps. "He was so fucking confident in himself that he implicated you. He just assumed you'd go along with it. Like, what kind of psychopath *does* that? And now—" She laughs, a wild look in her eyes. "I invited him back to my apartment, because I guess I fell for it, too."

I feel for her. I really do—enough that I give her one more kernel of truth.

"It's not your fault," I tell her gently. "Some guys are experts at hiding who they really are."

Guys like Axel, who dropped the suave act and called me a bitch the second he realized he wasn't getting laid. Like Trip, who lured me in with soft words and softer looks that made me feel like the center of the universe, only to throw it back in my face, asking what the hell he did to make me fall in love with him.

And maybe even guys like Colin. Guys who seem safe and kind and good—who make you think you could be good, too, right before they slide a knife across their best friend's throat.

"Yeah," Zoe says. "I guess they are."

Silence curls around us, a moment of understanding. I close my eyes, take a deep breath of cool air, but on the inhale, my head swims with images that feel all wrong, incompatible. The pool of blood. The knife in Colin's hand, dropping down into the river. His fist against the wall, the shout, but also his fingers brushing gently through my hair, touching my collarbone, settling into the dip at the base of my spine, and the smell of him on my clothes again, clean and sweet. The smell of Ben's room. The tang of meat, the sharpness of death.

"Jane?"

I open my eyes. "Yeah?"

"You okay?"

I think about lying. I should. But the words won't come out. Instead, I just shake my head.

"Hey." Zoe pulls me into a hug, so warm it makes my throat sting. "We're going to get through this, okay? If he really did this . . . we'll prove it. We won't let him get away with it."

Tears spill down my cheeks, quiet but uncontrollable, and it scares me that I don't know who they're for.

Colin is out cold. Seeing him curled up on the green velvet sofa, I wonder if Zoe really gave him those sleeping pills to help him rest, or if some part of her already suspected—if she wanted to make sure he couldn't hurt us.

Now, she sleeps next to me in the bed, her breath rising and falling in an even rhythm. Even in sleep, though, she seems uneasy, her eyes shifting beneath her lids, lost in some frantic dream.

Colin looks completely at peace. His face is free from the hard lines and angles that have plagued it all night, like a hand brushed over sand to smooth the surface. All of him is soft now: his breathing, the rumpled mess of his hair, the eyelashes on his cheek like little dark butterfly wings, longer than a boy's should be but somehow even more beautiful for it.

I should wake him up. This might be our best chance to be alone and talk this over. But Zoe would hear us leaving, and he's already lost in a pill-induced haze.

I'll let him sleep.

I tend to get epiphanies late in the night, understandings made more powerful by the fact that, if I'm not careful, they could slip away by morning.

Tonight, this is mine: it's lucky, having someone to watch while you sleep, standing guard against the monsters in the shadows, but it's luckier still to be the one standing guard. To have someone you love enough to stay awake for.

In her sleep, Zoe shifts closer to me. She grabs at the covers bunched around my shoulders and pulls them to her, clutching at safety in an invisible storm.

20

I don't realize sleep has found me until Zoe shakes me awake.

"We're going to New Jersey."

I blink, the world coming into hazy focus. Zoe stands above me, a look of fierce determination on her face.

"What?"

"Colin went home."

I sit up. "Wait, why?"

"Because he's running away," Zoe says, like it should have been clear from the moment she told me. "And he has to go to Ben's funeral, I guess, but when he told me this morning . . . I could tell. He's guilty, and he's freaking out. So, he's going back to New Jersey. And we're going after him."

On instinct, I fumble for my phone and click the screen awake. Nothing. Colin didn't text me.

Panic digs in. This wasn't supposed to happen. I was supposed to *talk* to him, make sure we're on the same page before he jetted off without a fucking text.

When I look up again, Zoe's already shoving things into a bag.

"Wait, hold on." I get out of bed. "Why are *we* going?"

"Because he killed someone last night, and we're the only ones who know it." Zoe sets the bag down. "Also, he asked me to come."

It's a fresh stab in my chest. *He asked her.*

"Obviously, I didn't want to leave with him alone," Zoe continues. "But he'd be suspicious if I flat-out refused. So, I told him I can't get out of the city until later. I'm leaving tonight, and you're coming with me."

I can't even respond, not with the hurt still reverberating through me. Colin asked Zoe to come, and he didn't even text me, when I'm the one who helped him cover up a murder. I'm the one he was *inside of* last night. Anger burns hot and fast, but I try to force it down.

"You told him I'm coming?" I ask.

"Not specifically. But you have to. I can't do this alone."

She can't do this at all, I think. Not when she's this certain that Colin is a murderer. Not when I don't know what either of them will do. I'm grasping for the right argument, some way to make this stop, but all of them freeze on my tongue when I see the desperation burning in Zoe's eyes.

"Jane, please," she says. "We can't let him get away with this."

Something like déjà vu prickles at the back of my neck. *We can't let him get away with this.* It's the second time she's said it since last night.

How the hell does she plan to stop him?

And I know, suddenly, that there's no getting out of this. Zoe knows Colin killed Ben, and she thinks we're the only ones who can prove it. Because, I realize, we are.

Zoe's right. We can't let Colin out of our sight.

And I can't let her out of mine.

"Okay," I say. "We'll go."

A relieved smile breaks through her intensity.

"I already booked us a rental car."

I head out quickly once we've hammered out the details. Zoe will pick me up tonight, which gives me more than enough time to get home, pack, and try to get in touch with Colin.

I send him a text as soon as I'm out of Zoe's apartment.

Everything ok? Call when you can

I check my phone frantically on my walk to the station, on the platform, but by the time the train rattles in, I haven't heard back. I call him as I get on, but it cuts to voicemail. Spotty service, maybe. I try again at the next station, but still nothing.

My heart starts to flutter, a small, frightened bird trapped between my ribs. I think of texting him again, but then it occurs to me that maybe Colin is just being smart. He doesn't want a record of our communication, anything that would tip off Zoe or the police to the cover-up.

No contact is good, I tell myself. I can be okay with no contact.

I have to be.

For the rest of the ride up, I busy myself with canceling work for the next couple of days, and then, once that's done, I focus on my plan. Even if I can't get in touch with Colin beforehand, I'll find a way to get him alone in New Jersey. Once I can finally talk to him, I'll know what to do next. Until then, I'll just have to keep an eye on Zoe, make sure she doesn't do anything impulsive.

By the time I get home, I'm feeling considerably less panicked. I throw some clothes into a duffel and then grab my phone. Even if Colin doesn't respond, I want him to know I'm coming. I type out a text.

Zoe told me you're heading home—we figured you might want some NYC company. See you tonight :)

It's vague enough that if someone besides Colin sees it, they won't suspect anything. I could still just be his *friend from Penn.*

I press send. For a few minutes, I watch the screen for his texting bubble, but nothing comes.

And then, I realize. There's no *delivered* message under my text. I turn my Wi-Fi off and on again, but nothing changes. No error message, but still, that little *delivered* is missing.

Quickly, I google "message doesn't say delivered." The first result is a highlighted clip from an article: *If your message doesn't say delivered, the recipient's phone or internet may simply be off.*

But then, just below that, another article clipping:

If you don't see "delivered" under your text, it may mean the recipient has blocked your number.

Blood rushes in my ears.

What the *fuck*? Panicked, I call him again. Voicemail.

Again.

Voicemail.

I throw my phone against the wall.

"Jane?" Anna's voice comes from her room. "You okay?"

Shit.

"Yeah, sorry," I call back. "Butterfingers."

I scramble for my phone, breathing out when I see that, besides a little scuff on the edge, my phone is okay. But I need to get it together. Keep it under control.

I am loved, I am whole, and he came back.

He came back.

All I have to do is get through this trip, be good for a few more days, and then he'll never leave me again.

21

Zoe is quiet as we drive. Our shitty rental car propels us across the George Washington Bridge, and she keeps her focus on the road, the golden-hour glow of Manhattan fading in the rearview as we zoom toward the rolling green nothing of New Jersey. Then, after cutting off a van in the next lane over and earning us an angry honk, she says, "I'm going to get Colin to confess."

I nearly choke on the stale cigarette air.

"How?" I sputter.

It's the first of many questions springing frantically to mind, but if Zoe notices, she doesn't let on. Her grip tightens on the wheel, her eyes still locked on the road.

"I'll talk to him," she says, like it's simple. "He trusts me. I mean, I'm still his girlfriend."

It's a jab in the wound, so acute I could almost believe she knows what she's doing.

"I won't come at it like I'm accusing him or anything," she continues. "But the guilt must be eating him alive. If I talk to him, make it seem like I'm on his side . . . maybe that's all he needs. And

I'll record it—without him knowing, obviously—but that way, if he confesses, we'll have something to bring to the police."

I'm gripping the seat so hard I'm surprised my nails don't rip clean through. It takes everything in me to keep my voice level as I ask, "Do you think that's a good idea, though? He could lash out. If he realizes what you're doing—"

"He won't." She glances at me, looking disappointed that I don't think this is a better idea. "And it's not like we have any other options. It's like you said: the police won't do anything until we have proof."

We emerge from the bridge onto the highway, a sprawl of lanes winding toward suburbia, and I ball my hands into fists. *Breathe.* This is a terrible idea, obviously, but even if I can't make Zoe see that, it's not the end of the world. I just need to talk to Colin. I'll tell him—what? *Don't kill Zoe when she accuses you of murder, because I can still fix this somehow?*

I check my phone again, but still, there's nothing from Colin. Suddenly, all the other cars feel too close, too many, and I'm overwhelmed by how doomed this plan is—walking into Colin's childhood home with his still-technically-girlfriend at my side, not even two days after Colin and I came back to each other. We still haven't had a chance to *talk*, and I'm half worried he hates me.

Barreling headfirst into New fucking Jersey, it's too easy to enter a dark night of the soul.

"Jane?" Zoe glances my way. "Are you okay?"

"Sorry," I say. Another automatic apology, the habit I still can't seem to shake. "Just . . . thinking."

She nods, her focus fixing again on the road. "I'm nervous, too. But we can do this."

When I can't bring myself to respond, Zoe turns to look at me.

The sun lights up her face and sets it aglow, turning the miniscule hairs on her cheek into glittering dew.

She tells me, sharp as a blade: "We're going to make him pay."

A chill run downs my spine. The way she's looking at me, rage burning like its own sun in her green eyes—I recognize it. I've *felt* it. And I wonder, not for the first time, where it's really coming from.

I wonder who is more dangerous: the killer we're driving to see or the girl with her foot on the gas.

Thirty minutes later, we pass the WELCOME TO UPPER SADDLE RIVER sign. It's royal blue, with curlicued lettering and a country club air that seems to scoff at our little Chevy Malibu. Or maybe it's not the sign so much as the gradual sprawl of mansions it announces that makes me feel inferior: nouveau-riche monstrosities with no unifying aesthetic besides *big* and *bright*, with their long driveways and wide green yards and square footage much too large for the parents, dog, and two-point-five children each one no doubt accommodates.

Zoe, however, looks unfazed. Probably because Upper Saddle River, New Jersey, has nothing on Greenwich, Connecticut. Her GPS orders us to turn right, and Zoe flips the blinker.

"It should be up here," she says.

I hold my breath as I take it in—the street with its stretch of houses so big and perfect, it's as if they were plucked out of thin air and dropped on the ground by some unseen hand, as precisely spaced as a Monopoly board.

For all I know about Colin, I didn't expect him to come from this type of wealth. He went to an Ivy League, and he's a software engineer, but he wears a North Face instead of a Canada Goose. He makes coffee instead of buying it, except on special occasions. None of him feels pretentious or *rich*. But this—this is Americana, backyard pools and hedgerows and too many cars in each driveway, all of them embla-zoned with bumper stickers for impressive, expensive schools. These are the kind of people who brag about their children at summer bar-becues and PTA meetings, proud to have borne them into a world where the cards are stacked so egregiously in their favor.

The GPS announces that we've reached our destination, and the Malibu grinds to a halt. This house isn't much different than the oth-ers, except for the divine glow radiating off it simply by virtue of its meaning: *his*.

Red brick, a shade startlingly similar to his apartment, only blown up to supersized proportions. Long stone driveway, two-door garage. Colonial, symmetrical. Neat little hedges leading up to a grand entrance, framed by columns. This is the house that grew Colin Hillgrove, sprouted him from the freshly mowed lawn. I feel it again, that thread between us, tugging me home.

Zoe still has her foot on the brake, chewing her lip. For half a second, I think maybe she's realizing this was a bad idea—until she turns, decisively, right into the driveway. It's a move bold enough to make anxious heat prickle under my arms and at the base of my spine, but there's no undoing it now. She parks the car, silences the engine.

"Ready?" she asks.

I have no choice but to be.

We climb out of the car and walk down the hedge-lined path to the front door. The welcome mat bears an *H* in fancy script, and this isn't the way I wanted to meet his parents, not when I'm sweating and vaguely cigarette-smelling and embroiled in a web of lies as intricate as the leaded glass on their front door.

Behind us, something moves, and I whirl around. A family of three deer on the lawn, their heads snapped toward us in mirrored panic. They dart away, scattering toward the neighbor's yard, but the image lingers. Their black, frightened eyes.

Lifeless eyes. Meat on a hook. The blood on his fingers warming my cheek.

It's a beautiful thing, watching something die.

I want to say something, stop this somehow, but I'm too late.

Zoe's already ringing the bell.

22

It's Colin's mom who answers the door. I like her instantly, probably because she's not the cold country-club type I was afraid she'd be. She's small, sweet-faced, and clearly the source of Colin's freckles.

"Oh, hi. How can I help you?"

She asks the question like she actually means it, not with the subtext of *Get off my doorstep*.

"Hi, Mrs. Hillgrove?" Zoe asks, even though it's obvious. "I'm Zoe, Colin's girlfriend. And this is his friend Jane. He asked us to come by."

Mrs. Hillgrove blinks, clearly a little thrown off.

"We were there with him," Zoe adds, casting her eyes downward, "after he found . . ."

"Oh," Mrs. Hillgrove says, understanding. "Oh, yes. Colin told us he had friends with him when . . . I'm so sorry, girls. Please, come in."

I don't miss that she called us both Colin's *friends*, and I like her even more. Obviously, Colin hasn't told his mom about Zoe. He hasn't even told her that he invited her here.

If Zoe's pissed, she hides it well.

"Thank you so much," she says sweetly. "It's so nice to meet you."

"You, too. It was Zoe, right? And . . ." Mrs. Hillgrove pauses, glancing my way.

"Jane," I tell her.

"Right, of course."

Her eyes linger on me in a way that makes my stomach flip— almost like she's seen me before, but she can't place where. Then, she ushers us inside.

Right away, it's clear what I should have known from the beginning: the Hillgroves' home doesn't have the harsh, unlived-in feeling that so many of these wealthy houses can't ever shake. It's warm, cozy despite all the space, and reminiscent of Colin's bedroom with its clean- but-not-tidy state: shoes discarded next to an open, overstuffed coat closet, framed photos of baby Colin and his older sister on the foyer table. I absorb these little fragments of him eagerly: school picture day, T-ball, beach vacation—a little shell in the foreground, Colin's gap- toothed grin behind, urging the camera to share in his wonder.

"Colin?" Mrs. Hillgrove calls upstairs. "Zoe and Jane are here." She turns back to us. Still lingering, I realize, on me. It sends a buzz of excitement and uneasiness down my back, the fact that I might be the more noticed guest, even standing next to Zoe Ember.

"Can I get you anything?" she asks us. "A drink, a snack?"

Before we can answer, a man appears in the doorway of the next room.

"Oh," he says, adjusting his glasses. "Hello there."

Something about his demeanor makes me stand straighter, like he's a school principal or some other mildly threatening authority figure from my youth. Colin's dad, I'm assuming.

"Jeff, this is Zoe, Colin's girlfriend." His mom hitches slightly on the word, the newness of it.

Mr. Hillgrove raises his eyebrows, clearly also surprised by this update to his son's relationship status.

"And this is Jane, a friend of his from . . . ." Mrs. Hillgrove looks to me for explanation.

"College," I say quickly, figuring I have no choice but to prolong the lie.

"Well, then! Lovely to meet you both." Mr. Hillgrove approaches with a gregariousness so unlike Colin that I'm momentarily thrown off. Still, I see traces of Colin in the color of his father's hair, the intelligent perch of his glasses. When he shakes my hand, his grip is firm but kind. "And please, call me Jeff."

"Helen," Colin's mom adds, like she's embarrassed to have forgotten before.

"So nice to meet you both," Zoe says with a smile that manages to be both dazzling and somber. "I really wish it were under different circumstances."

Colin's parents are both stoic, even though the grief is plain on their faces. They both must have watched Ben grow up alongside Colin, watched them play and make stupid jokes and graduate high school, and it hurts, knowing they can never know the truth. Knowing I have to look at them when I do.

Jeff clears his throat.

"Well," he says, "I know Colin will be glad you made the trip."

Helen climbs up the first few stairs.

"Col," she calls up. "You coming down?"

And then, there he is, standing on the second-floor landing with a sleepy look, and I want to rush up there and throw my arms around his shoulders, tell him it's all going to be all right. He sees Zoe, and his face melts into relief, only to harden into cool surprise when his gaze drifts to me.

"Jane?" he asks. "What are you . . ."

Zoe cuts him off, doing what I can't: running up the stairs, pulling him into a tight hug.

197

"I hope you don't mind that I brought backup," she says. "I figured you could use a little extra New York support."

Colin's eyes shift to mine again, unreadable except for the glaze of shock, and I know right away that he hasn't gotten my texts. I tried to warn him, and I failed.

Well, maybe he shouldn't have fucking blocked me.

The vitriol is so sudden that it shocks me, and I try to talk myself down. Colin is scared and hurting. It's not fair of me to blame him like this. Still, the feeling persists, an echo beneath the logic.

"So." Jeff claps in textbook dad fashion. "What would you girls say to some dinner?"

Two things I learn during my first family dinner with the Hillgroves: first, Colin's favorite comfort meal after a bad day is a large Hawaiian pizza, and second, meeting the parents might be one of the few things Zoe isn't naturally good at.

"It's really no problem," she insists, meticulously peeling each ham slice from her pizza and stacking them at the edge of her plate. "I know it's been a tough couple of days, so I don't want to make things difficult."

Colin's parents had already ordered the pizza before we got there, and when Zoe saw it had meat on it, she made sure everyone knew she was a vegetarian—even if, clearly, she's the kind of vegetarian who can still eat the pizza if she peels off the ham.

"And it's not like you knew," Zoe tells Colin's parents, with a distinct glance at Colin.

I don't know if it's a reference to her dietary preferences or the existence of their relationship, but either way, it makes me falter with my slice halfway to my mouth. Zoe has a right to be thrown off that

Colin didn't tell his parents about her, but to toss that back at him after everything he's been through in the past two days? It's bold, I'll give her that, but there's something else brewing beneath it, something I recognize: anxiety, bright in her eyes, the flitting of her hands. Despite her unshakable belief that their son is a killer, she wants them to like her, and it's making everything worse.

"So," Jeff says, heroically changing the subject. "You're an artist, Zoe? What kind?"

She smiles, wiping her fingers delicately on a napkin. "Mixed media. Painting, photography, collage, basically whatever I can throw on a canvas before someone stops me. I'm sort of a maximalist, which is funny, considering who I ended up with."

Ended up with, like this is endgame and not a two-month dating app relationship doomed to implode at some point in the next twenty-four hours. It's stunning, how quickly I swing between envy of Zoe's confidence and anger at how brazenly she flings it around.

Jeff laughs. "Our boy certainly is a bit of a minimalist, isn't he? I've always said Colin would live like a monk if he could. Assuming it's a monastery where they also have Hawaiian pizza."

He takes a bite, gratified with his own sense of humor, and I like him, even as Colin stares red-cheeked at his own plate. Colin's dad may be dorky and a little boisterous, but he's hardly the worst when it comes to the lottery of fathers.

"What about you, Jane?" Helen asks.

Nerves shoot through me, a sudden fear that she's read my mind, but I like her for bringing me back into the conversation—and perhaps for noticing the way the ham has stayed unpretentiously on my own slice.

"I'm a playwright," I say. No *but*.

"Oh, that's wonderful!" Helen brightens. "Jeff and I are always trying to stay on top of the new stuff whenever we get into the city. I'm a Shakespeare fanatic."

Colin never mentioned this to me, but it fills me with a bright, sunny warmth. I can picture myself sliding easily into their family dynamic, dinners in Midtown before an eight o' clock show, dissecting the play with his mom on the subway ride back while Colin looks on, amazed at how perfectly I fit.

It's that buzzing, hopeful image that leads me to say, "I'm actually working on a play right now. It's an adaptation of *Hamlet* but focused on Ophelia."

"Oh, *Hamlet* is one of my favorites," Helen gushes. "You'll have to let us know when we can get a ticket."

"Well," Zoe steps in, "we'll actually be premiering an excerpt at my art show next week."

Colin's grip tightens on his water glass. We still haven't talked about this, either, my debut at Zoe's show. I still don't know if he's upset about it.

"How exciting!" Helen glances at Colin, a little bit uncertainly. "Is that something we can get tickets for, or . . . ?"

"It's fine, Mom," he says. "You guys don't have to drive all the way up."

"Well, you're more than welcome to, if you'd like. But totally your call." Zoe smiles, but I can see a hint of iciness beneath it as she looks at Colin—barely a flicker, but there.

"You'll have to forgive us," Jeff speaks up. "Colin is never the most forthcoming about his life in the city. It's a wonder if we can get him on the phone for ten minutes a week."

"Just so busy with work," Helen says.

"And exciting artists and playwrights, clearly," Jeff echoes, giving Colin a fatherly clap on the shoulder. He glances at me, eyes narrowing. "You said you're a fellow Quaker?"

It takes me too long to realize he means the Penn mascot, and I hope the pause hasn't given me away.

"Yeah," I say. "Colin and I were—"

"We were in the same dorm," he interrupts.

I look at him, but he won't quite meet my eyes. Does he still not trust me to keep up with his own ridiculous lie?

Jeff looks momentarily hesitant, but he recovers quickly.

"Of course! I'm sure we've met at a move-in or Parents' Weekend. The old memory's so spotty these days. Must be all the beer."

He takes a sip, as if to prove the point. Colin and Zoe both declined when he offered us one, and even though I would have liked to soften at least some of my defenses, I did, too.

Dinner persists in a similar fashion: small talk, dad jokes, questions about our lives as young people in New York, and it would all be lovely, if it weren't for the truths we've been carefully avoiding like a rotting carcass on the side of the road.

Still, I do my best to sink into the warmth of it, to let it ease the tension all over my body while it can. And then, it's over.

"So," Jeff says, as we start to clean up the table, "will you girls be staying with us tonight?"

I hesitate, deferring to Zoe. The thought of imposing makes me want to crawl into a ditch and rot, but she didn't mention anything about hotel reservations.

"Oh," she says. "Well . . . actually, if it wouldn't be an intrusion, that would be great. Thank you so much, Jeff."

She gives him a bright smile, dimple on full display. Behind them, I watch as Colin scrapes his plate into the trash, jaw set. A tangled mix of worry and relief skitters across my skin. Clearly, he doesn't want her to stay here.

Unless it's me he doesn't want.

"Of course," Jeff says. "No problem at all."

"You girls can take the guest room." Helen gives Colin an uncertain look. "Or I suppose, Zoe, if you like . . . I mean, we're not exactly puritanical."

Zoe laughs brightly. "Sure. That okay with you, Colin?"

"Yeah," he says. "Fine."

With that, he storms off so abruptly that we're all briefly stunned.

"I'm sorry," Helen says when he's gone. "You'll have to excuse him. It's all been so . . ." Tears spring to her eyes, her voice going tight. "Ben was like a second son to us."

She breaks off into a small sob, and I feel like a stone sinking to the bottom of a dark pool. I know it wasn't *me* who killed Ben, but still, the truth eats at me.

"Of course," Zoe says, stepping forward to pull Colin's mother into a bold but gentle hug. "He was such a good guy. I didn't know him for long, but I thought of him as a real friend. And Jane . . ."

Over Helen's shoulder, Zoe gives me a sad, knowing glance, and I remember that I'm supposed to be the one who was dating Ben.

"Oh," Helen says, thinking she understands. "*Oh.* Jane, I'm so sorry."

Before I can answer, she pulls me into a hug, the delicate bones of her arms wrapped so tightly around me that, in spite of everything, I feel my own throat closing with tears.

"It's just a shame," Jeff murmurs. "A real shame."

After we've retrieved our things from the car, Colin's parents lead us upstairs, and for the first time, I bear witness to his childhood bedroom. Blue-striped bedspread, desk tucked into a corner, tall bookshelf topped with, adorably, a Lego model of a *Star Wars* ship of some kind. Besides the unmade bed and the duffel bag on the floor, the bedroom looks untouched, and somehow, I knew he came from a family who would keep things exactly the way he left them.

"Here, Jane," Helen says, "I'll show you to the guest room."

A reminder, gentle as her hand on my shoulder, that I'm the *friend*, not the girlfriend. That my supposed boyfriend has been recently murdered, and I am alone. A Bonnie without the dignity of sharing a bed with her Clyde.

I drop off my things in the lovely but devoid of character guest room and then meet Zoe, Colin, and his parents back in the hall. Jeff and Helen insist that we let them know if we need anything, anything at all, before disappearing downstairs. And then, we're alone.

"I'm going to shower," Colin says the moment they're gone, as if he can't handle the thought of talking to us without a buffer. He turns back into his room, speeding into the bathroom and closing the door behind him. The click of the lock is like pressure on a bruise, the dull ache of how badly I want to touch him.

"Come on," Zoe says, leading me toward the guest room. "We can talk."

I step inside, and she shuts the door behind us, pressing her back against it with a look of sudden worry on her face. I open my mouth to speak, but she holds a finger to her lips until the sound of running water comes from Colin's bathroom next door.

"Okay, so he's definitely thrown off by you being here," she says finally. "But this can still work. I'll give him some time to cool off in the shower, and then, when he's done, I'll ask him to go for a walk."

My heart leaps at the clear meaning in her expression. She's going to try to get Colin to confess *tonight*.

"Do you want me to come?" I ask. "It might be safer if we talk to him together."

As in, it's the only way I can be sure this doesn't end with Zoe dead. But she shakes her head, giving me an almost apologetic look.

"I think it'll be best for me to talk to him alone. You're his fake alibi, remember? He's already being weird and cagey around you."

It stings, as much as I know it isn't true. Colin's *weird and cagey* around me because we slept together, staged a crime scene, and now I'm here, watching as he pretends he's not about to break up with her.

"Maybe," I say. "I just—I really don't think this is a good idea."

Zoe stiffens. "You don't think I can pull this off."

She's right, but her disappointment feels like a slap in the face—maybe because I'm the one trying to save her life.

"That's not what I'm worried about," I argue. "I'm worried about the off chance that Colin sees you recording him and freaks the hell out."

"He won't hurt me."

"Zoe." I look her dead in the eyes, needing her to understand. "He killed his best friend to protect himself. Do you really think he won't do it again?"

The question is a jolt of electricity between us. Zoe flinches, and I realize, with a rush of adrenaline, what I've just done: for the first time, I've outright admitted that Colin is a killer. She watches me, her stare crackling with something I can't quite read. For a moment, I think she's about to agree that this is a terrible idea—but then she straightens her spine and smooths out her expression, like she's zipping herself into a costume of cool confidence.

"I know," she says. "That's why I have to do this."

Another realization, sharp and unsettling: at some point since our arrival in New Jersey, Zoe and this plan have switched from *we* to *I*.

"And I'm not afraid of him," she adds. "I mean, if nothing else, he's not going to kill me with his parents sleeping nearby."

She *does* have a point. Colin wouldn't risk getting caught, would he? I mean, he's not going to do it *again* in the span of twenty-four hours. Still, I'm grasping for a reason to stop this from happening when something shifts. It takes me a second to realize it's the absence of the running water.

Time is up. I'm too late.

Zoe glances at the wall between us and Colin.

"I should go," she says. "But everything's okay?"

She gives me a meaningful look, and I want so badly to scream that it isn't, but I'm weak, and she's unstoppable, and so I nod.

"Good." She squeezes my arm. "I'll let you get some rest."

Zoe leaves, closing the door gently behind her. I stare at the space she left, caught in the tailwind of a disaster in motion.

23

There's no way Zoe's plan will work. I tell myself that like some kind of affirmation: they'll go on their walk, but he won't confess to her, not when he wouldn't confess to me. And Zoe's right. He won't hurt her.

Not tonight, at least.

I wait in the guest room with my ear pressed to the wall, listening as Zoe suggests their walk, as Colin agrees. I wait until I hear his door creak open and their footsteps disappearing completely down the stairs. Another two minutes just to be safe. Then, I'm on the move.

I pad down the hall and slowly push open his bedroom door.

It's different, being alone here, in this shrine to the first eighteen years of Colin's life. It smells like him, mixed with the new smell of his house: linen with a touch of something warm and autumnal. I can picture him here, moving through the years in little snapshots of homework, laundry, music, and friends, maybe even girls. I'm sure there were girls. Some of them probably still think of him, sometimes, with the wistful wonder of what might have been.

It hits like a shot of sunlight straight to the chest: this is what I was looking for. *This* Colin, the real version, not the heartless killer

Zoe's made him out to be. And now that I've tasted it, I'm itching for a full-on high.

I explore the bookshelf first, a mix of school-mandated reads and other more fun choices, sci-fi and fantasy. The entire Percy Jackson and the Olympians series is here, but missing the first book, which I saw in his room in New York. I smile, knowing he's the type to hold on to pieces of childhood comfort. Sometimes I wish I'd been that way, too, instead of moving to the city with only the barest bones of my personhood, abandoning everything else, the things I can't ever get back. But it's not like I had much worth holding on to.

I let myself get lost in the pages, leafing through to find scattered dog-ears. Then, once I've put the books back, I go through his drawers. They're sparse, filled with clothes he's probably outgrown but never got around to getting rid of. His duffel, too: standard home-for-the-weekend fare, clothes that smell like him stuffed haphazardly inside. No more bloody knives wrapped in fabric—not that I expected any.

Still, to be safe, I check the closet. It's also mostly remnants from his childhood, empty hangers interspersed with some old sweaters, jackets, and suits he probably hasn't worn since someone's bar mitzvah.

It's because the closet is so empty, really, that I notice the shoebox on the floor. The other shoes here are lined up like poorly behaved kindergartners, tripping over each other, laces untied, but this box sits tucked at the very back of the closet, closed like teeth around a secret. Bending down, I take the box and sit on the floor. As I lift it, I can already tell there's something besides shoes in here. Several things, I think—small and light.

Carefully, I lift the top. The first thing I see is a bunched-up scarf—chunky knit, probably handmade, judging from the lack of a tag. I pull it out, set it beside me. The rest is a time capsule of little pieces, and I latch first onto a school ID, bright blue and red on top of the pile. University of Pennsylvania. The name: Leigh Carlsen.

My breath catches. *Leigh.*

The ID photo shows a girl with reddish hair and a bright smile, but that's all I can see of her face. Her eyes are scratched out, marring the plastic with ghostly white lines.

I drop the card and grab for the next thing I see: a tennis ball, the bright yellow-green fuzz matted, and I understand.

The Penn tennis quarter-zip, soaked in blood.

I dig deeper, hungrily, and the horrors take on new, ghastlier shapes. Three black hair ties, little strands still tangled in the elastic. A balled-up thong, pink and stained with something dark enough to be blood. A plastic retainer case. Like a final girl who can't help but open the door, I snap open the case, and there, inside, is a used retainer, the gum-colored plastic pockmarked with tartar.

And then, I see them.

The pictures. Printed Polaroids, oversaturated and ghostly but impossible not to recognize.

A girl tied to a chair, to a bed. Hands bound, cables around her wrists, her stomach. In every photo, her head is covered in a canvas bag, like whoever did this couldn't bear to see whatever awful look was frozen on her face.

I drop the photos back into the shoebox and run to the bathroom, the air still humid and sweet and with the smell of Colin's shampoo. Dropping to my knees on the tile floor, I pull my hair back and retch into the toilet bowl. Nothing comes out but strangled dry-heaving. I'm an empty husk, the sickness already spread too far to purge.

I thought I had prepared myself for this. But seeing it, touching it . . . The truth lands with another nauseating kick: Colin did this. He *killed* Leigh, and whatever part of me believed there was some explanation—some higher purpose that made it anything but base, brutal violence—is suffocated by the little trophies in that box.

The worst part, the dark Shakespearean irony of it all: I should have known.

Because there, in that box, is what I've been outrunning all my life.

It's a beautiful thing, watching something die.

He's not here—*not here*—but somehow, he's pulling me back to him, his big hand tugging me up by the shoulders and back, so far back, to the house just outside of Fairhope, Alabama. Down Cypress Lane, pavement and oaks and big green yards, houses far enough from the water that this isn't old money and far enough from each other that southern neighborliness only extends so far. Waves and pleasantries exchanged, questions unasked.

Yellow house, front porch trimmed in white. Rocking chairs, wooden swing, American flag flapping in the breeze. Homey clapboard, gray roof topped with two quaint dormers side by side—the kind of house that, on the outside, makes your mouth water for sweet tea and lemonade, barbecues in a backyard that rolls out into thick trees, the sort of near-wilderness that lends itself to make-believe.

And inside, terror.

But not always. It wasn't always that way. When Mom was still here, we teetered on the edge, but she kept us centered, a table balanced precariously on three legs. When he had his moods, she was there to bear the brunt, to absorb the shouts and the shattered glass while I hid at the top of the stairs, feeling both safe and wretched, frozen and hating myself for it. Knowing, somewhere deep inside me, that we were here because she'd chosen this. Because she didn't want to leave.

Because our house of horrors was, at least, familiar. Predictable. After enough times, you get used to the performance: this is where the jump scare starts; a scream here; there, a skeleton. Safe in the understanding that no matter how hard they try to scare you, it's all paint and lighting and stage blood. You're safe because they can't touch you.

Until we weren't.

The first night my father's anger turned on me, I was fifteen. He didn't hurt me, not really, but it was close enough. A shout, a fist slammed into the wall, only inches from my head, in a spray of plaster. Afterward, he disappeared. Going on a drive, he said.

It was the first time my mother ever called the police. I listened, ear pressed to her bedroom door, as she answered their questions. *No, he hasn't physically hurt anyone. No, he hasn't tried. But he—*

But my daughter—

No.

No.

All right.

Thank you. Her voice thick with unshed tears as I started to understand what they were telling her, what some part of me already knew. They can't do anything for the kind of abuse we get. Call back when he hurts someone.

Even though, by the time he did, it would already be too late.

As soon as she ended the call, Mom started to pack our bags. I felt a mix of hope and fear, watching as she handed me a duffel. Told me to bring only what I needed.

But then, he came back. And she never came to get me.

In the morning, my duffel still stowed secretly beneath my bed, there was a knock on my door.

We're going to the hunting camp, he told me, Mom hovering behind him like a spirit. *Family trip.*

It was an hour and a half outside of town, deep in the woods. He would go on his own, every so often, and it was always a respite for us back at home. For a moment, the house on Cypress Lane was quiet.

But this time, for whatever reason, he'd decided we would all go together. He always decided: he was the director, we the actors, and there wasn't, it seemed, any other way to be. And so, we took our already-packed duffels and put them in the car, like this was the plan all along.

It still looms in my mind like a nightmare, hazy bits and pieces stitching into more of a feeling than a shape: the double-wide trailer. A darkened room with scratchy bedsheets, the air thick with a dank and coppery smell. Blood, sweat. Deer heads, stuffed and mounted, watching as I slept.

That day, he took me out to the woods. A rare outing, just the two of us. He was peaceful—joyful, even—as we crunched through the dirt and leaves, rifle strapped to his back. It was there that he taught me how to kill.

Hear that, Janie? he whispered, hands over my hands, both of us holding the gun like one creature. *You listen close enough, you can hear how scared they are.*

I knew, even then, that the whole point of this was to make her angry. She hated guns, didn't think kids should be around them. It's why she begged him to keep all his weapons here. One reason, at least. Because she was scared of him, too.

Now, I also think some part of him might have been doing this for me—might have seen that spark of anger deep inside me, wanted to stoke it. Teach me the way he'd been taught.

Either way, I played along. I listened. I tried. But all I heard was the rustle of the breeze, the *thump-thump* of our hearts together.

I'm nervous, I told him. *I don't know if I want to.*

He laughed, squeezing my shoulder as if to loosen the tension.

It's a beautiful thing, he told me, *watching something die. One day, you'll understand.*

And then, like a prophecy fulfilled, it appeared: a buck materializing in the clearing, neck thick and pulsing. Time slowed down. The sun got brighter. Quietly, he helped me aim, breath on my neck, my heart galloping to a frantic *thump-thump-thump* as his finger curled around mine on the trigger. Poised.

Pulled.

But at the same moment, I shifted our aim, yanking it to the right. The bullet sailed a good two feet away from the buck, bouncing off a tree trunk with an explosion of bark. The buck ran, and I knew, in that instant, that I had broken whatever truce we had started to build.

Are you stupid? he'd exploded, ripping the gun from my limp hands. *What the hell are you doing, missing a shot like that!*

My apologies were too late. The balance had already shifted, the precarious peace disturbed. I'd ruined everything, and whatever came next, I knew it would be my fault.

He stomped back to the trailer a good six feet ahead of me, slamming the screen door before I had a chance to follow him in.

That night, it started as it usually did. A shout. A shatter. In the stuffy dark of the bedroom, I closed my eyes, tried to be somewhere else. A different play, a different world. The door slammed just like it had only a few hours before, and I thought, *Good. It's done.* But then it slammed again. She followed. The shouts continued outside the trailer, and I closed my eyes tighter, hummed quietly to drown out the noise.

A shot rang out.

I snapped my eyes open, wondering if I'd dreamed it, but no— there it was again, a loud decisive pop. I held my breath as a heady, almost manic feeling stretched through me like the antler shadows on the walls. There, in the dark, I had a fleeting thought: *Good.* Now they'll know. Now there will be proof.

And then, hurtling back to myself, I understood. Two shots followed by silence, only one logical end to that story. I threw off the covers and walked into the hall—slowly, quietly, that *thump-thump-thump* of my heart beating fast and uncontrollable.

I pushed open the screen door.

My mother lay on the grass. Her hair was splayed around her like Ophelia in the water, chin tipped to the stars, two little rosebuds blooming from the bullet wounds in her chest.

It was an accident, Janie. I didn't mean to.

For once, his voice was soft. But there, barefoot on the deck of the double-wide, I could see it on his face: that same look he got whenever he shot a buck. Glassy-eyed wonder. Awe.

I thought about it. I really did, in enough detail that I could picture it perfectly: charging at him, pulling the gun from his hands, turning it toward him and scrambling for the trigger until I felt that pull. There would be heat, smoke, kickback. I would watch, in slow motion, as the bullet broke through his skull in a rain of blood and brain matter.

Come here, he said. *Come here.*

And all of those evil thoughts dissipated. Like a ghost trapped on the same path from the moment its soul left its body, I walked to him. He held me close.

That's my girl. Be a good girl, Janie. We're all we've got now.

I held him tighter, tuning out his whispers, his apologies, everything but the *thump-thump* of his heart against my ear, the taste of blood at the back of my mouth.

I was fifteen and old enough to do the math. I had three years to endure this alone. To be his good girl.

Then, I would escape.

I'm aware, first, of the cold wet of the bathroom tile against my cheek. I press myself up from the floor until I'm on all fours, head rushing. My face is feverish from the steam left over from Colin's shower, my hair damp, and I don't know how long I've been lying here. For a moment, I barely know why.

Then, all too quickly, it comes: ten years and nearly a thousand miles away, I'm somehow no farther from that wretched fifteen-year-old girl—retching here on the bathroom floor, brought to my knees by a love soaked in blood.

Sound. Voices from below. Feet on the stairs.

It snaps me back into my body, the understanding like a cool, clean blade: I didn't lock the door.

I push myself off the floor and run, heart ricocheting, back into Colin's bedroom, where I gather the box haphazardly, burying its sickening contents beneath the lid. I could run, I should run, but the voices and footsteps are closer now, louder, and it's too late. I'm a deer, animal heart beating, and all I can do is dive into the closet, closing the doors as quietly as possible to hide myself in the dark, the box still clutched in my hands.

The bedroom door creaks open.

24

At first, only footsteps. They move deeper into the room, toward the bed.

"You need to use the shower or anything?" Colin asks.

"Yeah, I will in a bit."

My grip tightens on the box. This mundane conversation isn't at all what I expected—unless Zoe didn't confront him after all. I can't be sure how long they were gone. Time has become an elusive thing, fuzzy and malleable, and my heart is beating so loudly that I'm sure they can hear it through the closed closet door.

Hear that, Janie? You listen close enough, you can hear how scared they are.

"I was thinking we could decompress for a minute, though," Zoe adds. "It's been a long day."

"Sure, whatever."

Thump-thump.

Thump-thump.

Someone sits on the bed, a little squeak of the springs giving.

"Can you—" Colin stops himself. "Never mind."

"What?"

He sighs. "Outside clothes on the bed. You know I have a thing."

"Yeah, sorry. Let me change."

I know Zoe's clothes are out there and not in here, but as I hear her get up, the *thump-thump* picks up speed, terror spreading in thick roots from a blackened pit in my center.

A duffel unzips.

"It's so quiet here," she says. "It's nice, I guess, but I don't think I could ever get used to the quiet, you know? And the dark."

Silence, as if to prove her point. Too much space for my wild heart to fill.

I can't stay here all night. If they go to sleep, then what? I'm so sick with panic that I almost want to kick the door open, give myself over to all that will follow, if only for a lungful of air that isn't so close and stuffy.

Logic takes over as I remember my phone. Slowly, I reach for it, and the screen comes to life. Fighting to keep my sweaty grip on the phone, I open our texts. I try to remember if Zoe has her phone set so that messages show up on her lock screen or not, but my mind is foggy with panic, untrustworthy. I have to settle for something that could reasonably be explained away if Colin sees it. Hurriedly, I type.

Is it weird that I always check the closet for monsters when I'm sleeping in a new place?

I press send, squeezing my eyes shut like more darkness could make me disappear. In the quiet, I listen for some sign that she's seen it, but nothing comes.

"I'm pretty beat," Colin says. "I think I might want to get to bed early, if that's okay."

Still soft and gentle, but now, I hear something else humming beneath it—a quiet anger, bees in a tiny enclosure.

And then, Zoe shakes the hive.

"I really think we should talk," she says. "I'm worried about you, Col."

It's his mom's nickname for him, foreign on Zoe's tongue, and it must be a step too far.

"Fine," he snaps. "You want to talk? How about the fact that Jane fucking *followed* us here?"

I freeze, gripping the box so tightly its edges nearly cut into my palms.

"I asked her to come," Zoe says. "I didn't want to drive up from the city alone."

"But it's not just today. This whole time, ever since you invited her to my birthday, she's just—"

He stops, and my heart is its own animal, now, jumping at the walls of its pen. He's about to tell her how he really knows me. Part of me wants to slap a hand over his mouth, but another, wilder part wants to hear him say it, to bask in the wake of the explosion.

"I think she's into me," Colin says finally.

For a moment, Zoe is quiet.

"What?" she asks. "Why?"

"Because it's obvious."

The words are three arrows shot into my chest—a ghost pain, the sort of empty numbness that comes with the shock of a mortal wound.

"Look," Colin goes on, "before you invited her to my birthday, I hadn't seen her in months. We're not close. I went along with it because I didn't want to hurt her feelings, but now . . . she's wormed her way back in. She made friends with you just to stay close to me, because she's obsessed with me, and she's got this crazy idea that I'll leave you for her. Do you seriously not see it?"

Zoe is quiet, and the numbness starts to fade, like cold thawing into pinpricks all over my skin, growing until it's a full-fledged burn. I want to scream. I would, but I can't breathe.

"Whatever," Colin says, when Zoe still hasn't answered him. "I'm going to bed."

Footsteps thud on the floor.

Footsteps moving in my direction. And I remember, too late, Colin's clothes hanging just above my head.

"What are you doing?" Zoe asks.

The footsteps stop.

"Changing," Colin says flatly. "Is that okay with you?"

Another step. Only a few more and he'll be here. I picture his hand on the knob, pulling it open, finding me here in the dark with his box held tight to my chest, like a real monster in the closet, and I shut my eyes, a child playing hide-and-seek. *You can't see me if I can't see you.*

And then, just before the creak, the flood of light—

"Wait."

At Zoe's voice, the steps halt again, and there's a small flutter of hope in my chest. Did she see my text?

"What?" he asks.

"If you don't want to talk, then—" Silence, stillness. "Then let's not talk."

A catch of breath, maybe my own. And then, a new sound. One I recognize.

She's kissing him. And he's kissing her back.

Even now, after all the ways Colin just betrayed me, this is the worst of it. Envy is a cord wrapped tight around my heart, and I can still feel the ghost of his mouth on mine. Colin makes a low, guttural sound, and my throat tightens with the impulse for a sob or a scream—I'm not even sure which. There are footsteps backing away from the closet, and then the creak of the bed, one body settling into the mattress and then another. I consider pressing my hands to my ears like a child, trying to dissociate, but a sick, twisted part of me wants to hear all of it, to log every sound as a clear image in my mind.

Colin lowering Zoe onto the bed. Her fingers winding into his hair, his hand on the curve of her waist, trailing down. His mouth finding her neck, her back arching as she gasps with pleasure.

Wait, she gasped. Why did she gasp? I strain for more sounds, more data to sift through to determine whether Zoe is actually enjoying this. And then, another moan. She has to be acting, trying to distract him so I can escape, but I can't deny the glimmer of truth in that sound, and an even darker thought breaks through it.

Maybe Zoe isn't trying to help me. Maybe she just wants me to hear this.

The part of my body that logic can't conquer wants to push the closet door open, catch them in the act just so I can see the looks on both of their faces. I'm inching toward the door, almost pressing my ear against it—foolish, mad—and then I hear her.

"Want to take a shower?"

"I already did," he says, confused through the fog of longing.

Another pause, another caught breath, and I can't even tell whose.

"Well," she says. "I'm dirty."

And that's enough. Colin makes a sound I've never heard him make, almost a growl, and the bed squeaks again—they're on the move—and is this what he wants? Dialogue ripped from a poorly scripted porno? I try to imagine myself saying something like that, and I can't. I'd burst out laughing, and he'd laugh, too, but that's what I'll tell our kids one day when we give them the talk—that they should find someone they're comfortable enough to laugh with, because it's all a little ridiculous, really, but it should be *fun*. Because that's what we have.

It was. It is. Colin only said all of that to Zoe to make her question herself. To protect me. The pieces don't quite fit together, but they will. They have to. They—

The bathroom door shuts. A few seconds later, I hear the shower rush on. This is my escape hatch, I know, but I hesitate with the shoebox in my hands. If I take it, Colin might notice it's gone. If I don't, it's evidence lying around for anyone to find. Do I want them to find it?

Maybe I do. Maybe he deserves it.

I set it down. But as soon as it leaves my hands, I know I can't bear the thought of leaving Leigh in this makeshift grave, shoved between a wall and a faded pair of sneakers. I pick up the box and push the closet door open, crawling out. The shower patters, and then there's another moan, and I could stay here all night, bathing in my own torment, but I have to go.

I take the box and run into the hall, not bothering to close the bedroom door behind me. My feet know before I do that I can't stay in this house. I slink down the stairs as quickly and quietly as possible, and then I slip on my boots, which are still sitting next to the door with the Hillgroves' shoes. With something like a prayer that Colin's parents won't hear, I grab the rental car keys, unlock the front door, and step outside.

It's blessedly cold, a shock of night air on my flushed cheeks. Wet with tears, I realize. I don't know when I started crying.

Besides the lights in the Hillgroves' house, the street is completely dark, and I'm suddenly terrified of what might be waiting in the shadows. I run to the car like a child from a nightmare and press the ignition. It shudders to life, too loud in the silence.

I hesitate again. Is Zoe safe if I leave her behind? But she has to be. Colin's parents are there. He won't hurt her.

Still, I'm not sure if it's the comfort of that thought or the memory of her gasp as he kissed her that propels me out of the driveway and onto the street.

I don't know where I'm going. Only away, the shoebox sitting in the passenger seat like precious cargo. I could ditch it, destroy it, or maybe just bring it straight to the police, get Colin the help—or the punishment—he really needs. It's too stuffy in here. I reach for the air, but the rental is unfamiliar, and I'm still fumbling with the controls when I see a large object directly in my path.

I slam on the brakes, the tires squealing. The car stops a few feet away from the thing, and I grip the wheel, pins and needles prickling in my hands from the adrenaline.

It takes me a few seconds to understand the mass illuminated in the haze of my headlights.

A deer, dead. Crumpled. It was dead before I got here, I know, but I can't shake the feeling that this is my fault. Its neck is bent to face me, eyes lifeless, but somehow still pleading, accusing.

I throw the car in park and get out, the engine still running. It's a doe, all lank and downy, blood matted in its fur. My legs are shaky beneath me—fawn legs—and I crumple to the road, my knees against asphalt.

I'm sorry, Janie. His voice again, or maybe it's Colin's. They blur and hitch, stitching into one terrible being. *I didn't mean to.*

I scream until the open mouth of the darkness swallows it up.

A light grows from behind me, setting the deer's body aglow. For half a second, I think I've created this somehow, a divine gleam borne from my vigil, but then a car door shuts.

"Jane?"

Zoe.

"Jane, oh my god."

She runs over, and then I feel her hands on my shoulders, anchoring me back to myself as she crouches beside me.

"What happened?" she asks.

"The deer," I manage. "I didn't hit it. It was already . . ."

I choke out a sob, and she pulls me close, her fluffy-pink-cloud smell engulfing the blood and the damp.

"Are you okay? Where were you going?"

I finally turn and notice the car Zoe drove here, parked behind the rental with its hazard lights blinking. It must belong to the Hillgroves.

"I just needed to go."

I'm aware of how nonsensical and childlike I sound, but Zoe nods like she understands.

"We should get out of the street," she says.

I stand slowly, a little lightheaded, as reality settles back into my bones.

"We can't go back to Colin's," I tell her.

She hesitates. "You were hiding in his closet, weren't you?"

I nod, bracing myself for what comes next—the moment she confronts me, when she forces me to answer for all of my lies.

"I didn't believe him," she says. "All those things he said . . . I know he was trying to manipulate me. I didn't believe him for a second."

It takes a second for it to settle into something I can understand. Zoe still believes me. She's choosing me.

"And I didn't want to do it," she adds, "what I did back there. But I saw your text, and it was the only—"

"It's okay," I tell her. I'm not sure if it is, but right now, it feels like it. Zoe believes me. Zoe's my friend.

And Colin betrayed me.

Colin is a killer.

And then, I remember the box.

"Can we go somewhere to talk?" I ask. "Not here. I—" I force myself to look at her instead of the deer's body, head rushing as I understand the severity of what I'm about to do. "I found something."

25

I follow Zoe to an abandoned drugstore parking lot, where she parks the Hillgroves' car and then climbs into the rental with me. She shuts the passenger door with a decisive click, and we're alone, enclosed in the cigarette smell.

It's not until now, when we're away from the deer and all that it dredged up, that doubt creeps in again. If I tell Zoe about the box, she'll insist on going to the police, but I still don't know if that's what I want. I still don't know what's safe.

"Do the Hillgroves know you took their car?" I ask. I'm stalling, and I'm sure she knows it.

"Not exactly." She bites her lip. "As soon as I noticed you leaving, I might have made up an excuse to ditch Colin and grabbed the first pair of keys I saw by the front door."

"Car theft," I say flatly. "For me?"

It was a joke, a weak one, but Zoe looks at me seriously.

"I needed to know you were okay."

A shot of guilt melts slowly into something like warmth. Zoe is looking out for me. She's always been looking out for me, even when that means sleeping with a man she thinks is a killer. Even when I've been going behind her back with him this whole time.

And so, I do what I've known I have to ever since she lifted me back to my feet: I give her the truth, or at least the part of it I can spare.

I reach for the shoebox.

"I found this in the closet."

It feels so innocuous, this little cardboard thing, but the way Zoe looks at it, it's like she can already tell what's inside.

"Here." I hand it over. "But just—maybe take a second. It's really bad."

Zoe nods, her jaw tensing. She looks down at the box and carefully lifts the lid.

I keep my gaze on her face, trying my hardest not to look at each item as she sifts through them. It's a journey of emotions I've already taken: confusion, shock, disgust. And then, she gets to the Polaroids.

For a moment, she's silent. Still, except for the slow flipping of picture to picture.

She drops them back into the box and slams the lid back on it. "Mother*fucker.*"

"Zoe . . ."

"Fuck!" She buries her face in her hands, her shoulders shaking with sobs.

I reach awkwardly across the console to touch her, rubbing her back like fucking Trip in the common room or someone trying to burp a baby, but it seems like it's all she needs: for me to let her cry. To let her know I'm here.

When she's finished, she sits up slowly, sniffing and wiping her hands over her face. I brace myself.

"You said before that you were in a bad relationship," she says. "That you called the police about it."

Every surface of my skin stands at attention. She knows, I think.

Somehow, she knows—but I don't know about what. My father. Colin. All the lies I've been telling.

"How did you get out of it?" she asks.

Her voice is so soft, so afraid, that I tell her the truth.

"I moved."

"And he never came looking?"

I shake my head.

"That's really brave of you," she says.

I scoff, an impulse. "Running away?"

"No." Her eyes burn, green and serious. "Taking control of your life."

It's more than I can process. I've never told anyone about this before, not even Colin, and to feel it received with such admiration . . . it's like a weight lifting off my back, sun breaking through the clouds, all of the idioms we collect like puzzle pieces, hoping they'll fit together into some approximation of the real thing.

"Thank you," I breathe.

For a moment, there's nothing but this new lightness, so unfamiliar it's almost heavy. Then, Zoe looks out the window, cheek cast in a red glow from the drugstore sign.

"Do you think that was really her we were DMing? Leigh?"

"No," I admit. "I don't think so."

For a moment, the contours of her face warp with horror. Then, determined, she reaches for her phone.

"What are you doing?" I ask, the panic surging again despite everything else.

"Searching for Leigh," she says. "We have her full name now, from the ID, so we can find out for sure if she's . . ."

Dead. I hold my breath. I should have thought of this first. There's still a chance, however small, that she's still out there. That Colin didn't kill her.

Zoe narrows her eyes as she scrolls, and my heart lurches.

"Anything?" I ask.

"Some LinkedIn and Facebook profiles for other Leigh Carlsens, but nothing that looks like her."

Zoe scrolls some more, and just as I'm starting to relax, she gasps.

"Wait, here," she says. "There's an article."

Her voice has gone small, her face haunted, and I know, even before she holds it out for me to see, what it will say.

University of Pennsylvania student found dead.

It's from what looks like a campus news site called the *Daily Quaker*, posted in April, nearly three years ago. Zoe angles her phone so we can both read.

The University of Pennsylvania community is mourning the loss of Leigh Carlson, an engineering major and student athlete who was due to graduate this June. On Friday evening, Ms. Carlson's boyfriend, Collin Hillgrove (senior, computer science), found her unresponsive in the bathtub of their shared off-campus apartment. Despite the efforts of paramedics, she was pronounced dead at the scene. At this time, police have not released an official cause of death, but they have not yet ruled out homicide.

I read it twice, three times, each new reading like sinking to the bottom of a river—my *garments, heavy with their drink,* pulling me down, down, down, to the muck and grime below. The paragraph is brief enough to leave me breathless. Beneath it is a photo of Leigh, the first clear one I've seen, and it feels like the end of this watery dive.

Leigh, smiling in a University of Pennsylvania tennis quarter-zip.

Leigh, with her whole face visible now, so that I understand one thing: we could be related. Same pale skin, hazel eyes, freckled nose, right down to the now-matching auburn of our hair.

An invisible weight rams into my chest, knocking the wind out of me.

"Jane?"

"It was Colin," I force out. "He's the one who told me I'd look good with red hair."

Zoe's mouth drops open as she holds her phone closer, making the same connection that I just did. "Oh my god."

I dig my nails into my thighs, trying to breathe, trying to see through the murk of this.

But only one explanation bobs to the surface: Colin wanted me because I look like Leigh. Colin told me I could pull off red because he wanted me to look *more* like Leigh.

"I can't—" I start, but I don't know where I'm going. "I don't—"

"Wait." Zoe has been scrolling, and now, she shows me her screen again. "Look. They spelled her last name 'Carlson' with an *o*, but wasn't it Carlsen with an *e* on her ID?"

I glance down at the box as Zoe reaches inside. Dread hardens on her face as she checks the ID.

"Yeah," she says. "Carlsen with an *e*."

"And they got Colin's name wrong too," I realize, squinting at the screen. "Two *L*s instead of one."

Some part of my brain wants to believe that this is proof of any other version of the truth—some other Collin, two *L*s, some other Leigh, that none of this is what it seems so undeniably to be.

But then, Zoe says what we both know is true.

"He scrubbed everything. That's why there were no other search results. He got rid of everything, but this one must have slipped through because of the typos."

For a second, we're both quiet. Stunned.

"How would he even do that?" I ask.

Zoe gives me an uncertain look. "You know his family is, like, a big deal, right?"

I frown. Sure, Colin's house is a little grander than I expected, but his parents seem as warm and down-to-earth as he is. As I thought he was. But the way Zoe says it, *a big deal* sounds like some kind of crime.

"How do you mean?"

"Like, they're loaded. His dad basically retired at forty after selling his software company. And I'm sure they know plenty of people who could make things disappear."

It's a small detail in comparison to everything else, but still, jealousy scratches at the back of my neck. Maybe it's the fact that Zoe knows this at all. Did Colin tell her more about his family than he told me?

But so what if he did? He didn't even tell his parents about Zoe until she appeared on their doorstep. It doesn't mean anything.

And then another voice whispers from somewhere smarter: *Why do you care?*

I let my head fall against the car seat, suddenly exhausted.

"What are we going to do?" I ask.

I realize I'm desperate for her answer. Because I don't have any, not anymore. All of my control has been sapped like the life from the broken doe's body.

"We have to confront him."

Instinct makes me bristle. "But—"

"The police won't help us." She gestures at the box. "This isn't enough, especially not if Colin's parents have some kind of pull with them. We need a confession, and the supportive-girlfriend route clearly didn't work. So, we'll tell him what we know, straight-up. Shock him into confessing, or even attacking—something concrete. Something we can prove."

My stomach lurches at the wild gleam in her eyes. *Attacking?* This is too far. This is doomed. It's—

"Jane." She grabs my hand, cutting through my racing thoughts.

"You were right. I shouldn't have tried to get him to confess alone, but if we work together, we can do this. He can't stop us."

But he will, I think. All he has to do is tell Zoe the truth about us. It's all it will take to turn her against me, and I'm afraid of what will happen when she does. Mostly, though, I'm afraid of the fact that I don't want to stop her.

Because, for the first time, some bruised, broken part of me wants Colin Hillgrove to burn.

The thought is shocking enough to send me grasping for purchase, some way to stall the inevitable.

"Not tonight," I plead. "I need to get home. I can't be here right now. I just—"

"Of course." Zoe squeezes my hand and then lets go. "We'll do it when he gets back to the city. It'll give us some time to get ready."

Her understanding is a fresh ache, because I don't think I'll ever be ready. It's all catching up to me, the lies, and no amount of planning could prepare me for their impact.

But I'm so tired, and Zoe's so certain, and is it so wrong, for tonight, to lull myself into a different reality? It's what she's taught me, anyway: *manifesting*. Molding worlds.

Maybe this one will become real.

"Okay," I tell her. "Let's go."

26

We have to leave our things behind. It's the price we pay for fleeing New Jersey in the dead of night, since we didn't want to risk waking Colin. And, though I didn't tell Zoe, I wasn't sure if I could go ahead with this if I saw him again, asleep, his face soft and innocent.

I stay at Zoe's. She offers casually on the drive back, but I think we both know that neither of us wants to be alone.

When we get back to her studio, I'm too tired to even care that I don't have a toothbrush. We stow the shoebox safely under her bed, and Zoe lends me pajamas, which I change into while she goes to make tea. She puts the kettle on—an actual kettle, adult and evolved from my perspective as someone who's always just microwaved the water—and I curl onto the green velvet sofa, limbs heavy. When I press my face into the cushion, it still smells like Colin.

It's no longer a reprieve. Now, it only riles up my stomach acid, burning my throat.

Still, I start to drift off before the kettle even whistles. Just as I'm about to fade completely, I'm aware of a chunky-knit blanket draped over my body, and I curl into it, anchoring myself to one thought: soon, Colin will answer for his betrayal.

Soon, he won't be able to run.

I let it pull me under.

After a night like the one we've had, you either sleep like the dead or not at all. For me, it was the former. But when I get up around eleven, the studio already smells like coffee, and I find Zoe in the kitchen, looking like she's been up for hours.

"Hey," she says. "I didn't want to wake you up. You seemed like you needed it."

"Yeah." I drop into one of the dining table chairs. "Did you sleep?"

Instead of answering, she lifts her phone.

"I texted Colin early this morning that there was an emergency with the gallery and we had to get back to the city. He didn't seem suspicious, but who knows. He said he'll be back on Friday, after the funeral."

The funeral. Somehow, I'd forgotten. Nausea lurches through me as I think of all those people watching Ben as he's lowered into the ground.

And then, wading through the murk of that thought is another, pulled up by the mention of the gallery.

"Friday," I say. "That's your show."

Zoe nods. "Yours too, now."

A small smile flickers on her face, but I can't bring myself to return it. Somehow, I'd almost completely forgotten that my professional New York debut is less than a week away. I already sent over the scene selection and got the approval from the gallery, and last week, when my roommate Harmony caught wind, she promptly volunteered herself and her actor boyfriend Garrett to perform. All that's left is an audience.

Call it a twisted sort of dramatic irony, but I know what Zoe's about to say before she does.

"I think we should do it there."

"Confront him?" It's obviously what she meant, but I ask anyway.

"It'll probably be the first time we have the chance," she explains. "He's not getting in until late afternoon, so he'll have to come straight to the show after he drops his things off at home."

My heart starts up a frantic beat, an animal with the scent of a predator in the air.

"Won't it be dangerous to do it in front of everyone at the gallery?"

"We can pull him aside after," she says, "somewhere private. But we'll at least be safer with people nearby."

I search for an excuse, but I come up short.

"There's no perfect time to do this," Zoe adds. "I think we should do it as soon as we can, before we lose the nerve."

In those words, I hear an echo of what she said last night—*shock him into confessing, or even attacking*. It could have been an offhand remark, a throwaway idea, but in the harsh clarity of morning, I don't like how familiar it feels: that masochistic wish for violence, if only for the proof. The small relief in the pop of the gun.

"What if he doesn't confess?" I ask, skirting that fear for a new one. "He could deny it all. That would be bad. We wouldn't have proof, and then he'd know we were onto him."

And the other question trying to claw its way out: What if he doesn't deny it? What if he looks in my eyes and says he meant every word of what he told Zoe back in New Jersey—that I'm obsessed? That he doesn't want me?

I don't know which I'm more afraid of: brutality or the part of me that craves it—because pain, at least, is better than apathy.

"Jane." Zoe's voice is strong enough to pull me out of the tidal wave of panic. "I know you're scared. I am, too. But we can do this together. We *can*. And I think the show is the best time to do it. Because no matter what, we've both made some fucking phenomenal art, and people deserve to see that. We need to be heard—by Colin and every other man who's ever thought he could silence us."

For a moment, I forget the fear, the guilt, everything except the sunlight emanating from my very core.

Zoe's right. Playwrights feed on an audience—and suddenly, I'm ravenous.

That night, when I'm alone again in my small, empty room, Colin calls me. The ring jars my heart into a gallop, and I scramble for my phone, cupping his name in my palms. My thumb twitches over the answer button, but just before I press it, I stop myself.

We need to talk, obviously. He needs to *hear* me—but not now, like this, when he could so easily sweet-talk me back into submission. I can't talk to him until I can see his face. Until he's seen my play.

My play.

For the first time in a long time, it's a phrase I think with pride.

I let it ring.

27

On Friday night, I get dressed early. It feels right to take my time, build my armor with care.

When I'm finished, I stand in front of my cheap bedroom mirror, considering my reflection in the slightly warped surface. I'm in the outfit Zoe bought me again, black tights thrown under to fight the chill. I run my fingers through the soft waves I ironed into my hair, pulled half-back with my bangs falling over my forehead. I look good, I think. Better than I have in a while.

I look, still, like Leigh.

I try to shake off the thought, and wonder instead if I put on too much eyeliner, but I have to leave soon, and there's no time to wipe it all off.

I grip the rosemary necklace, closing my eyes and taking a deep breath in and out.

I am loved, I am whole, and I release you.

The mantra has lost some of its meaning, now that I know Zoe as a real person instead of just a fuzzy TikTok ideal, but still, it feels like a life raft, her unshakable confidence buoying me up in a churning sea.

I open my eyes and check the time. A little after six. I should go if I'm going to meet Zoe there by seven like we planned. I consider grabbing a heavier jacket, now that the November chill is really setting in, but in the end, I shrug into my denim one. Old faithful, a protective skin.

I have a feeling I may need it.

I give myself one last look, one last breath. And then, I swing my tote over my shoulder and walk out of my bedroom.

On my way, I text Zoe from the kitchen. Just after I send it, something stops me. My gaze drifts to the knife block on our counter. With a glance over my shoulder to make sure neither of my roommates are around, I go to the block and pull out a knife, burying it like a secret in my inner jacket pocket.

In the theatre, it never hurts to be prepared.

As soon as I see Zoe at the gallery, I wonder why I even bothered with my own outfit. She's stunningly ethereal in a flowing white dress, bright flowers weaved into her wild curls. It's an obvious nod to Ophelia, which, on anyone else, might be corny or overkill. But as she walks toward me, fabric billowing out around her as if held up by water, I can't imagine that she would be wearing anything else.

"You look amazing," she tells me, pulling me into a hug.

"You, too."

"Thanks." She releases me with a smile. "How are you feeling?"

I take a moment to absorb the gallery around us. Even though I was here just yesterday, when we rehearsed the scene with the actors, it feels like a new space entirely. The lighting is dim and shadowy, with bright spots illuminating each piece on the wall. I tend to think of art galleries as cold, harshly lit spaces, but this one gives the feeling of being in a watery grotto.

And there, in the center of the space, is the bathtub. A real one, claw-footed and filled with water, my stage directions brought to life. We rehearsed with it yesterday, too, but it feels different now in the wash of blue-green light, with the buzz of opening night in the air.

"It's incredible," I say.

Zoe looks around us, proud, no knee-jerk need to deflect that comment.

"I know," she says.

Maybe some people would diagnose it as vanity—I might have, too, when I first met her—but now, I understand Zoe's self-assuredness for what it truly is: a weapon. A superpower. And I've never admired her more.

Zoe's gaze falls back to me, and she reaches for my arm. "Here. Let me introduce you to everyone."

She pulls me around to each of the gallery employees, introducing me as *the playwright*, imbuing it with every ounce of her own confidence. Eventually, Zoe leads me to a supermodel-tall woman with olive skin and sleek dark hair, who shakes my hand.

"Jane, so nice to meet you. I'm Mara, the organizer of tonight. I read your piece. Really fantastic work."

A little burst of pride goes off in my chest. "Thanks."

Mara doesn't let the compliment linger, launching straight into business.

"So, we're thinking we'll start the performance at eight forty-five, so guests have had time to get drinks and take in all of Zoe's wonderful work," she explains. "The tub is filled and good to go. We'll also be setting out some rugs and cushions for the audience to sit on once the piece begins. We thought it could give it a nostalgic, comforting feeling, only to have that comfort called into question by the incisive story you've crafted here."

I glance at Zoe, who's looking hopefully back at me, almost like she's worried I won't like the suggestion.

"It's perfect," I say honestly, because I can't quite describe the weight of what I'm feeling, something growing, stretching past the bounds of my chest. It's been so long since someone brought my words to life with such care. Since I've been called *incisive*. Since I felt, truly and deeply, like I have a story that needs to be told.

For the briefest of moments, I forget Colin entirely. There's only this feeling, burning bright.

And then, another employee comes up to Mara with a question about programs, and she goes off to handle whatever needs to be handled, telling us not to hesitate if we need anything. Zoe and I are alone in the blue-green light hanging over the bathtub.

"Thank you," I say. "For letting me be a part of this."

Zoe gives me a look. "Of course. Why wouldn't I?"

"I just—this is your show. Your stuff is incredible, and it deserves to be the center of attention. Tonight should be about you."

I gaze at the walls, genuinely floored by the beauty around us. Zoe watches me for a moment, dimple rippling across the blue-lit surface of her cheek.

"It *is* about me. And you." Her stare floats around the room. "It's about Leigh, too. And any other girl who's fallen under the spell of someone they shouldn't have." For a moment, I think I catch a flare of worry in her eyes, but when they land back on mine, they're blazing green and furious in the strange, watery light. "Tonight is exactly what I've always wanted my art to do: knock them off the pedestal and claim it for ourselves. And I'm really fucking glad you're here to do it with me." She smiles. "Now, come on. Celebratory preshow drink?"

I glance at the bar table, still setting up. "So, we're really over the no-alcohol thing, then?"

She shrugs. "After this week, I'm starting to feel like that was pretty much bullshit."

I laugh, trailing in her wake as she leads us to the bar. The bartender pours us each a glass of champagne in a small plastic cup, and I glance at the side of the room, where a white curtain hides the entrance to another offshoot of the gallery. I didn't think much of it yesterday, but now they've strung blue lights around it, so it looks like a part of the show.

"Is there more in there?"

Zoe grins, taking the drinks and handing me mine. "A surprise."

"I don't like surprises," I say, only half joking.

She quirks an eyebrow. "This one, I have a feeling you'll like." She lifts her champagne. "Cheers."

We tip our plastic cups together, and then I take a long sip, trying to quell the uneasiness stirring low in my gut.

When it's finally time for the gallery doors to open, people are already lined up outside, waiting. I watch as Mara and another employee welcome them, passing out programs, one of which I snag for myself. The design is minimalist, sans serif font on a white background announcing the title.

Zoe Ember: Be All My Sins. I recognize the title instantly, pulled from a quote Hamlet says to Ophelia.

And beneath that: *featuring a short theatrical piece by Jane Williams.*

My nerves swirl. I think about getting another drink, just to have something to occupy my hands, but I want to be clear-headed for this. I watch the line of artsy Brooklynites streaming in, my pulse jumping every time I see a lean man upward of six feet, but none of them are Colin. Not yet.

I catch sight of Zoe near the entrance, shaking hands and radiating artistry. I'd feel less nervous if I went over and joined her, but I won't. This is her moment, and I want it to be all hers.

I scan the room for my actors. They're by the bar, dressed in the costumes Zoe cobbled together for them both: for Harmony, a white sundress; for Garrett, a white T-shirt, jeans, and a short-sleeved button-down with blue stripes. The shirt I recognize as Colin's, and my stomach tightens. He must have left it at Zoe's.

Seeing me, Harmony waves. A little begrudgingly, I cross over to them.

"How are you feeling?" she asks. "This is, like, such an exciting crowd. I'm so nervous."

"Don't be," I tell her. "You're going to kill it. Both of you."

They will, I think. I watched their run-through just before the doors opened, and despite my nerves, I'm feeling confident. Not only in the work itself, but in the plan. This really might work.

"She always kills it," Garrett says, kissing her cheek.

Harmony laughs, swatting him away. "Okay, stop being cute. You're going to make me actually *enjoy* being murdered by you."

The word is like a signal flare, and I glance around the room, worried that somehow, someone's overheard. That they understand just how real it is. But I'm being ridiculous. To everyone but me, Zoe, and Colin, tonight is nothing but theatre.

I endure some more small talk with the actors, until finally, it's eight thirty. Fifteen minutes to places, and still no sign of Colin. I watch the clock anxiously, minutes stretching to impossible lengths. Mara and the gallery people start to lay out the rugs and pillows, letting everyone know that the show will be starting soon.

At eight forty, when I still haven't seen Colin, I'm panicked enough to consider pulling Zoe away from whatever art person she's talking to.

But then, the door opens, and there—Colin floating in with a chill of night air.

He's in my favorite sweater again, and the sight of it is enough to make me almost forget all of the ways he's hurt me. He's nervous—I can tell from the way he pushes his hair away from his freckled forehead, how he adjusts his glasses, and a silly part of me still wants to run to him, take his hand and pull him out of the cold. He scans the room, his face softened by the light, and I watch him take it all in.

And then, as I hoped and feared it would, his gaze lands on me.

My breath catches, my mouth opening like I might say something he can hear from all the way across the room. But then, Zoe appears at his side, pulling him in for a kiss before handing him a glass of champagne. She takes his hand in hers, guiding him toward an open seat at the very front of the audience.

My heart takes up a frantic beat, more intense than any preshow nerves of my life. Colin settles into the soft cushion on the floor, and we can't do this. I'm suddenly certain that it's all too much—this performance, this spectacle, our plans to corner him when it's finished.

I'm about to go to them, tell Zoe we have to stop this, but then she's giving Colin a final kiss on the cheek and coming my way.

"He's here," she mutters when she gets to me, as if I didn't already know.

I nod, mouth dry. "I think—"

Her hand darts to mine, squeezing suddenly and intently.

"Don't," she says. "No second-guessing. We'll think about it when the show's over. For now, all we have to do is sit back, relax, and enjoy."

I'm silent, drowning in the rush of my own dread. I focus on the anchor of her hand, and slowly, it starts to pass.

"Ready?" she asks.

"Ready," I manage.

I'm not sure if it's true, but Zoe's already giving my hand one last squeeze, and I have no choice but to believe it.

Mara catches her eye from across the room, and Zoe nods.

"Showtime," she whispers to me, stepping forward.

Mara moves to the front of the audience, her presence commanding them to a hush.

"Good evening, everyone. Thank you so much for coming out tonight to 'Be All My Sins.' I'm Mara Diaz, the organizer of tonight's event, and on behalf of FOCAL, I'm so thrilled to welcome you. I trust you've been enjoying the exhibition so far, and now, you're in for a real treat. I'll let our artist and playwright take it from here." She gives us a smile. "Everyone, allow me to introduce Zoe Ember and Jane Williams."

There's a soft rush of applause, like a crackle of a bonfire, and before I have time to really think, Zoe is pulling me into the center of it.

"Hi, everyone." She waves, graciously waiting for their warm welcome to fade. "I'm Zoe, and I truly can't thank you all enough for being here tonight. I feel a little as though I've opened the doors to my soul, and you've all treated it with such kindness and care." She presses a hand to her heart. "Those of you who know me know that my philosophy has always been throwing as much as you can at the wall and seeing what sticks—sometimes literally." A smattering of laughter from what I assume is a group of Pratt alums. "So, tonight is no exception. The short theatrical piece you're about to see is a more recent addition to tonight's program, but as I've gotten to know its creator, I knew tonight just wouldn't be complete without her voice."

Zoe grins at me. "It may have been a boy who brought us together—hi, babe." She wiggles her fingers at Colin, charming, prompting another peal of laughter, before turning back to me. "But I feel truly grateful now to call Jane a collaborator and friend. I said I welcomed everyone here tonight into my soul, if you'll forgive me beating this metaphor to death, but with Jane . . ." Another smile, wide and dazzling. "I feel like she's been here all along."

The audience applauds again, and I let my gaze slip to Colin. His face is impassive as he takes a long sip of his champagne.

"Jane?" Zoe asks. "Want to say a few words?"

I swallow the sudden dryness in my throat.

"I'm, uh. I'm a playwright by nature, which means this sort of thing generally makes me want to crawl into a ditch and dissociate."

Laughter, maybe polite. Maybe genuine. I straighten my shoulders, try to assume Zoe's bold spine until it feels like my own.

"But I can't thank Zoe enough for including me tonight. Seriously, I'm still pinching myself that someone so cool and talented decided to take me under her wing. And, you know, lend me half her closet. We're talking a lot about souls, and I don't know much about those, but, um . . ." I give her a small smile. "I think Zoe's is a pretty cool place to be. And I hope she lets me stick around."

I flush, a little embarrassed at my own earnest use of the metaphor. I look back out at the crowd.

"So, Hamlet," I continue. "Hamlet says that 'the purpose of playing . . . is to hold as 'twere the mirror up to nature.' But that's basically pretentious bullshit."

More laughter, letting me in on it, too—that warm glow I thought only Zoe could pull out of them.

"We all know that theatre is a weird mix of reality and fiction. The harder part is knowing which is which."

I can't help another glance at Colin. He looks back at me, his eyes warm and honey brown behind his glasses, and I feel the pull of the cord, tugging me closer to the edge, to losing my nerve.

I look away first. Stand up tall.

"So, without much more ado about nothing . . . here's a play."

Another crackle of applause as Zoe and I take our seats on the cushions that have been saved for us. The lights go down, and the audience falls to a hush, gathered around the fire of our own making.

28

OPHELIA PLAY

By Jane Williams

A room somewhere, indistinct except for the bathtub at its center.
OPHELIA enters, holding a letter. As she reads, the room fills with
the sound of a faucet slowly dripping.

OPHELIA: To my mother: I hope this letter finds you well. I hope it
finds you at all. I haven't figured out how to send a letter to the dead
just yet, but I've tried a few things. The post office felt too bureau-
cratic. Burying it felt wrong, too. But don't worry—I'll find a way.
We always do.

I miss you. It's been hard, with you gone. Father is angry, often
with me, but I think we both understand that it's really with himself.
I'm angry, too. To be honest, I'm angry with you. For leaving me here
with him.

Things are getting better, though. I'm trying to keep busy. Reading, learning. Baking. Father says my crème brûlée is divine, but I

don't think I've mastered the texture, and anyway, I found it all a little boring, as much as I'm afraid to tell him.

Also, I've met someone. And I know, I know. It's never good for a girl to get too excited. But I can't help it. He feels right.

I found a new sort of flower in the garden this morning, and I haven't learned its name. I'll fold it up in my letter. Maybe, if it reaches you, you can tell me what it's called.

OPHELIA places a sprig of rosemary in the center of her letter, which she folds up into a simple paper boat. She sets it in the bathtub and watches it float. There's a sound like pebbles at the window. She goes to look down, smiling when she sees who it is.

OPHELIA: You can come up!

HAMLET enters through the window. He kisses her.

HAMLET: Soft you now, the fair Ophelia.

OPHELIA: Is that poetry?

HAMLET: Maybe.

OPHELIA: My father told me to never trust a poet.

HAMLET: Your father had a point.

> The audience is enjoying it, I think. I hear their laughter, amused at the characterization of Hamlet as a pretentious fuckboy, but I don't register their faces, not fully. I'm too

focused on Colin. He's staring blankly at the bathtub, the water rippling on the surface.

I had no idea how Leigh died—I wrote this play before I even knew she existed—and maybe it's another cosmic connection between us, proof that we should be together.

Or maybe that's bullshit.

Either way, I want him to see it, and it's not until now that I realize why: I want to *see* him see it. Because, even though he's betrayed me, I know him. And I'll know, from the look on his face, if he did it. If he meant it.

If he deserves what's coming to him.

I glance at Zoe and find her staring at Colin, too. She looks over gives me a small nod.

The play goes on.

HAMLET: I have a game we can play.

HAMLET produces a rope.

OPHELIA: Jump rope?

HAMLET: Something like that. Here, sit. Put your hands behind your back.

She does. He starts to wind the rope around her.

OPHELIA: This is supposed to be a game?

HAMLET: For most men, yes. It's all a game. They'll tell you all the pretty things you want to hear, but they don't mean a thing. Every moment is just another chance to trap you before you wise up enough to run.

OPHELIA: And you?

HAMLET ties the rope. He kisses her.

HAMLET: I'm keeping you safe from them.

Everything freezes. OPHELIA addresses the audience.

OPHELIA: To my mother: I'm not a fool. I can see what he's doing. I know, because I've grown up on it. I've watched it happen to you: rope wound so slowly and gently that each tug felt more like a kiss on your wrists, on the delicate bones of your rib cage. He's wrong—it's not safety. Not quite, but it might be close enough.

I have some questions for you.

Did you know what was happening when it started? Or was it too gradual for you to notice, water quietly turned up to a boil?

Did you try to stop it? Or did it feel easy, like sinking to the bottom of a river?

Or maybe you felt some echo of what I feel now, what might be wrong and twisted but undeniable.

Did you start to like it?

Did you start to crave the sweetness of the burn?

HAMLET unfreezes.

OPHELIA: You can go tighter.

HAMLET: What?

OPHELIA kisses him suddenly. She holds out her wrists.

OPHELIA: Tighter.

For a moment, they stare at each other, a standoff.

HAMLET: No.

OPHELIA: Why?

HAMLET: *(Disgusted)* Because you're not supposed to like it.

It happens so quickly that I'm shocked, even though I know it's coming. I wrote it that way. Still, when Garrett lunges forward and hoists Harmony up to standing, the violence takes my breath away.

I look at Colin, and he's stunned—unmoving except for the quick, almost imperceptible rise and fall of his chest.

I watch him watch it. Garrett is Hamlet, dragging Ophelia to the bathtub, monologuing about how she's wrong for wanting him, for wanting the pain he causes her. Water splashes as he forces her to step inside, to sink down until she's submerged from the shoulders up.

Colin's eyes widen, and I glance back at the stage.

Harmony—Ophelia—*Leigh*—is looking out at the audience.

Looking directly into Colin's eyes.

"God have mercy on his soul," she says, quoting Ophelia's final line in *Hamlet*. Her stare is unflinching, like she can see right through him. Like she knows. "God be with you."

He pushes her under, and the lights go black.

For a moment, we're all submerged. The audience gasps in the dark. I feel Zoe squeeze my hand.

And then, the lights come up again.

We're back in reality now, but still, I'm watching from under-water. There's applause, hands moving but somehow muffled, silent. Harmony gets out of the tub, alive again, and joins Garrett. They bow together, Harmony's hair and dress dripping water, making little rivulets on the ground.

Colin watches for a moment, completely still as the hands flutter around him. The light shifts in his glasses, two clear, swirling pools reflecting the actors as they dive up from their bow.

And then, he moves. He flees as quickly as he can, which isn't very—it's awkward and cumbersome, Colin nearly stepping on skirts and toes as he makes his way out of the audience, pushing toward the exit and into the night.

It hits me as the door swings shut: *I don't know.* I thought I would know from his face, but I don't. There was no undeniable shadow of guilt. All I see, when I conjure that expression mere moments after it's gone, is hurt. Like he can't believe we did this to him. That *I* did this to him.

I don't know what to do with that.

I start to move after him, but Zoe grips my hand, hard.

"Not yet," she whispers.

"But—"

"We still have the surprise."

Before I can respond, Zoe steps into the center of the space. She directs her own small round of applause to Harmony and Garrett as she murmurs some congratulatory words I can't hear. Then, she ad-dresses the audience.

"Thank you, everyone. Give it up for our playwright, Jane Wil-liams!"

She turns to me, beaming again. The applause is a sudden roar in my ears, or else it's my heart, my blood rushing. Zoe waits for it to die down, but even when the clapping stops, there's still that low rumble in my skull.

"Now, we have one more surprise for all of you tonight," she says. "If you'll follow me into the second gallery, I'd like to present our grand finale."

Zoe gestures to the doorway, where Mara is already pulling back the curtain. The audience members get to their feet, moving toward it with a low, intrigued chatter. Through the current of motion, Zoe stays planted, a tree with billowing white branches.

Her stare is locked on me.

"You coming?"

I glance at the exit, where Colin just disappeared, and Zoe wades toward me, reaching for my hand. Her touch is cold.

"Come on," she says. "We'll find him after. You don't want to miss this."

There's something in her voice, the willow-green flash of her eyes, that makes dread pool in my stomach, rising like a flood as she pulls me toward the door. Once we're a few steps away, she lets go.

"Go ahead," she says. Her smile is small and demure, a porcelain-doll smile, like she's suddenly embarrassed or worried I won't like whatever's waiting inside. She adds, at a whisper: "This part's just for you."

Mara is gone now, the white curtain waiting for me to pass through alone.

And so, like an actor playing out a scene of Zoe's creation, I draw back the curtain and step inside.

29

The first thing I notice is the light—stark, so bright it makes me squint. It takes me a few seconds to adjust, but when I do, there's no mistaking it.

Even in darkness, I would recognize the woman on the walls.

I step deeper into the room, my heart making a slow crawl into my throat as I confirm what I already knew.

It's me. I'm the star of the show. The walls are covered in photos, ranging from small to poster-sized, and I am the subject of every single one. There's a sick twist in my gut, like I'm looking at something I shouldn't be seeing—a secret kiss, an open wound. Still, I can't fight the pull, my feet carrying me to the first wall with the grim inevitability of the gallows.

There I am, at that East Village bar where everything began, only I'm not with Colin. I'm sitting across from the very first pawn in my plan: Henry, or maybe Harry. I don't even remember. We're photographed through the bar's front window, both of us in profile. Henry-maybe-Harry is caught mid-monologue, and I'm smiling politely, gaze drifting over his shoulder.

Right beside that photo is me on a date with the next boy, and then the next, and the next—eight weekends' worth of first dates, all the boys I endured while I waited for Colin to finally appear.

I feel the sideways glances of a few gallery patrons, probably struck by the resemblance, but their looks are fleeting. Different hair color, a face that's hard to remember.

I move on to the next wall.

It starts as a small, crackling fire in my core, branching out, licking through every part of me until my whole body is a furnace. The understanding of what she's done.

Shots of me outside of Colin's apartment, phone pressed to my ear and staring intently out of the frame. That outfit, the fear on my face—I recognize them. It's the day I found the knife.

And then, the photos get more personal, diverging from Colin altogether. There I am on the subway, headphones in, digging for something in my tote bag. And here I am walking into my apartment building, glancing over my shoulder.

Me, frozen in my fifth-floor window, reaching up to close the curtains, shot from the darkened street below.

Zoe took these. All of them. This whole time, I've thought I had the upper hand, thought I was the one doing the watching.

But she was watching right back.

I whirl around, but I can't find her in the crowd. She didn't follow me in.

And then, as I'm scanning the space, I land on a piece in the center of the room. Another tub, identical to the one in the first gallery.

There's nothing but the thump of my heart and a slow dripping sound, like a faucet leaking, as I approach it. I move slowly at first, and as I get closer, I realize the dripping isn't in my head—it's coming from the bathtub, a speaker affixed to the bottom of it. I move quicker, closer, until finally, I'm looking over the edge.

There's a canvas inside, shaped to fit the full area of the coffinlike surface. On it, a girl lies dead. Her body is painted in a long white gown, her pale hands clasped around a bouquet of flowers—real ones, rising up from her two-dimensional body. Her hair is painted auburn, flowing out around her as if she's really floating.

But her face. Her face isn't a painting. It's a photo of a real girl, from the shoulders up, cut out and collaged onto the rest of her. Pale skin, freckled nose. Hazel eyes open wide. Lips parted, revealing slightly over-bitten teeth.

And dangling in the delicate space above her collarbone is a rosemary necklace.

But the girl in this photo isn't me. Her nose is narrower, her eyebrows thinner.

Leigh.

I step back from the bathtub, the dripping incessant, raging like a flood in my ears. Because now, I understand. Leigh isn't wearing my necklace. I'm wearing *hers*. And Zoe gave it to me.

It wasn't just Colin who noticed our resemblance, who told me I'd look good with red hair. Zoe did, too. She's the one who dyed it.

Zoe has been watching me, taking me under her wing, all in the name of turning me into a dead girl reincarnated.

I turn around, scanning the room, but Zoe's still not here. She couldn't even stay to watch me experience her sickening finale.

I storm away from the bathtub, from the dripping, and push through the white curtain and back into the main gallery. Still no Zoe. I keep walking, slamming through the front doors and out into the night. Somehow, the dripping is following me, echoing in my skull.

"Stop it," I whisper.

I fumble for my phone. No new messages. Nothing.

Shoving it back into my pocket, I walk down the street. I don't know where I'm going, only away from the dripping, but still, it's following me.

"Stop it," I mutter. "Stop it, stop it—"

"Jane."

I turn around, and there she is, materialized on the street corner like a spirit. She has that same worried look on her face, like she's not sure if I'll like what she's made for me.

"I can explain," she says softly. "Let me just—"

"Did you kill her?"

This isn't the question Zoe was expecting. She stares back at me, a flash of that same hurt I saw on Colin's face.

"No," she says. "Why would you think that?"

"I don't know, Zoe, maybe because you've been stalking me for months and trying to turn me into your—your little *copy* of a dead girl!"

She blows out a careful breath.

"Okay, so, I can see how this would all be jarring. But this was the only way I could explain it to you."

"Explain *what*?"

We stand there, locked in a battle of stares. A gust of wind blows, lifting Zoe's curls and dress, floating them around her like water.

"Leigh was my best friend," she says, her voice as light and soft as the breeze. "We grew up together. She was more like my sister than anything. Our moms were best friends, too. In all my earliest memories, Leigh is just there. My own special person."

I don't say anything, just wait for her to go on.

"We were inseparable until college. I went to Pratt, and she went to Penn. Which is where she met Colin." She takes a shaky breath, and now, the lightness is gone. "I first heard about him at the beginning of our sophomore year. She was *obsessed* with him. I was excited for her, because she'd never had a real boyfriend before, but I was also a little jealous. I already felt like she was slipping away, and then here's this random boy from Nowhere, New Jersey, trying to make her his.

But I relaxed a little when I finally met him over Christmas. It was a few months into their relationship, and he was . . . great. Sweet to her, polite to me. I thought, *Okay. She's still Leigh. Maybe this will be fine.*"

Zoe's face turns cloudy. "I don't know exactly when it started to change. It was slow. Gradual. Leigh was calling me less, hanging out with Colin more. At first, I figured she was just busy, whatever, but then a whole month went by, and I didn't hear from her. I reached out to some of her college friends, and they all said the same thing: she's just busy with Colin. They're adorable. *So* happy together. But I knew something was wrong. So, after sophomore year, when she'd decided to stay on campus with Colin for the summer, I went up to visit. She almost wouldn't see me. Said she was 'too busy.' But finally, I wore her down. And when I saw her . . ."

Now, her expression darkens from cloudy to a full-on storm. "She'd lost weight. She looked exhausted. The whole time we were at this coffee shop, she was frantically checking her phone. I called her on it, and she tried to play it off, but finally, I got her to admit how bad things had gotten. Colin was isolating her from her friends, wouldn't let her do anything without telling him first. Even when she told him where she was going, he'd be out of his mind with jealousy. So, eventually, she just stopped doing anything without him."

My teeth start to chatter, the chill biting through my denim jacket. Zoe seems dead serious, no trace of a performance. But this doesn't sound like Colin. Despite all the wrongs he's committed, he's never been possessive, never abusive. Zoe even said so herself. And how can I trust her, now that I know she's been lying to me for months?

"I tried to help her," Zoe says. "I told her she could come stay with me, that I'd help her leave him, but she freaked out when I brought it up. She insisted that she *loved* him. It was like because Colin never physically hurt her, she was convinced there was nothing wrong."

A flash, sharp and biting, of the hunting camp—that fleeting thought after I heard the shots. *Now they'll know. Now there will be proof.* I press a hand to my ribs, like that might hold me together.

"And all her friends seemed to think he was this perfect guy," Zoe continues. "Even her parents. The whole damn school. Leigh swore he was just protective. That everything he did was because he loved her so much." Her lip curls. "Eventually, she just got up and left the coffee shop, left me there alone. But I wouldn't give up. I called her again and again until she blocked me. Then, I started calling her Penn friends, too, but they all brushed me off. I even tried to report Colin to the police, but they basically laughed in my face. They told me, *actually* told me, that it's not a crime for a guy to be in love with his girlfriend."

She hugs her arms tightly around herself, and I mirror her, both of us standing unmoored in the cold. This whole time, she's known it, too. What it's like to ask for help and be silenced. To pay the price.

"Eventually, I had to go home," she says. "Leigh still wouldn't talk to me. I kept trying, but she blocked me everywhere. And so . . . I let her." Zoe shudders, tightening her grip on her elbows. "I thought eventually, she'd come around on her own. But she didn't. They moved in together junior year. And then, when I heard that Leigh had quit the tennis team her senior year, I knew. She was in too deep. It was her favorite thing in the world, and he made her quit. But there was nothing I could do. And I was just so angry. I mean, my best friend, my person, threw out everything she ever cared about for a *boy*. That's not the Leigh I knew. And I figured maybe that's for the best. Maybe it's not the Leigh I *want* to know."

She grits her teeth, face twitching with grief, and I know what's coming.

"And then, I got the call from her mom. Colin had 'found' Leigh in the bathtub. The second I heard, I knew he'd done it. He'd finally taken it a step too far, and now, it was too late. Leigh was this strong, amazing person who never used to take shit from anyone, and I couldn't save her. And she couldn't save herself."

A tear falls down her cheek, and she wipes it away with the back of her hand. Her face hardens into a stone mask, like she's determined not to let one more tear escape. Like she's lost too many already.

"I called the police again, but no one believed me. They thought it was suicide, maybe accidental, but either way, end of story. They barely even investigated. But I could tell something was off, so I pulled it out of one of the younger cops: there were some people on the case who thought things seemed fishy with Colin, but the chief of police refused to entertain it. I'm almost positive it's because Colin's parents paid him off." She scoffs. "Or maybe everyone was just so taken by his grieving boyfriend act that they didn't even have to."

I turn away from her, pressing a hand against the nearest building to steady myself. This is too much. I can't do it, sift through the murk of it all to separate my own gut instinct from Zoe's manipulation.

"You don't believe me," she says quietly.

"I don't know what to think," I snap, whipping around to face her again.

"You saw those pictures. The box. He *did* this, Jane. Even his parents knew. They scrubbed the whole internet of everything about her."

I know. I know the pictures were real, and the box, but so were Colin's lips all over my body. The way he held me close.

"What does this have to do with me?" I force out.

She's quiet for a moment.

"When I realized Colin was going to get away with what he did to Leigh, I shut down. I mean, I was a shell of a person. I barely got through the rest of school. I had this sick, twisted need to keep track of him, but all of his social media was private. I couldn't find him anywhere. So, I tried to forget, but he was always there in the back of my mind." She laughs, almost ironically. "Actually, that's when I got into all the manifesting stuff. I would fall down these rabbit holes, doing all these exercises, just desperate for the universe to make him appear. You get that, don't you?"

When she looks at me, it's not mocking. She's dead serious, desperate, and I understand. Zoe thinks we're the same. I used to believe it, too.

But we're not. I was desperate, yes, but it was all for love.

Zoe is desperate with hatred.

But are they really that different? asks a voice in my head. One that sounds a lot like my father's.

"When a year went by and I still hadn't found him, I started to lose hope. So, I gave up. Tried my best to forget it all. And for a while, it worked. Things were picking up in the art world. I started my TikTok—because even if the manifesting wasn't working for Colin, I *was* pretty good at it. And people would pay for coaching. A lot of money, actually." She laughs drily, but her face quickly turns serious. "But it didn't matter. I was like a ghost haunting my own life. *Nothing* mattered. I didn't feel anything. Until one day, it happened." A small smile flickers on her lips. "I was just swiping through the apps, looking for someone to help me feel more numb . . . and there he was. Here, in the city. In the palm of my hand. He'd already liked me on the app."

Goosebumps raise on the back of my neck.

"Colin only ever met me once, but back then, he knew me as Zee Miller. Leigh always called me Zee. She liked that it rhymed, Leigh and Zee. I'd changed Miller to Ember for college—it's a much better stage name. Anyway, I figured maybe Colin didn't remember me. So, I matched with him. We started messaging, and pretty soon, it was obvious he didn't. And that's when I came up with the plan."

"The plan?" I echo.

"The plan to get close to Colin," she says simply. "And ruin his little life."

All at once, I understand.

"You were the one calling him," I say. "Harassing him."

She nods, and the weight of it crashes into me full force, a wave.

"Oh my god. The bloody knife and Leigh's sweater . . . you left those in his drawer to screw with him, didn't you? That was never even real."

"It was real," Zoe snaps. "Maybe not the blood. And maybe he didn't kill her with a knife. But he killed her. That's *real*."

My breath feels thin, too weak and empty to fill up the cavern in my chest.

"What did you think would happen?" I demand. "Someone would find the fake murder weapon and bring it to the police, and they'd believe it was real? Or did you think all this would be enough for Colin to snap and confess on his own?"

She looks almost hurt.

"It was working. He *was* snapping. We both saw it." She gives a small sigh. "But no, that wasn't the whole plan. That didn't come together until I met you."

Another chill shudders through me. "What?"

"I've known about you a long time, Jane." She looks down, almost apologetic. "Colin and I were already messaging before he ended things with you."

It's like she's dragged a scalpel down my middle, opened it up to let the insides hang out.

"So?" I ask, trying as hard as I can not to betray the hurt. As far as I know, she's still lying. Trying to get me on her side.

"It's not your fault," she adds. "I think you were always doomed with him. No matter how hard he tried, you would never be Leigh."

The worst part is the kindness in her voice. Despite my best efforts, my pain is clear as day, and I hate her for it—for thinking she can fix it. Zoe waits, that terrible sympathy still emanating like fumes, but when it's clear I'm not responding, she takes a small breath and goes on.

"On our first date, I snuck a look at his phone when he went to the bathroom." She rolls her eyes. "He's unbelievably careless with that thing. Anyway, I saw some texts from you come in, so I looked through them. He was planning a date with you that weekend at the Brooklyn Botanic Garden."

My stomach roils. The Brooklyn Botanic Garden. The date that led into our first night together. The date before he broke my heart.

"So, I thought I'd check you out," Zoe says. "Get a sense of my competition. Well, imagine my surprise when I see him there with a brunette Leigh. I almost thought I was hallucinating, but no. There you were." She looks at me, almost awed. "I watched you both the whole time. Followed you to dinner, and then all the way back to your apartment. I don't even know what I was doing. I couldn't stop myself." She glances away, like she's embarrassed. "A few days later, when I saw him again, I just knew. He'd ended it with you."

Another sickening roll of hurt, raw as it was on the day that he broke things off.

"But I couldn't let go of you," Zoe continues. "You just looked so much like her. So, I got an idea." Her expression turns pleading. "You have to understand, I didn't know you yet. All you were was this girl who looked so much like Leigh, and I . . . I just thought, *If I could get Colin to snap, then . . .*"

The pain morphs into a cavern, wide and bottomless.

"You used me," I breathe, gripping the rosemary necklace like I might tear it from the chain. "You never even gave a shit about me, did you? I was just another little pawn for you. All you wanted was—"

Like a final kick to the stomach, I understand. What this really means.

"You wanted him to kill me."

A tear drips onto her cheek.

"He was going to get away with what he did to her," Zoe says quietly. "He never would have gone down for it, so . . ."

"So you needed another murder to pin on him," I spit.

"I never would have let it happen. I swear, Jane. The second I saw you together at the waterfront, I—"

"You were there," I cut her off.

She nods, and one understanding comes after another, a chain of explosives.

"Oh my god. It was *you* on Leigh's Instagram all along. You set up the meeting. You got Colin to come. How did you even—"

"I texted him from your phone," she says gently. "The first night you stayed at my apartment. I pretended to be you, and I told him that you knew about Leigh. That he had to meet you there, or else you'd go to the police."

It leaves me breathless, my head swimming. The way Colin looked at me. *Come on, Jane. You already know.* Because Zoe made him think I did, and she hoped he'd kill me for it. We both showed up to that meeting as unwitting pawns in her game, because we always have been. This was her plan all along: get Colin pinned for murder, even one he didn't commit. Even one like—

No.

As soon as I have the thought, it seizes my whole body. It's impossible, *mad*, but still, I have to say it out loud.

"You killed Ben."

Zoe's face warps, but not the way I think it will. Not with guilt. She looks like I've struck her a fatal blow.

"No." She shakes her head once, sharply. "No. That was all Colin. That's what I've been trying to tell you. Even if I could have gone through with the whole plan, I wouldn't have needed to. Ben was clearly onto Colin. I don't know how—maybe Ben found the knife and everything, or maybe he'd had his suspicions all along. I mean, he must have seen Colin and Leigh together. Known what they were like."

A haunting echo of what Ben told me after our date: *I just think you should be careful. Sometimes, there's this other part of him that comes out.* I hug my arms around my middle, clenching my teeth to keep them from chattering.

"Either way, Ben must have threatened Colin," Zoe says. "And Colin killed him."

Looking at her now, I'm certain: she believes what she's saying. Even I knew it the moment I saw Colin standing over Ben's body, the knife dripping blood.

But he was so adamant that he didn't do it.

I'm flailing, falling, grasping for something to hold on to. Someone to believe.

"You know it's true," Zoe presses. "I've known it from the moment I heard the break-in story. And you have, too."

"Yeah?" I snap, like a petulant child. "Why are you so sure?"

She looks at me sadly. "Because you helped him cover it up."

My skin burns with the shame of her accusation. I don't have the strength to deny it.

"If you knew this whole time," I start, "then why even bother doing all this? Why not tell the police what I did?"

"Because we both know they wouldn't have done shit."

It's my own words thrown back in my face, my insistence that she shouldn't call the police. Zoe folded, not because I was convincing, but because she'd already been through it, too.

She laughs bitterly. "I mean, they wouldn't even suspect him when he was standing over the body." Her face turns serious again. "But even if I thought they would help, I wouldn't have gone to the police. I wouldn't do that to you, Jane."

"Then why not just tell me the truth?" I demand.

"Because you wouldn't have believed it. I knew as soon as I saw you together that night. You were like Leigh—in too deep. You wouldn't have listened to me, so I had to do for you what I couldn't do for her. I had to show you."

It's like a shock of cold air to my lungs. She's right. She's right, and I hate her, and I can't be here, but I can't move.

"That's why you made me come to New Jersey," I say. "You really thought we'd get him to confess. And the box, the pictures—was that even real?"

"Yes," she says sharply. "That was all true. I didn't find them on his computer—he was smart enough not to keep them there—but I knew they existed. Leigh told me about them before she decided she couldn't trust me anymore. She said it was something Colin wanted to try, some sort of bondage thing, but I knew better. And I'm glad you found them. It wasn't enough, me telling you. You had to see them for real."

It's like I'm watching us from above, floating up with the streetlights. Zoe knew about the pictures. This whole time, she's been sitting on this, *knowing*, testing me until I passed by whatever metric she decided. And suddenly, I'm hurtling back into my body, taking control of it again. I turn and walk away.

"Jane, wait. I'm not judging you. I'm trying to tell you I get it. I *know* you."

I spin to face her.

"No, you don't. You don't know me at all."

"I do." Her eyes flash. "It's like I've been saying: we're the same. I know what it's like to love someone so much you can't let go. What it's like to hold all that rage inside you, rage that terrifies you. I know it, and you do, too. So I thought—" She hesitates. "I thought if anyone would understand what I've been trying to do here, why I had to do it, it would be you."

I stare back at her, dread coming cold and undeniable.

"Why?"

"Because . . ." There's a small hitch in her voice, a hesitation before plunging over the edge. "I know what you did to your father."

30

The world around me stutters, shimmers. Images flicker over each other in a sickening slideshow: Zoe, here, looking at me. The deer on the road. My mother on the ground.

My mother, my first dead body, but not the last.

"How?" I manage. "How do you . . . ?"

"I did my research." There's a self-satisfied glimmer in her tone now, like she's proud. "I found my way into some NYU alumni records. I had to dig for it, but your home address was there. Cypress Lane. Fairhope, Alabama. From there, it was pretty easy."

The edges of my vision go fuzzy. I drop to a crouch on the sidewalk, pressing the heels of my hands to my eyes, but it's all there, memory clear in the blackness. The scenes I've tried my hardest to forget.

The house on Cypress Lane.

The inevitable.

But I didn't know it then. I had just turned eighteen, and my three years were up. I'd been so good, so careful, and finally, I could escape. My ticket: an email acceptance to NYU.

I waited three whole days to tell him. I needed him to be drinking, but not drunk yet—still on the happy and generous side of the border, not yet tipped over into angry. He'd had a good day at work. He told me all about it over dinner, how well his company was doing, the good quarter they were having. When he was one scotch in, I dropped the bomb.

I got some good news today, too.

I showed him the email. Watched, heart knocking against my chest like a hummingbird in its cage, as he read it.

As his face turned from jovial to surprised to blank. Cold.

And I knew, even before he said it, that I had chosen wrong.

That school's a joke, he said, passing my phone back to me like he was sending a meal back to the kitchen. *No use spending tens of thousands to live in a tiny, dirty box.*

I can get financial aid, I tried. *Not a full ride, but it's something to—*

You're not going. End of story.

I should have left it there. But I was angry, so angry, and sick and tired of walking around a house full of invisible land mines, performing this same delicate dance on my way to a finish line that he, with the swiftness of a bullet, had just destroyed at the kitchen table.

Then I'll get a loan, I said. *In my name.*

And who's going to help you do that?

I'm eighteen. I don't need your help. I can do whatever I—

The glass sailed out of his hand and shattered on the wall behind me. He stood up, chair scraping on the ground, and came close enough that I could smell the scotch.

You're an ungrateful little bitch, he shouted, spit flying onto my face. *You think you're going to pack another little duffel and hide it away? Try to run off like your mama? Well, how'd that work out for her, Janie? How'd that go?*

It started that night. I was in my room, shuddering in my bed with anger. I just needed to think. Find a way out.

And then, I heard him coming up the stairs.

I heard my lock click from the outside. The scrape of a chair sliding against my door.

That night, my bedroom became my cage. It always had been, really. Now we'd just stopped pretending.

He kept me there for days. He even bolted the windows from the outside. The only time he came in was to bring me dinner, just one meal every day. For the rest of the hours, I cried. I disappeared into the plays on my shelf.

And then, on the third day, I made a plan.

It would begin, once again, with being good.

I was grateful, so grateful, for the dinner. And I was sorry, so sorry, for thinking I wanted to leave. He didn't believe me at first, but little by little, my goodness wore him down. I was his daughter again, soft and sweet and healed of the rage he'd seen inside me so early on.

One night, after dinner, he locked me in as he had for days—only this time, I didn't hear the telltale scrape and thud of the chair sliding against the door. It was working, I knew. He was trusting me again.

For another week, I lived in my cage. I said thank you for my dinner. I behaved. And still, the chair didn't come.

In the third week of my captivity, I was allowed back into the house again. A few days later, I was allowed in the yard.

And then, at the beginning of the fourth week—three days before my NYU deposit was due—I asked if we could take a trip to the hunting camp.

Just for a few days, I reasoned. *It's so cramped here, and I could use a change of scenery.*

Even after all I'd endured, some part of me was certain it wouldn't work, that he'd know exactly what I was planning. But the thing I didn't count on, the thing that saved me: he wanted this illusion to be real as much as I wanted him to believe it.

And so, we went. For the first day, I kept it up. He wouldn't let me near the guns, not yet; we spent the night playing cards and watching movies, making hot dogs on the grill. I could almost tell myself this father-daughter bond *was* real, not an illusion at all. It made me ache, to see this softer side of him. To know what I still had to do.

The second day, he took me to hunt. It was an echo of that day three years ago: quiet woods, shoes crunching. Sun-dappled path. Gun strapped to his back.

This time, when the buck appeared, I was ready. He steadied the gun, hands over mine. Finger curled over the trigger. Breathing. Heart beating.

And then, I pulled.

The buck fell, knees crumpling. The moment it hit the ground, he cheered, wrapping me in a hug and lifting me up, swinging me around. *Good girl! Got your aim from your daddy, didn't you?* For a moment, I was blinded by his pride, warmed from the inside out.

He pulled me out into the clearing, where the buck was twitching, bleeding from the bullet in his neck. We got close enough to see the pulsing of its veins, the wild, darting panic of its deep black eyes. He wanted me, I understood, to watch it die. To see its beauty. But all I felt was a numb sickness growing out from my core.

You know what this means, right? he asked when it was finally done.

I did. He'd told me about it, the old tradition: you make your first kill, you get bloodied.

We dragged the body back to the cleaning shed. He was in a good mood as he hung it up to bleed. As he dipped his fingers in, walked toward me dripping red. It was warm as he painted it onto my face. The smell dug deep into my nose, my throat, and I tried my hardest not to choke on it.

I tried my hardest to smile. To let him think that I was proud.

Once we were done, we went back to the trailer. He cracked open a beer. I started toward the bathroom.

Where d'you think you're going? he asked, still jovial. *Blood's got to stay on all night. It's tradition.*

I gritted my teeth. He handed me my own can of beer, and I took it. Said thank you. We sat at the table, drinking together, as he regaled me with stories of growing up just outside of this camp, of coming here with his father. He went through a second beer, and then a third. We watched a movie. Two more beers. By the sixth, he was sleepy. Foggy.

When he was snoring, I crept to his room. The gun I'd used to kill the buck was hanging on a hook by the door.

The gun that had killed my mother.

I took it and walked back to the living room. As I passed, I caught a glimpse of myself in the stained, rusty bathroom mirror. A bloodied girl. It had caked on my face, drying enough to crack. It brought out the green in my hazel, I thought. All that red.

I walked, as quietly as possible, to my snoring father. Holding my breath, I reached out, positioned the gun in his hands. He was out cold, so far gone that he didn't even notice. I prayed—maybe the first time I'd ever really prayed—that he would stay that way.

And then I slid the barrel into his mouth.

For all he'd shown me about the beauty of it, it turned out that in the end, I couldn't watch.

The rest moved quickly. I took our phones and his keys, and, just before walking through the screen door for the last time, I noticed his old denim jacket hanging on the back of a chair, untouched by the blood. I considered it for a moment before slipping it on. It felt good. Like armor.

Like a pelt.

I drove to the nearest police station. I had thought about washing the blood from my face, but I figured it fit our story better. I shot a deer. That's why my prints are on the gun, why some stray blood might have ended up on my clothes.

I got bloodied. I have to wear the blood all night.

It was all coming together, the play exactly as I'd imagined. As I drove, I allowed myself the briefest smile before locking back into my character. A grieving girl. A girl soaked in blood.

The police were shocked, at first, to see me at their doorstep, like a horror movie creature. And then, they realized I was just a girl. A sobbing girl, a girl in shock.

I told them what my father had done to himself.

The other story beats played out exactly as I'd scripted them.

I washed off the blood. I went home. Our neighbor, Mrs. Hutchinson—who had always, I think, had her suspicions, but never once acted on them—came to watch me, not that I needed much watching. I was eighteen. I was free.

I submitted my NYU deposit.

I learned, as I suspected, that my father had left me everything.

I used some of his savings to plan the funeral. I went. I cried. I didn't have to force myself, either. I was sad for him. Sad to see how empty it was. Sad because, as wrong as I knew it was, I missed him— missed him the way a moth misses a flame, circling its artificial sun and dreaming of one more second in its warmth, the sweetness of the burn.

After it was all dead and buried, I sold the house. It went more quickly than I'd thought, but for less than I'd hoped. Figures, I guess, when it's a death house, even though neither one actually happened there.

I took the money from the house and added it to the savings.

I packed what little I wanted to keep and moved to New York.

And everything before that was irrelevant.

Only, it never was, no matter how expertly I convinced myself.

The story stuck. Even if people back home had their suspicions—which they no doubt did—there was never any proof. I left, and they forgot me. The city swallowed me whole. At school, I never mentioned where I came from, and no one ever really pushed. A name like Jane Williams yields too many search results to ever close in on one story in Fairhope, Alabama—and even then, all that story would say is that my father killed himself three years after the hunting accident that killed my mother.

But I couldn't make the truth disappear from my own memory. I pushed it down, drowned it in other stories, but it was always there, lurking beneath the surface.

It was right there for Zoe to find.

"I tracked down your neighbor," she explains. "Sally Hutchinson. I called her, told her I was doing a background check on you for a job. She told me what happened to your dad, but she didn't seem to believe it. When I pressed her, all she said was, 'I was there, in the days after. And that girl . . .'" She pauses, and it's like Mrs. Hutchinson is really here, her Alabama accent. Zoe's an actress, after all. "'I know her daddy put her through a lot, and I don't like to speak ill of the dead. But what I'll say is that girl never seemed to miss him too much.'" She looks at me with deep tenderness, Zoe once again. "So, I did some more research. Tracked down the hunting camp, found the nearest neighbor. Some guy named Rick."

Rick. I don't remember a Rick.

"He lived about a mile from the camp," Zoe explains. "But he was on the road that night. Said he remembers seeing a little girl driving toward town, covered in blood, with a smile on her face."

"I shot a deer," I argue, even as the truth reveals itself in the heat under my skin. "When you shoot your first one, they paint you with its blood."

"Which is why Rick didn't ever go to the police," she says calmly. "Why no one's come after you. It's all circumstantial, right?"

I take a step back.

Zoe holds her hands up, like I'm a frightened deer and she doesn't want to spook me. She has no idea.

The knife is weighty in my pocket, but I force myself to keep my hand at my side. If I touch it, I'll give myself away.

"I'm not going to turn you in," she says. "Not even close. I'm trying to tell you I understand. I would have done the same thing."

Her words are so soft that for a moment, I want to curl up inside of them, forget her indiscretions and let her certainty rock me to sleep. But I can't. Zoe is a monster, and so am I—and maybe so is Colin. But right now, after all that we've done to him, he might be the most innocent.

"Where is he?" I ask.

"Do you still not trust me?"

I pull out the knife.

"Where's Colin?"

My hand shakes, the blood rushing loud in my ears, and I hate how it feels. I hate that she doesn't look more afraid.

Zoe just stares at the blade, her lips pressing into a sharp line, looking strangely brokenhearted.

"Is that what you need?" she asks. "To hear it from him?"

"Where is he?" I tighten my grip.

"Fine." Zoe lifts her hands in surrender. "I'll show you."

I lower the knife a few inches. With a final glance at the blade, Zoe turns and leads me around the corner. We walk about a block before she stops at what appears to be an abandoned warehouse, much like the one across from her apartment: crumbling brick, concrete,

271

flickering light. She leads me up a set of rickety stairs to a locked door and pulls the key from her pocket, slotting it into the lock. The door opens with a metallic creak, echoing into the large and darkened space.

Zoe holds the door for me.

"Go ahead," she says, and I wonder if it's because she's suddenly afraid to turn her back to me.

It's good, every so often, to remember that I can be the monster in the night. The reason to look twice over your shoulder.

Tightening my grip on the knife, I step inside. My boots echo on the concrete floor. It takes a moment for my eyes to adjust, but even in the darkness, I can pick out the shape in the center of the large, high-ceilinged room.

I can feel his fear.

"Colin?" I whisper.

Lights hum to life overhead, washing the space in a harsh industrial glow.

The sight of him is enough to still my breath. He's bound to a chair with tight cord, his hands and ankles tied, his mouth gagged. He lifts his head groggily, and I notice his glasses are gone. It takes me another second to spot them on the floor, cracked.

"He doesn't actually need them, you know," Zoe says, following my line of vision. "They're literally blue-light glasses."

I don't know why, but it's this piece of information that makes me truly enraged. Not just because Colin is apparently a pretentious phony—but because Zoe is so holier-than-thou, so convinced I'm some lovesick girl who barely even knows the object of her affection.

Do I?

Colin whimpers, and despite everything I know now, protectiveness takes over.

"What did you do to him?"

"Just some pills in his champagne," Zoe says. "Perfectly timed, honestly. He barely made it out of the gallery before passing out on the street. Made the whole thing pretty easy. He's kind of a beanpole, so it wasn't that hard to carry him." She smiles at him, his binds and gag. "I like to think of this as my own artistic interpretation of his photoshoot with Leigh."

She's monstrous, smiling there in her Ophelia dress, that dimple scythed into her cheek.

"Don't worry, though," she adds, strolling lazily over to him. "He should be perfectly fine to answer some questions. Aren't you, Colin?"

She slaps him hard in the face, and he jolts fully awake. He mumbles something frantic into the fabric between his teeth. Zoe rips it out of his mouth. His stare is wide and panicked, fixing on me.

"Jane."

The sound of my name in his voice nearly makes me weak in the knees. I move toward him.

"Please help me," he whimpers. "Please—"

And then he sees the knife in my hand.

"No." He tries to scoot the chair backward, almost tipping it over. "No, no, no . . ."

"I'm not going to hurt you," I tell him, barely disguising my own pain. All this, and he still doesn't trust me.

Well, no wonder. I'm standing here with his kidnapper and a weapon.

Zoe's watching me still, an almost intrigued look on her face.

I let out a breath. I don't love her methods, but there *are* things I need to ask him, and it's not like he can run away from confrontation now.

I kneel in front of him, hiding the knife back in my pocket, and deliver the biggest, most clichéd understatement of my life.

"We need to talk."

31

He's the one tied to the chair, but still, anxious heat shudders down my spine. The entire world is balanced on the knife's edge of this conversation, this moment, and I have to do it right.

I take a breath.

"I want you to tell me about Leigh."

Colin blanches. He glances over my shoulder, at Zoe, and I shake my head.

"Don't worry about her. We're talking right now. Me and you."

His eyes snap back to mine, and I hate the fear there as much as I love the rush it gives me—knowing that I'm the one in control.

"You think I killed her," Colin says finally, his voice raw. "I know she told you I did. But you can't trust her. She's a liar." His pitch rises in panic. "I didn't put it together until she *drugged me*, but Zoe's real name is Zee Miller. She was Leigh's friend, and for some reason, she has this fucking crazy idea that I—"

"Colin." It comes out cool and sharp enough to silence him instantly. "I know who Zoe is. I know her side of the story. Now, I want to hear it from *you*."

He nods, chewing on the inside of his cheek.

"Okay. Okay, I can do that."

For another few seconds, he's quiet, gathering himself.

"Leigh was my first serious girlfriend," he says. "I'd had one or two in high school, but Leigh was the first person I really considered a future with. I . . . I loved her."

He sounds almost nervous to say it, like it might hurt my feelings, but relief washes through me. For the first time, it feels like he's really being honest.

"But I always felt like she was holding back," Colin continues. "She prioritized other things over us. Tennis, school, friends that were bad for her." He glances up at Zoe, then back at me. "When I'm in something, I'm in it a hundred percent, and Leigh . . . she wasn't always like that. But I understood. She had some issues she was working through."

"Issues?"

He nods. "Mental health stuff. Trust. Self-consciousness. She was also using pills, but I didn't know it until the end."

"Bullshit," Zoe says.

I turn to look at her, the pure, disgusted rage boiling in her glare. She stayed composed even when Colin threw insults her way, but clearly, he's struck a nerve with Leigh.

"Let me finish," I tell Zoe, level. "Please."

She blows out a breath that might as well carry smoke with it, but she nods.

I turn back to Colin. "Zoe says you were possessive. Cutting Leigh off from her friends and family."

He glares up at her before looking at me again.

"That's not what it was like. She's framing it like I'm some abuser, but . . ." He shakes his head. "I just loved her. And when I love someone, I start to lose my head sometimes."

The door of my heart creaks open. *You and me both.*

"So, yeah," Colin continues. "Maybe I was a little hurt that I felt like she wasn't as committed as I was, but I never forced her to do anything. I didn't make her stop doing tennis or seeing certain people. She just understood that if things were going to work out with us, then we both had to make some compromises. Cut out toxic people."

I nod slowly. It sounds reasonable, rational, enough that a new version of this story starts to play out in my head. Clearly, Zoe's no stranger to toxic behavior. What if she really *was* the problem, the possessive one? What if Leigh was better off without her?

But I can't deny the other evidence, cold and objective.

"What about the pictures?" I ask him. "You're saying you didn't hurt her, but I saw them. They were . . ."

I clamp my jaw, disgust rolling in my stomach.

Colin looks down at his bound hands.

"I know. I know what they look like. But it was . . ." His cheeks burn pink. "It was consensual. We both wanted to, you know . . . explore some things. It was honestly her idea. She could be surprising that way."

His tone warms, an echo of the boy who loved her. I'm aware that this contradicts Zoe's story—she said the pictures were Colin's idea, not Leigh's—but I understand if Leigh wanted to take them. I know what it's like to be enthralled by the pain, to think of it as the sharpest kind of love. It's an explanation I considered from the beginning, but still, there's a tug of resistance in my gut.

"So why keep them?" I ask, a little more harshly than I mean to. "Why keep any of the stuff in that box?"

"Because I missed her," he says. "Toward the end, I think we both knew it was never going to work out long-term, but then she was *gone*. Forever. And I just . . . maybe it's messed up, but I wanted to remember her. The part of her I loved."

"You needed her retainer and bloody underwear to remember her by?" Zoe interjects. "And what about the ID? You literally scratched her eyes out. That doesn't seem like someone who's fondly reminiscing."

I want to argue, but she has a point. Colin's jaw sets, his face turning grave.

"I guess I was angry, for a while," he says. "For the way that she left me."

My stomach sinks.

"How did she die?" I ask quietly. I still don't know, not what the official cause was, and I'm afraid of his answer—of how convincing it will be.

"Pills. They don't know if it was intentional or accidental, but she took a bunch, got in the bath, and just . . . drifted." His voice turns strained. "I knew she struggled, but I never thought . . ." Tears well in his eyes. "She looked so peaceful, lying there."

I can't go any longer without touching him. Reaching out, I cup his cheek in my palm, wipe away a tear with my thumb. He leans into my touch, his skin warm.

"I swear, Jane," he murmurs. "I didn't kill her."

We're so close that I can almost feel it: leaning in, kissing him, falling into our own little world until it drowns out the rest. It's been barely a week since we last kissed, but the distance between now and then feels like a cruel, impassable gorge. His hands in my hair, my back against the railing. The hungry growl of his voice.

Come on, Jane. You already know.

I pull my hand back like his skin has burned me.

"Why did you come to the waterfront that night?" I ask.

Colin blinks, dazed, like he'd been lost in the memories, too. "What?"

"Zoe pretended to be me and texted you that I knew about Leigh. You thought I was going to the police. Why would you come if you didn't kill her?"

There's a current of something in his eyes, surprise or panic, and it scares me that I can't tell which.

"I thought you knew about the pictures," he says finally. "And the box. That's all I meant. I was embarrassed. I didn't want you to think I was some obsessive creep."

It rings false, a little alarm bell in the back of my head—enough that I have no choice but to ask him the question I've been dreading.

"Then why did you tell Zoe I was obsessed with you? That you didn't want me?"

The hurt sharpens me, hardens me, but then he's searching my eyes, and I'm drowning in honey.

"I didn't mean any of it," he says. "I was worried she was onto us."

That word again. *Us.* It's a new, glistening promise, and I want to believe it.

"You understand, don't you?" he pleads. "We're the same, Jane. You and me. We fall fast and deep, and sometimes, that means we make impulsive decisions, or we do things other people wouldn't understand. I *know* you."

It's all I've wanted to hear from the moment I met him. Every atom of my being wants to pull him close and tell him I understand, to let our hearts beat together. But that doubt won't stop humming at the back of my mind, a bee buzzing around the honeycomb.

"Jane." My name again, an incantation, and I have no choice but to hear him. "Zoe's manipulating you. She's trying to turn you against me. You have to believe me. I would never have hurt Leigh, or Ben, or anyone. I—" He steadies himself, his gaze burning deep into mine. "I love you. And nothing else fucking matters."

The words echo through me, undeniable. *I love you.* In all the years I've been searching for this, I don't think I ever quite prepared for how it would feel. I'd imagined trumpets, butterflies, liquid sunlight—loud things, moving things, bright things. And it's still that, in some ways.

But it's also this: sweet, quiet relief. A warm house after miles in a winter storm.

"He's lying."

Zoe's voice slices through the moment like a dagger, and just like that, it's gone. Even this, she's stolen from me.

I rise, my head rushing with fury, but Zoe stands firm, cold and unafraid, with her arms folded over her chest.

"He's been lying to you this whole time."

"So have you."

The words burn through me like acid, and Zoe's mouth opens in surprise, her hands falling to her sides. I expect her to fight back, but instead, her eyes well, their green glowing even brighter.

"I know," she says. "And I'm sorry. But please, Jane. You can't fall for this. You can't let him get away with this again." She moves closer. "I understand. I know exactly what it's like to want love so much because you never got it anywhere else. I know because I've been there, too. And I still fucking believe in love. But this isn't it. This isn't real."

Something about her words claws under my skin, scratches at the marrow. She's right. Isn't that what I've been doing from the moment I saw my mother lying on the grass? Searching for the love she never had. I told myself I wouldn't end up like her. I would choose love, bravely, but not *that* kind, the love that's really possession. I would find safety in softness, in kindness, in men who see me as a person with goals and things to say—not as something to own, a delicate jewel locked away for safekeeping until they decide to smash it just because they can.

But then there's the other truth, swimming just beneath that one: Zoe's giving me too much credit. I'm not some Freudian disaster, scouring the earth for the antithesis of my father.

I'm his daughter. His darkness runs thick in my veins.

And I am not capable of being good.

I take the knife out of my pocket.

32

Here we are: the final scene. The inevitable.

It was always going to end like this.

Love stories always do.

I move toward her, and her eyes widen with fear, but she doesn't run, doesn't even flinch—like she knows this is inevitable, too. My heart *thump-thumps* in my chest, the hunter but also the deer, and I know, in this moment, that I love her.

I've always known that love is a choice. Sometimes a brutal one, always a sacrifice. And sometimes, you have to let it go.

It's a beautiful thing, watching something die.

For so long, I've been trying to deny it, to tell myself that it was never inside me, but here I am, living proof. Zoe even helped me understand it: I could never be good.

It's time I stopped pretending.

I am loved, I am whole, and I release you.

I raise the knife.

"He doesn't love you."

This time, her voice is so calm it startles me. I freeze, blade poised, and still, she doesn't run. She keeps her eyes locked on mine, like she needs me to understand this one thing, even if it's the last thing she ever does.

"A person who loves you doesn't start messaging someone else on a dating app when you're together. A person who loves you doesn't break things off after six dates." It's not malicious, not even pleading. She says it simply. "Jane, he doesn't love you."

I'm shivering. I don't know when it started. Doubt has burrowed into my chest, made itself a home there.

"I have the proof on my phone," Zoe tells me. "I'll show you right now."

I turn back to Colin, the question in my eyes.

And that's all it takes.

"Yes," he blurts. "But it didn't mean anything. It was a mistake. She was manipulating me."

I take a step toward him, the knife still in my hand.

"Whoa, wait," he says. "Are you seriously about to turn on me for *this*? I thought you loved me."

"Colin." His name scratches in my throat. "I need you to be honest with me."

"Why?" he explodes. "You won't believe me anyway. You already think I killed them." He laughs—wild, almost manic. "She got to you. Oh my god, I can't believe this. I love you, Jane. I love you, and she's a fucking psychopathic bitch!"

He screams it, spit flying from his mouth, and my grip tightens on the knife handle. He's breathing hard, a vein bulging in his neck and hate in his eyes, and there he is: the monster from the stairwell, the twin of the one that lived in my house.

For the first time, I wonder what would happen if our roles were reversed—if I was the one in the chair, and the knife was in his hand.

But then all at once, the monster is gone.

"Please," he whimpers. "Please don't kill me."

I come closer, close enough to touch him, but I don't.

I kneel before him.

"I have one more question," I tell him, surprised at the calm that overcomes me. "I need you to be completely honest with me. Okay? That's all I need."

He nods quickly, grasping at this final chance for absolution.

I study his face. Honey eyes. Dark lashes. The hair curling gently on his forehead, damp with sweat. The freckles all over his face like a sky full of stars, sprinkling all the way down to his lips. I memorize every inch of it, composing a map in my mind, because I know, even as love crushes my heart in a vise, that our entire world hinges on his answer.

"Why did you end things with me?" I ask.

For a second, he's quiet. Surprised.

"Honestly?" he asks.

"Honestly," I echo.

Determination sharpens his features. He's going to tell the truth. And for once, no matter what it is, I'm going to accept it.

"I just got overwhelmed, I guess." He sighs, a release of pent-up panic. "Maybe I wanted you to be Leigh. But that wasn't fair. She was this lightning-in-a-bottle type of person, like—like I couldn't even believe she'd choose to be with me. And you're great, obviously, but . . ." His face crumples, like it's a relief to finally say it. "Sometimes, you made it too easy. And that's always been kind of a turn-off for me."

I laugh. It surprises him, clearly, as much as it does me—the automatic jerk of it, this sudden bubble of humor. *Too easy.* It's the epitome of Zoe's logic, hers and all her manifesters': *Attract, don't chase. Don't be too available.*

I look at her now—this beautiful, ethereal woman, with her curls and her flowers and her ability to manipulate the universe, to weave reality like a friendship bracelet and dangle it from her delicate wrist. This is what Colin wanted, I think. What the boys always want: to tame that power. Make it theirs.

Zoe looks back at me, balanced somewhere between apology and acceptance, and it surges up from my core with a painful certainty: rage, bright and hot and familiar.

There is only one way to let it go.

The knife thrusts forward, and Zoe gasps.

Colin, his eyes widened, is too stunned to make a sound. He just looks, burning with betrayal, at the blade buried in his stomach.

When his stare finds mine again, I keep my grip firm, loyal, watching as he twitches and gurgles. Until he finally stops altogether.

I let go of the knife, still embedded. My hand has barely left the hilt when Zoe materializes to wrap her arms around me, pulling me close. I'm crying, I realize. But not sobbing—the tears fall freely, easily. A release. Zoe strokes my hair softly, like a mother.

"You're okay," she says. "You're okay."

And I am. What I can't find the words to tell her, as I take one last look into Colin's eyes—milky soft, unburdened—is that my father was right.

It's all a little beautiful.

SIX MONTHS LATER

There's a knock on the door, three quick raps.

"Come in," I tell her, winding the last lock of my hair around the curling wand. "I'm almost done."

Zoe opens the door and gasps dramatically.

"Okay, shut *up*. You look so good!"

I smile, releasing the curl to bounce onto my shoulder. "Thanks."

I've gotten better at this lately—accepting compliments instead of looking for ways to deflect or reject them. I've even started to believe them.

"So do you," I add, taking in her outfit. Zoe, as always, is stunning. Opening night is no exception.

She stands at my side, admiring our reflection. "Thank god these people have such a hot playwright and director."

"It's a gift," I joke, playing at overly humble. "It would be wrong of us not to share it, really."

"Naturally." Zoe grins, dimple deepening. "How are you feeling?"

"Good," I say. "Nervous."

"Me, too. Like, I know it's going to be great, but it's always nerve-wracking putting your work out there. Especially when you're doing something new."

Since our collaborative debut at her art show, Zoe has cemented *director* in her list of multi-hyphenate titles. She's good at it, too—even if I like to think there's something special about our specific alchemy, the way she brings my words to life. Tonight's opening will be our first since that night. It's at an off-Broadway theatre, a fact that still has me pinching myself every ten minutes. Some days, I'm almost certain I'll wake up to an email informing me that actually, this was all a mistake, and they're pulling the plug.

"What?" Zoe asks.

She can read my thoughts as well as she can read my plays.

I sigh. "Do you ever feel like none of this would have happened without . . . you know, everything?"

It's still hard for us to talk about it. *Everything* has become our shorthand for Colin and all that's happened since. And, in a way, I know I'm right: the recent surge of interest in Zoe and me as artists isn't *unrelated* to the true crime mystique of it all. We're two girls who unwittingly uncovered a killer—one who mysteriously disappeared on the night of our collaborative debut.

That's the official story: Colin Hillgrove hasn't been seen since he walked out of the art show in a guilty daze. Shortly thereafter, his parents received an email from his account confessing to both Leigh's and Ben's murders. This prompted a search of Colin's apartment, which yielded evidence to support his confession: the Leigh box, Colin's laptop—the one he reported as "stolen" in the supposed break-in—and his phone. There, they found not only the threatening texts that must have pushed Colin over the edge, but something that had nothing to do with me or Zoe at all—a log of abusive messages from Colin to Leigh in the weeks leading up to her death. Demands to know where she was, wild accusations that she was cheating, and then, the final nail in the coffin: a text on the afternoon of her death that read only, *When I get home, you're going to regret this.*

Colin's body was never found. He's still technically a missing person, but at this point, everyone knows he's gone. *Presumes.*

If there's one thing I'm good at, it's telling stories, and it seems like everyone believes this one. Probably because, despite some theatrical embellishments, it *is* the truth. Colin killed Leigh and Ben. He may never have confessed, but we didn't need him to: I understand, now, that he was always a liar. A manipulator. He was, at risk of sounding like a ubiquitous TikTok post, a *gaslighting narcissist.*

Whatever you call him, the core of the matter is this: he was none of the things I believed him to be.

Still, I miss him. The person I thought he was. What we could have been together.

I'm learning to be okay with that.

Zoe leans against the counter, tilting her head thoughtfully.

"Maybe," she says. "But that doesn't mean we don't deserve it."

I smile. "True."

We both believe it, I know, but there's still an undercurrent of worry between us. There are people out there who don't buy our story. Mostly, they're the types who lurk in Instagram comments and Reddit threads, no one really credible. When it came to law enforcement, Zoe and I benefited from the same privileges Colin did, if in a slightly different way. We're two pretty white girls with a unified story—and, this time, enough evidence to pass their test. Of course they believed us.

And they should have, because our story was true. At least in all the important ways.

"Oh, shit." Zoe frowns. "I meant to get champagne for everyone to pop after the show." She checks the time on her phone. "I'll run to the store."

"Do you want me to come?"

"No, you finish getting ready. I'll be back in ten minutes. Don't worry a bouncy little curl on your beautiful head."

She starts toward the door.

"Can I borrow your lip gloss?" I call behind her.

"Yes, totally. It's on my dresser, I think. Feel free to run in and grab it."

"Thanks," I call, but she's already flitting out the door.

I touch up a few stray pieces of my hair and turn off the heat. Then, I step out into Zoe's studio.

It's strange, how quickly I felt at home here. The green velvet sofa is almost like a second bed to me, thanks to all the nights I've passed out there after we hit the Brooklyn bars or stayed up way too late working on script revisions. At first, I felt like an imposition, but slowly, I started to understand that Zoe actually means it when she says she likes having me here. Now, the chaos of her things makes an intimate sort of sense to me, the scattered clothes and canvases like their own site-specific work of art.

It does make it difficult to find the lip gloss, though. It's not on her dresser with the other makeup things, so I scan the floor to see if it's fallen there somewhere. When that proves unsuccessful, I try the top drawer, just in case Zoe put it there without thinking. She does that, every so often—phone in the fridge, AirPods in the kitchen cabinet, things placed thoughtlessly while her brain is elsewhere, dreaming up things more important than the three-dimensional.

Inside the drawer, though, all I see is socks and underwear. I'm about to give up when I catch something else shoved into the mix: a beaten-up copy of *Hamlet*. I take it out. And I know—by now, I should have learned to leave other people's things alone, especially their underwear drawers. But I'm a playwright. I have a curiosity about other people's inner lives that I can't quite shake.

I open the book. It's heavily annotated, and I'm about to start thumbing through the highlights and sticky notes when I notice something pressed between the pages. I open it up to the bookmarked scene. The announcement of Ophelia's death, Gertrude's monologue. Tucked against the spine is a white piece of paper, folded up to a thick little square.

I unfold it.

A newspaper clipping, I realize. A Philadelphia paper. And then, when I notice the headline, my breath catches.

Death of Penn Student Sheds Light on the Opioid Crisis.

There she is, in a grainy photo, smiling in her tennis uniform.

Leigh.

I read on, heart thrumming.

As the University of Pennsylvania community mourns the loss of student Leigh Carlsen, we are also facing yet another reminder that the opioid epidemic is closer to home than we might think. On the surface, Carlsen was hardly the picture of someone struggling with addiction: an engineering major and tennis star from Greenwich, Connecticut, she was described by friends as a devoted student and athlete with an undeniable joy for the world around her.

"She was always the most positive person on the team," says former tennis coach Jennifer Smith. "Even when we lost—which we rarely did with her around—I've never met anyone with a deeper love of the sport."

Carlsen left the tennis team before her senior season. Just a few months later, she was found dead in her off-campus apartment from a fentanyl overdose.

I read it again, like there must have been some mistake, but the cause of death is loud and clear in black print. A fentanyl overdose. But the article Zoe and I found online, the only one that mentioned Leigh at all, said the cause of death hadn't been released yet. It said they hadn't ruled out homicide.

And then, I realize. Zoe and I didn't find that article together. *She* found it.

I whip out my phone. What was the name of the site? *Penn Daily? Quaker Daily?* No, the *Daily Quaker*. I google it, and nothing comes up.

I refresh, like that will help, but nothing changes. As far as I can tell, the *Daily Quaker* doesn't exist.

An idea starts to drip into my head, shifting and churning like ink in water. Zoe could have created that article somehow. A website she made herself, disguised to look like a real newspaper, the misspelled names a convenient explanation for its sudden appearance.

But no. That's ridiculous. If that was all a lie, if a murder investigation was never on the table, then why would Colin's parents have worked so hard to scrub Leigh from the internet?

The answer becomes clear as soon as I reach the bottom of the article, his name sticking out like a beacon.

Among those reeling from Carlsen's death is her boyfriend, Colin Hill-grove.

"I had no idea she was struggling like that," he says. "It's something I'll have to deal with for the rest of my life, knowing this was all going on and I didn't know."

Hillgrove, along with many of Carlsen's friends and peers, has pushed university administration to take action—although not without opposition.

"We wanted to set up a fund in her name to help educate and prevent opioid-related deaths," says Maddie McMichael, a teammate of Leigh's. "But her parents didn't want Leigh's name attached to it."

Carlsen's parents could not be reached for comment.

The words on the page start to bleed together, morphing into a dangerous understanding.

It wasn't Colin's parents who scrubbed her death from the internet.

It was Leigh's. Because they were ashamed, maybe. Embarrassed.

But why would Zoe lie to me?

I force myself to take a breath, be logical. Maybe Zoe really believed that Colin's parents scrubbed everything. She told me that some of the cops thought Colin was suspicious. Maybe that was true, too. Or maybe Zoe just needed to tweak the narrative, make it easier for me to see who Colin really was.

I read his quote again. Free from any other context, he comes off as a grieving boyfriend, a good guy unfairly blaming himself for the tragedy. Another expert manipulation, I think. Colin told me himself that he was obsessive, possessive. He made Leigh sacrifice her *toxic friends* and everything else she loved to be with him, his own twisted idea of compromise. He was an abuser. He *killed* her.

But what if he didn't?

Suddenly, my dress is too tight, the air hard to breathe. I stuff the article back between the pages and dig again through Zoe's drawer, hoping—perhaps madly—for some other secret, stowed-away evidence to make this all make sense.

And then, as if I willed it into existence, it comes.

A phone, shoved in the very back corner beneath a bundle of socks.

Already, I recognize it.

With a quivering hand, I lift the phone and turn it on, telling myself that maybe I'm wrong. This isn't what I think it is.

After what feels like an eternity, I'm starting to think the phone is just dead when, finally, it blinks to life, greeting me with a low-battery notification above a familiar smiling basset hound.

Ben's phone. Here in this half-hearted hiding place, almost like Zoe wanted me to find it.

Slowly, the lights go up on a new and frightening version of the truth, playing out on a stage before me.

Colin's apartment, Ben home alone. Zoe, beautiful and unassuming, even with the kitchen knife hidden behind her back. Before Ben knows what hit him, the blade is slicing across his throat. And then, with his body still warm, Zoe takes his phone and texts Colin to lure him to the murder scene, her trap. She texts me, too, a message she knows I can't ignore. It's all so easy, isn't it? Because Zoe has done this before.

Ben isn't the first ghost she's impersonated.

I think of the fire in her eyes that night as Colin slept sweetly in her apartment.

They've got him at the scene of a literal murder, she said, *and still, they think some crime show bad guy is more plausible than the guy who was standing over the body.*

It's staggering, the obvious simplicity of it. Zoe practically told me herself: the police would never arrest Colin for Leigh's murder. What she left out was the possibility that Colin never killed Leigh at all—even though it's likely, almost certain, that Leigh was driven to those pills by his abuse. He *was* guilty, just not in a way that could be prosecuted. Zoe wanted nothing more than justice, even when that meant framing Colin for killing someone else. Even when, at one point, that person would have been *me*. Zoe didn't give up on her ridiculous, reckless plan.

She just found a different victim.

My phone lights up with a message from Zoe.

Champagne acquired!!!!

I sit down, press my forehead to my knees, and try to breathe, force my mad, racing heart into submission.

Okay.

Okay.

I, of all people, know that the truth can be complicated. Contradictory realities can exist side by side. Colin was a monster, but he was also quite possibly the love of my life. He may not have been a killer, but he didn't deserve to get away with what he'd done.

Zoe tried to kill me, but she's my best friend.

And both of us have killed, but we did it out of love.

For Leigh.

For my mother.

For ourselves.

For each other.

Because we understand what makes life and death so beautiful: they can both be under our control, if we're brave enough to take it.

Closing my eyes, I press the pendant of my necklace between my fingers. For a moment, I stay there, breathing. When I open my eyes, the rosemary has etched itself into the soft pad of my thumb. I watch it slowly fade.

Then, I get up and put the phone and the book back in the hidden corners of the drawer where I found them.

And I slide it shut.

ACKNOWLEDGMENTS

Three books in, writing acknowledgments doesn't feel like any less of a pinch-me moment, especially when this one in particular means so much to me. *So Happy Together* has already changed my life: not only is it the book that made it possible to achieve the dream of writing full-time, but it also feels in some ways like the most vulnerable book I've ever written, and I truly can't contain my gratitude for the people who made it happen.

First and foremost, to my agent, Claire Friedman, and my editor, Alex Sehulster: thank you so much for seeing the potential in this book and shaping it into the best version of itself, one that I truly can't wait to share with the world. Jane, Zoe, and Colin have been in the most expert of hands, and I couldn't have manifested a better team if I tried.

Huge thanks also to Sarah Grill for seeing that initial spark, and to Jennifer Enderlin, Kelley Ragland, Cassidy Graham, [TK other names??], and the full team at Minotaur Books for your support, enthusiasm, and expertise. You're making my dreams come true!

To Florence Hare, my wonderful UK editor; Jemima Forrester at David Higham; and the team at Quercus—thank you for championing this book across the pond! I'm so grateful to have y'all on board. Another huge thank-you to the rest of the team at Inkwell Management, with whom I know my books and I are always in great hands.

Of course, one of the biggest thank-yous will always go to my family and friends: Jane spends a lot of this book feeling painfully alone, but I count myself unbelievably lucky to have such a wonderful support system around me. Your love and belief in me mean more than I can say, I couldn't possibly do this without you. Also, I'd forgive you for murder, probably.

A special shout-out to all my failed New York City Hinge dates for the inspiration, and to Mitchell for being the success story (I'm really glad you messaged me back).

Finally, the biggest, most heartfelt and undying thank-you to *you*, the reader, for giving this book a chance. And if you relate to any part of Jane's story, I'm sending extra hugs from afar.

. . . . And a reminder that, to paraphrase Chrissy Chlapecka, he's probably not the love of your life. He's literally just a guy! (But maybe don't hit him with your car.)

ABOUT THE AUTHOR

Sub/Urban Photography

Olivia Worley is an author born and raised in New Orleans. A graduate of Northwestern University, she now lives in New York City, where she spends her time writing thrillers, overanalyzing episodes of *The Bachelor*, and hoping someone will romanticize her for reading on the subway. She is also the author of *People to Follow* and *The Debutantes*.